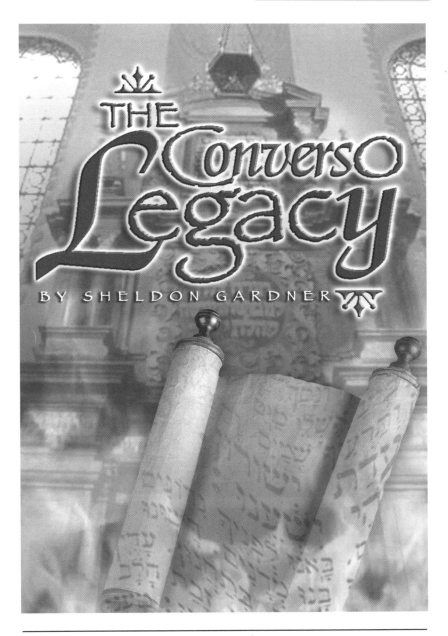

THE Converso Legacy

BY SHELDON GARDNER

Jerusalem

PITSPOPANY PRESS

New York

The Converso Legacy

Published by Pitspopany Press

Text Copyright © 2004 by Sheldon Gardner
Cover and Book Design: Zahava Bogner
Editor: Allison Schiller

Hard Cover ISBN: 1-932687-18-1
Soft Cover ISBN: 1-932687-19-X

Email: pitspop@netvision.net.il
Web Site: www.pitspopany.com

Printed in Israel

Dedication

To my wife, my three children, and my seven grandchildren.

You are my ties to immortality.

Acknowledgements

The folks who helped me are too numerous to list. However, I would be remiss if I failed to acknowledge the help of my wife Carole, my granddaughter Sheina, my good friends Russell Pelton, Charles Sandler and Robert Peck, my writing instructor Lisa Didier and our classmates.

Table of Contents

Chapter One: Hate in the New World 9

Book One: Samuel's Journey 11

Chapter Two: Life in the Shtetl 12

Chapter Three: Going to America 24

Chapter Four: The Goldeneh Medinah – The Golden Land 39

Chapter Five: Across the Great Country 57

Chapter Six: Survival 78

Book Two: Arrival in the West 85

Chapter Seven: A New Home 86

Chapter Eight: Mi Casa es Su Casa – My Home is Your Home 99

Chapter Nine: A New Way of Life 112

Chapter Ten: Evil Afoot 123

Book Three: The Plot to Save Ciudad Blanca 134

Chapter Eleven: Envy 135

Chapter Twelve: Potatoes and Politics 142

Chapter Thirteen: The Fast of St. Esther – The Festival of Purim 155

Chapter Fourteen: The Guarantor 162

Chapter Fifteen: A Trip to the Fort 166

Book Four: The Plan Must Not Fail 175

Chapter Sixteen: The First Victory 176

Chapter Seventeen: Hannah 184

Chapter Eighteen: Passover 191

Chapter Nineteen: The Dowager of the Carvellos 197

Chapter Twenty: A New Pattern of Life 202

Chapter Twenty-One: Evil Abroad 208

Chapter Twenty-Two: De Navarro's Revenge 212

Chapter Twenty-Three: A Victory Parade 217

Book Five: Coming Home 222

Chapter Twenty-Four: Romance 223

Chapter Twenty-Five: The Carvello Heritage 229

Book Six: Home at Last 235

Chapter Twenty-Six: The Quandary 236

Chapter Twenty-Seven: A Challenge to His Faith 241

Chapter Twenty-Eight: Alfred and Hannah 244

Chapter Twenty-Nine: Reuven's Return 247

Chapter Thirty: A New World 250

Chapter Thirty-One: Esther's Resolution 255

Epilogue 261

Hate in the New World

CHAPTER ONE

C hased by three boys, Sholom ran as fast as he could. They called out, *"Zhid,* Jew, we will catch you and break your head. We know where you live. Even if you get away this time, someone will always get you next time." His speed increased to an almost superhuman pace, fueled by fear. As his pursuers closed in, he could see his home. Entering the house, he slammed the door and barred it just as his tormentors arrived.

Samuel awakened, sweating from his fearful dream. In a daze, he stared around. He was not at home in Belkov; he was thousands of miles away in the dusty town of La Rosa, New Mexico in the United States. Looking out from his bed into the little store, his eyes took a moment to adjust. The boarded windows robbed the store of the morning sunlight. He could see well enough for his consciousness to return to the present. He thought to himself, *"How strange that this recurring dream of violent pogroms comes to me here in the New World. It must be because of the raid yesterday. I'd better get up and write to tell Momma and Poppa that I won't be able to send money home for a while."*

Samuel washed in a bowl of cold water. He threw on his clothes and moved to his desk to compose his letter home. It would be painful to write about the raid on the store. With the loss of merchandise and the expense to fix the windows, it would be even longer until there would

be enough money to send for his parents. He paused to
look out at the store to make sure no customer had come
in. No one was there.

   Dear Momma and Poppa, he wrote, then paused
before adding, *It's going to be a long time before I can send
money home.*

   He stopped again and thought, *"How shall I tell them about
the raid?"* His mind went back to the Russian pogroms, but
then he thought, *"I never allowed myself to imagine anything so
terrible could occur in America, not in 1886."*

   Samuel crumpled his letter and threw it into the
garbage. He just couldn't tell his parents of his defeat, not
after they had sacrificed so much to help him escape the
shtetl of Belkov in the Ukraine. Life had been perilous,
and America was their only hope for escape from the
Czar's tyranny. This attack shook his belief that he could
survive in this non-Jewish world of the New Mexican
frontier. Could he, as a Jew fleeing Czarist Russia, find a
home in America?

BOOK ONE

Samuel's Journey

Life in the Shtetl

CHAPTER TWO

S amuel's ancestors wandered throughout Europe until the thirteenth century when the king of Poland invited Jews into his country to work as artisans, merchants, and tax collectors. This invitation brought prosperity as Jews purchased surplus crops from the peasants. The introduction of cash into the economy began a departure from serfdom.

In the eighteenth century, Austria, Prussia, and Russia devoured Poland. Russia absorbed much of the Jewish population. As in the past, the government placed restrictions on these new Jews from Poland, keeping them in an immense ghetto known as the Pale of Settlement. The word *pale* means picket, and like a fence, it enclosed the nearly six million Jewish inhabitants in small, poverty-ridden villages known as shtetls.

The Russians planned to eliminate two-thirds of the Jews through emigration, death, or assimilation. Russia's policy of conscription of young Jewish men was part of its plan to wipe out Jewish identity, as the soldier, during endless years of military service, would be pressured to convert to the Russian Orthodox Church.

Samuel's family despaired under these vile policies. Sholom, as Samuel had been known, was rapidly approaching draft age. His family desperately searched for ways for him to escape the loathed military service. Leaving Russia was the only way.

Sholom walked into his wooden home, barely large enough for six family members. Weatherworn, the windows rattled against fierce winds and biting cold. The log walls were of little help. The fire in the fireplace provided a small amount of heat and light. He saw his mother, Fayge, sitting in the dark at the kitchen table preparing green beans. As his eyes adjusted to the room, he again noted that she looked far older than her thirty-seven years.

The tiny, careworn woman smiled. "Sholom, *mine kind,* my child, Poppa wanted me to tell you that he has bought your ticket to America. You, my first-born child, have been a great help to us; it will be hard to lose you. But you must leave next Monday. It now feels more real for us since we bought the ticket. Poppa wrote my cousin, Abe Schneider, in New York City. He will guarantee that you will have a job and not be a burden on the government. You will live with him."

She put down her work as her small, wrinkled face lit up. "It's hard for me to lose you, but you must go. Jews may no longer live in Russia. Poppa and I won't let you be drafted into the Czar's army. In America, life will be better. I know that God, who has not forsaken his people, Israel, will watch over you." She hugged Sholom close as she wept.

Sholom embraced his mother. "But how did you buy the ticket? Just last week, after borrowing from everyone, we were still twenty rubles short for all the expenses. I had given up hope."

"Poppa sold one of our cows, Maidel. You will turn eighteen in a few weeks. If we don't act quickly the Russians will draft you and turn you into a *goy.*" Her tiny body shook as she wept. "At least, if you are lost to us, you will remain a good Jew. In America you will marry and raise a Jewish family."

"But Momma," protested Sholom, "how will you live with only two cows? Selling milk from three brought in less than four rubles a week. There's never enough food."

"God will provide. We ask only two things of you. When you get to America, send back whatever money you can, to provide for passage for your brothers and sister. But, most important, remain a good Jew, no matter how hard that is in your new home. For you to leave your faith would make all of our sacrifices in vain. Many have changed their names, and you will have to learn to be an American, but never lose your Jewish soul." She wiped her tears away with her worn apron, pulled him to her, and whispered, "Now go and wash up. It's time to eat."

Suppertime brought the family together. It was *Shabbes*, the Sabbath, and no matter how difficult, there would be a special meal. The small home smelled of cooking food. Momma and Hannah placed the meal on the table just a few feet away from the iron stove that cooked food and heated the home. A white cotton tablecloth covered the wooden table. First, there was a bowl of watery soup. In addition to the soup, there was a small chicken, potatoes boiled in their skins, some green beans from their garden, and a platter of pumpernickel bread. Finally, their good fortune was a small slice of sponge cake with a cup of tea for dessert.

At the head of the table sat Poppa, a big man, whose quiet, unassuming manner belied his physical appearance. With his loving presence, he led the *brakhos*, the prayers that preceded each meal, which thanked God for their meager sustenance.

Sholom swallowed a mouthful of soup and then turned to his sixteen-year-old brother. "Nathan, maybe before long you'll follow me to America?"

A stocky young man, Nathan was well over six feet tall. He took a few small potatoes and passed the plate. "Our family can't afford to sell another cow. Jews must learn to live here and protect themselves against Ukrainians and Cossacks. You go. But my friends and I will make sure our people are safe here. We will be ready for their violence and will defeat them."

Poppa cut in. "That is a cruel remark. Sholom does not want to leave, but if he stays, they will take him in the army. Gone from us forever."

"Nathan, you're a strong young man," added Momma, "but you don't help your father." She passed the platter of chicken. "You spend most of your time in the streets with your ruffian friends, no different than the goyim. Big men, calling themselves the Guardians of Israel! Better you should go to *shul* and pray to God. He alone is the Guardian of Israel!"

"The people will no longer live under this oppression," Nathan lectured his audience. "Marx and Bakunin tell us of the revolt of the proletariat. Bakunin favors the use of violence to accomplish this end. The socialists and the anarchists will unite to defeat the autocrats. The only way we can live here, Momma, is with revolution. And I know we will not fail."

Poppa laughed. "You have accepted all the arguments of the revolutionaries without understanding what they mean." He took a piece of chicken, passed the platter on, and continued. "Because Jewish radicals like you are eager to join them and provide strength, your Gentile allies will use you to begin the revolution. Then they will turn against you with the same Jew-hatred as the Czar.

"Your radical friends have caused enough harm, bringing the Russians down on our heads. It is less than three years since the anarchists assassinated Czar Alexander II. The reactionaries have used the fact that one of the assassins was a Jewish woman to heighten the peasants' hatred of us. As if that was not enough, the new May Laws have increased the restrictions on how we may live. Soon we will not be able to survive."

Fifteen-year-old Isaac, a tiny, wizened boy with the look of a *Yeshiva bucher,* a rabbinical scholar, had been silently eating his meal. "I agree, Nathan, that God has abandoned the Jews here in the Pale and that only the fanatical dedication of the old men praying in shul has kept us from rebelling. But I disagree with your solution. Merely to reject the faith of our fathers as an answer to our problems and militantly oppose Czarist repression will not save the Jews of Russia.

"The only solution is to return to our homeland, Palestine. We will never be able to survive as Jews in Czarist Russia. We will never be allowed to live in peace except in our own land. Only when we return to *Eretz Yisrael,* the land of Israel, and assert our right to be a Jewish nation, will we be secure. Those settlers who have made *aliyah* by returning to Israel are showing us the way. That is the only salvation for the Jewish people, and I will join them." Then with a smug look, he resumed eating.

"If only the rashness of youth were accompanied by the wisdom of age," sighed Poppa. "Isaac, your love of *Torah* has changed to a love of Israel, but there is no Israel without God. The Jewish people have survived through the ages not by rashness, but by keeping their faith. If you go to Israel, how will you survive without work or food? The land is barren."

He looked over at Nathan who was busy eating. "Because you are big like a Cossack, you have become rebellious. Your strength makes it difficult, if not impossible, for you to submit to the forces of the Czar. But never forget that violence is not the way Jews solve their problems. We must rely upon our belief in God."

Sholom looked around the table, first at his father, then his mother, and finally his brothers and sister, struck by the differences within the family. Poppa and Momma were traditional religious Jews, who knew no other world than that of the shtetl. But Nathan, strong as a bull, was a warrior. As the Lion of Judah, he was proud of his strength, and his strength would lead him to violence. Isaac, the Hebrew scholar, transferred his intensity and single-mindedness from the *Yeshiva* to Yisrael. Both of his younger brothers had some schooling infected by the advent of the enlightenment into Eastern Europe, with its new ideas as to rationality. They had become alienated from their community and were beginning to separate their Jewishness from their religion. Sholom feared the unknown world outside. He knew his brothers could be hurt.

Hannah did not appear to understand the family's concerns as she cleared the remains of the meal from the

table. A scraggly young girl of fourteen, she helped
Momma in the kitchen by washing dishes and preparing
meals. She listened quietly to the family debates.

Knowing of his imminent departure, he sought to keep
the memory of this last Shabbes in his mind.

Poppa interrupted his thoughts. "Nathan and Isaac,
you two will have to take over for Sholom once he leaves
for America. I will need your help in caring for the cows
and selling milk."

"But Poppa," replied Nathan, "I need time for the
Guardians of Israel. We must be ready when a pogrom
threatens Belkov. I must be there to help my comrades."

"God will watch over us and protect us," murmured
Momma.

"Jews must watch out for themselves," added Isaac.

Early in the morning, the day after Shabbes, amidst
the clucking of the chickens and the mooing of the cows,
Sholom joined his father in the barn. Although it was
unusual for Jews to own land, they had a few acres
adjoining their home, where they grazed their cows and
grew a little hay to help them through the winter.
Momma and Hannah had a little garden where they grew
green beans, cucumbers, beets, carrots, onions, garlic, and
horseradish, so essential to their cooking that they were
called Jewish fruits.

They lived at the edge of town, just inside the wall
surrounding the shtetl. Belkov was an enclave of some
two thousand, mostly Jews, in a rural region of Ukrainian
peasants. Although it had been a fortified town centuries
ago, today only the broken walls remained as a reminder of
its former glory. Originally constructed to protect the
town from outside marauders, the wall now enclosed the
Jews in the shtetl, separating them from the Gentile farmers. The danger of marauders attacking from outside the
walls was long past, but the ever-present danger of
pogroms by their Gentile neighbors never ceased.

The shtetl Jews lived on an island within the larger
Gentile world of Eastern Europe, spending their entire
lives in their little towns without ever having been
exposed to the outside world. Yiddish, the everyday lan-

guage of the Jews, contained German, Slavic, and Hebrew words, and used the Hebrew alphabet for both print and script. More than a mere language, it was the mortar that bound together the Jewish culture of the shtetl, as essential as Hebrew was to the Jewish religion. It was sufficient to fulfill all their needs, excepting business relationships with outsiders.

The wall defined the shtetl, crowding homes within. For Jews, the market square and synagogue further delineated the area inside the wall. Without the market, Jews would have no place to sell their goods and no money to buy food. They would be unable to survive. Without their synagogue, they could not survive spiritually.

After the cows were milked and fed and the stalls cleaned, Poppa and Sholom went off to shul for morning prayers. Orthodox Judaism provided the structure for Jewish life in the Pale. Every shtetl had at least one shul, a synagogue where Hebrew was used in prayer. In Belkov, the shul was a large wooden building three stories high, built in the unique synagogue architectural style of the Polish Jews. Its sanctuary was filled with worshipers engaging in daily prayer. Over his shoulders, each man wore a *tallis*, a prayer shawl. He wore *tefillin*, phylacteries, on his forehead and arm, and a *yarmulke*, a skullcap, on his head. Each congregant engaged in individual repetition of the daily prayers. The prayers, uniting in their appeal to God, created a chorus with little melody but great enthusiasm.

Rabbi Moshe Mendel looked out over his reading glasses at the rows of men seated on benches and then called Sholom to the *bima,* the dais where the Torah is read. Placing his hands on the young man's shoulders and looking into his eyes, he began, "May the God of our fathers and our forefathers bless you and keep you. May He watch over you on your journey to America." Removing his hands, he added in a whisper, "Please wait for me."

After services, the *shamash,* the synagogue custodian, collected the books and put them back on wooden shelves while each worshiper folded his tallis and placed it with his tefillin into his cloth bag.

Rabbi Mendel walked over to Sholom. He looked up at the youth. "You are going to America. It's hard to be a good Jew there. Remember you have had a *Bar Mitzvah* and are a Jewish man. Do not eat food that is not kosher. Say your prayers three times a day. Do not forget our holy days, especially Shabbes, the most holy of all. God has made you a Jew. Therefore you have a duty to carry His message to the world by the life you live." He embraced the young man.

Sholom looked at the holy man, whose worried eyes peeked out over his full beard. "I will try my best to be a good Jew, Rabbi." Then he glanced at the barren room and the small bima with its threadbare velvet cover, whose Hebrew letters had long since faded. Behind the bima, he saw the elaborately carved wooden ark that enclosed the Torah, and above it, the *ner tamid,* the eternal light, an oil lamp that burnt perpetually. Abandoning his thoughts, he replied, "Thank you, Rabbi, for your concern and advice." He paused only for a final look at the shul, now fully realizing that he would soon be leaving Belkov and might never see his home or family again. Catching his breath to regain control over himself, he hurried down the dirt road past his neighbors' homes and soon caught up to his father.

"My son," said Poppa, "I know the good Rabbi advised you of the dangers of life in America. Of course, he is right. But if you can't keep all of the *mitzvos* required by God, just remember that our great sage, Hillel, reduced their essence to this one rule: what is hateful to you, do not do to another. That is the whole Torah. The rest is commentary."

"I don't want to leave. I enjoy working with you and going to shul. I love my family and want to stay here. I don't know any other life," implored Sholom. "I'm afraid to be out in the world all by myself."

Poppa put his hands on the shoulders of the trembling boy. "My son, there is nothing I want more than to have you remain, but there is no life for us here. The Russians hate the Jews as much as the Romans did when they destroyed the Holy Temple, or the Spanish when they expelled our people. Soon no Jew will be able to remain in Belkov, or the Ukraine, or anywhere in the Russian Empire. If we cannot save our children by sending them to America, our line of descent from Abraham and Sarah will soon be gone."

He gave his son a hug. "You're a good boy. You work hard and never complain. You live a Jewish life. Remember, God is always in your heart. Our love is always there. You will overcome your loneliness in America and marry a Jewish woman and have a family. We will survive the Russians because you will carry on the Rabinowitz family line and keep the Jewish religion alive. If you can, help us to follow you, but don't neglect building a life for yourself. Remember we love you and shall accept any decisions you make. Always do what is right."

Father and son walked to their home where they entered the small barn. As Poppa cleaned the stalls, Sholom brushed down the cows. He knew Poppa had always wished for a few more cows, so they could make butter, cottage cheese, and sour cream. Maybe someday they might even own a horse and wagon. Then he would be a real dairyman. But instead, things were becoming worse. Now, with only two cows, making a bare living would be difficult. They'd be lucky to earn enough to keep the family going.

Sholom poured the fresh milk from the bucket into a large metal container with a ladle chained to its side. Placing the container on his handcart, he left to sell to the customers on his route and hawk the balance in the market.

His home was on one of Belkov's three unpaved roads that came into the town through openings in the wall. To the north, a road came from Moscow, the ancient capital of the Russian Empire. To the east, a second came from Kiev, the seat of the provincial government. And finally, to the west, a third came from Brod, a city across the border in Austrian Galicia. They all converged in the market square, the center of Belkov with its town hall, church, and police station.

After a heavy rain, even the best of these dirt roads was transformed into a muddy rut. Most homes lined these streets, but some poor hovels were located in alleys that ran off to the side. Even a new building looked ragged after a couple of winters in its everlasting war with the rough Russian weather.

Pushing his handcart down the familiar route, Sholom passed the home of his next-door neighbors, where he saw Gittel smile at him. Small but full-bodied with long red hair and sparkling eyes, she was the prettiest girl he knew. Returning the smile, he quickly moved on, not wanting to stop because he didn't know how to tell her of his departure. He just couldn't handle saying goodbye. He shivered thinking of her, his only female friend and source of his adolescent fantasies, unsure of the details but sure of the delight. In his Orthodox world, sex was reserved for marriage.

Sholom called out his wares as he traveled down the narrow road. "Fresh milk for sale! A liter, only five *kopecks!*" He ladled out milk as his regular customers came out with their pitchers. Able to make out the church tower and city hall in the distance, he soon arrived at the market square.

The sounds of customers and vendors hit his ears. The market was crowded, but there was a place for every farmer, artisan, or peddler. Gentiles rarely worked as artisans or peddlers, while Jews were generally excluded from farming. Peasants had small farms, whose fields grew grains and vegetables and whose orchards produced apples, pears, and other fruits. These products were sold or traded for what Jewish artisans made or what Jewish peddlers brought to their stalls. As cash was scarce, barter was common.

Jews worked as cobblers, tailors, hat makers, blacksmiths, tanners, butchers, or any other occupation the Czar allowed them to enter. They sold shoes, hats, clothing, and other items crafted from cloth, leather, wood, or metal. Peddlers sold anything they could lay their hands on. Husbands joined wives, who helped in the family business. If he was a scholar, she might run the business while he studied Torah. The market was filled with a cacophonous symphony of Yiddish, Ukrainian, Russian, and other languages.

Sholom had about a quarter of his milk left when he arrived at the square. Finding a space, he set down his cart. Three Ukrainian peasant boys came by and taunted Sholom. "Zhid, Jew, we will see you at the next pogrom where we will break your head." They went on to describe what they would do to his sister, Hannah, conjuring up and spewing out every obscene term in their vocabulary. He ignored them, knowing that they would do nothing as long as the Russian soldier, serving as a policeman, was nearby.

But in a pogrom, it would be another matter. The word pogrom was Russian for riot, but connoted much more. It was a time when the authorities created an open season on Jews, like for hunters of wild animals. Last year the Rabinowitz family hid in their cellar until the violence ended. The mere memory chilled his body and made him shudder. Unlike Nathan, he feared a confrontation. Pogroms usually took place shortly before Easter.

Sholom knew very little about Easter, only that it was the time when Ukrainian Christians focused upon the crucifixion and resurrection of Christ and upon Jews as Christ-killers. Then, Gentile peasants, fired up by vodka, circulated a story of a lost Christian child kidnapped by Jews, whose blood was drained and used in the making of Passover *matzos*. Only fools believed such a story, but it circulated every year. Not much more was needed to fan the peasants' ancient hatred of Jews as the killers of Christ and as their economic oppressors under the old Polish rulers. This led to violent rampages where drunken peasants joined by barbarous Cossacks and Russian soldiers attacked defenseless Jews, maiming or killing men and raping women.

Sholom saw no relationship between the two holidays. For him, like all Jews, the Passover tradition celebrated Moses leading the Jewish people out of Egyptian slavery into Eretz Yisrael, and this made them even more mindful of their need for a new exodus.

"Sholom, do you have some milk to sell?" A customer's voice brought his mind back from his frightening thoughts to the more pleasant reality of the marketplace. He sold the last of the milk and hurried home. It was getting late, and daylight was fading. If only for the time he had remaining in Belkov, the rising storm could be forgotten. Even then, he did not know how long he and his family could survive in this land ruled by hatred.

 Going to America

CHAPTER THREE

*E*arly Monday morning, February 11, 1884, Sholom woke, looked out the window, and saw the glow of a kerosene lamp in the barn. Poppa must be milking the cows, he thought as he threw on his clothes and hurried to the kitchen.

Momma made a special breakfast of two eggs, black bread, and hot tea. "*Ess, ess mine kind.* Eat, eat, my child. You have a long way to go and should start out on a full stomach." She looked at him as if she wanted to hold his image in her mind forever. She always said that he looked like her father, of blessed memory, for whom he was named, and that his warm, friendly face reminded her of her childhood days. She handed him a small photograph of the family. "Keep this. It's from the fair last summer. It will help you remember us."

He put the photograph into the little cloth bag that hung around his neck. The deep sorrow in her eyes was agonizing to him. Swallowing his last mouthful of bread and washing it down with the remaining tea, he put on his jacket and hurried out to the barn.

The pleasant smells of cows and chickens filled his nostrils. Beginning his morning tasks, he fed the cows, cleaned out their stalls, and swept the dirt floor. He took a lingering last look and walked to the house, where he filled his backpack with a change of clothing, a bar of soap, a towel, and a comb.

"*Sonnelle,* my little son," called Poppa. "Come here."

Sholom put down the pack and walked over. Standing alongside Poppa, he was almost as tall as his father and, beginning to fill out, almost as big.

Poppa put his hands on his son's shoulders, looked into his hazel eyes, and implored, "Please, write us often. A letter will ease our minds, not only assuring us of your well-being, but also allowing us to accompany you on your journey. Then, God willing, when we follow you, it may be a little less strange." He paused, lowering his voice as he added, "If your mother or I die, please say *Kaddish* for us to keep our memory alive."

"Don't say that, Poppa, but if it makes you feel better, I promise I will say it."

Sholom walked away in anguish, not daring to look back for fear that tearful eyes would meet. Indelibly stamped upon his memory was the image of his father wearing his white dairyman's cap, jacket, and drab work pants and his mother in her bright red babushka and faded blue apron covering her simple cotton frock, both of them smiling to cover their breaking hearts.

He then felt a small, bulging object that Poppa had slipped into his hand: a tiny coin purse. Feeling the few precious coins, he mused that this was the last gift of love from his family.

He headed due west and walked for hours on this beautiful sunny day. The cool air invigorated him and offset his weariness. He bedded down on a pile of hay at a farm alongside the road. Feeling lonely, he looked up at the star-filled sky and thought to himself, *"I've never been away from home for as much as one night. I even miss Poppa's snores. Will I ever again have a home and a family? Jacob must have felt the same way when he left his parents, Isaac and Rebecca. God will be with me and protect me as He did Jacob."* Suddenly, feeling a desire to cry, he chided himself. *"If I'm almost old enough to serve in the Czar's army, I must not act like a baby."* He began to recall happy scenes from last Passover, less than a year ago. He saw the family around the table, heard their prayers and songs, and tasted the food. With a smile on his face, he fell asleep.

He and Poppa had planned for every mile and every kopeck, and prepared for every contingency. His father's last gift of a few coins, while unaccounted for, would help if any unexpected problem occurred. Others in Belkov, whose relatives and friends had written home, advised, "Trust no one. Don't be afraid of those *mamsers*, bastards, who shake down immigrants. They can't afford to make a fuss." He knew about the unscrupulous people waiting at every turn for their prey. His friend, Sol Goldstein, had been cheated out of his money by a trickster in league with a policeman and had to return home.

In three days Sholom walked seventy-five *versts*, about fifty miles, from Belkov to the Austrian border. He joined a caravan of Jews who, like him, gathered their meager savings, borrowed from family and friends, and fled Czarist tyranny. This human convoy included bearded men, old women wearing babushkas, and young men and women holding children in their arms or leading them by the hand. Carrying their few belongings, they poured out of Russia, walking down roads that passed through farm-lands, heading for freedom in the new Zion, America.

That night, as a smuggler met his group of emigrants where the woods obscured the border, Sholom snuck in behind the others. He saw the guide pass money to the guard, who then turned his back as the clients were guided into Austrian Galicia. As a man of draft age, Sholom knew that he must avoid the Russian guards. If discovered, he could be immediately inducted into the army. However, he was still unwilling to part with any of his coins. He had to reach the ship at Hamburg in nine days' time and wanted to conserve his money for any problem that might arise. Sholom followed the group through the forest and around several small hills. Avoiding the guide's angry looks by hiding behind trees, he followed as closely as possible to mix in with the others as they crossed over into Galicia.

Over the border, the young traveler found a road leading to Brody. Seeing a horse and wagon, he begged a ride
to the nearby town. As they traveled together, the driver,
a big, gruff man, told him, "Each day as many as a thousand Jews pour into town, looking for a place to stay until
they catch the train. They are put up in homes and on
the floors of factories and stables for the night."

As they entered the town, he was struck by the chaos.
Large numbers of refugees, with their families and belongings, crowded over the grassy areas in the town square.
They sought to secure a small spot to make into a temporary home. An old man sat down, removed his shoes,
and massaged his feet. A mother fed her small children.
A father sought water for his family. It was a town within
a town.

Sholom went to the Jewish Aid Bureau at the Hotel
Rainer, where Brody's Jewish volunteers helped emigrants
continue their exodus. A pleasant matron explained,
"Philanthropists, like Baron Maurice de Hirsch and Sir
Moses Montefiore, as well as the French and Austrian
Jewish aid societies, finance our work."

They directed him to a textile factory owned by a Jew,
where he slept on the floor, on blankets set out in the
aisles between the machines. Early the next morning, the
foreman came in and announced, "Clear the floor so we
can get to work." Sholom rose and continued his journey.

While waiting at the station for his train, he wrote
home by the light of a fire in the station fireplace.

Dear Momma and Poppa,

*I have made it safely to Austria. Once inside this
country I saw a man driving a big wagon. Because he
looked like any other Jew, I called out to him seeking
directions and a ride. His name is Sandor Warshawsky
and he lives in Brody.*

*Poppa, do you remember when you used to remark
that the people of Galicia, the Galitizianers, were smart-
alecks, chochims? Well that is so true. When I called
out to him, "Hey mister, is that town, Brody?" he
answered, "What else could it be? You must be a professor*

*to hazard such a guess." And then he offered me a ride.
I accepted the invitation and was soon sitting next to him.
When I tried to introduce myself and tell him, "I'm..." he
finished my sentence "...going to America."*

*Everything I said about home, he answered that it was
better in Brody and in Austria. When I told him about
Belkov, he told me that Brody was a fine city, that the
Austrians let the Jews work in any occupation, own land,
and travel, and as a result, everyone benefits from the
prosperity that the Jews helped create.*

*When I said Jews could not go to cities like Kiev with-
out a permit, he boasted that he made his living by haul-
ing rope, cloth, and metal products made in Brody all
over, even as far as Moscow, and that he had no problem
going anywhere in Russia because they wanted his goods.*

*Responding to his questions as to what I knew about
Galicia, I told him all I knew was that it was once a part
of Poland like the Ukraine and that many of our ways are
similar and that, Brody being so close to the border, it had
many Russians and many Russian ways. He replied,
"You are right in the little you know. Brody is a city of
twenty-five thousand mostly Yiddishe menschen, Jewish
people. Since the Austrians don't oppress us like the
Russians do, we have prospered. But unlike the ignorant
Orthodox of the Russian shtetls, here we are a modern
people who keep up with all of the new ideas spreading
across Europe."*

*My train is coming so I must finish this letter, ask the
station master to mail it, and be on my way. I miss you
all, but we will soon be together in America.*

Love,
Sholom

In the morning, dark smoke announced the coming of
a large locomotive. Sholom boarded his train for the two-
day trip to Hamburg. He and Poppa had planned for him
to arrive at least a couple of days before the ship departed
to allow time for any problems that might arise. The train
went first to Krakow, where it arrived late, and he rushed
to catch the train to Berlin. Just making it as the train

prepared to leave, he sat on a hard seat by the window, catching his breath. As he saw neat farms and great cities roll by, he thought of the contrast to his little town of Belkov. Viewing the outside world for the first time, he chastised himself for his provincial attitude, assuming that everywhere would be the same as in the Pale. Sholom peered out of the window as the train pulled into Hamburg and thought, *"What a large city! I could never imagine anything like those giant buildings."*

He overheard someone say, "Three thousand of us pour into Hamburg each day. We're all going to America. The Germans have even constructed temporary wooden barracks to house us. If these are full, we can sleep in the park."

Walking from the railway station, Sholom called out to a plump, rosy-cheeked boy, "How do I get to the port?"

The boy, who appeared to be about the same age as Sholom, paused for a moment from munching on an apple, then looked at the young traveler as if he were having difficulty understanding him. Finally appearing to have comprehended, he answered in German. *"Bist du ein Yid?* Are you a Jew? *Sind nicht Deustch du sprecht.* It's not German you're speaking. *Bist Yiddish?* Is it Yiddish?"

Sholom hesitated, concerned by this stranger asking if he were Jewish. Unsure if the inquiry came from a hostile or friendly source, he paused and then responded, "Yes, I'm a Jew."

"I'm Hans Bloch. I, too, am Jewish, but first I'm a German. I've never known a Jewish boy from Russia. We Germans stick close to our own." Then, looking closely at the rumpled boy, whose face showed homesickness and fatigue, Hans's curiosity had the best of him. "But I would like to know you better."

Little by little, the two began to communicate, Hans speaking German and Sholom, Yiddish. Because of the close relationship of the languages, the two were soon able to converse. Sholom pondered: *"How strange. He's a German who is a Jew, but I'm a Jew who is not a Russian. Had I been born here, I might have shared his opinion."*

For the next few days, the two youths explored while waiting for the ship to depart. The young emigrant slept in the park, eating food that Hans brought from home. While not like Momma's, it was good home-cooked food. His friend had taken food from his plate and snuck it into his pocket. The beef, potatoes, and green beans arrived mashed but Sholom did not care and used his hand to shovel food into his mouth.

Hans spoke of a world unlike the Pale, where a Jew could live relatively free from hatred. He told Sholom of the Warburgs, a great Jewish banking family. Then he admitted, "However, Jews are not quite full citizens in Germany."

Sholom responded, "I can't imagine a world that would allow us equality."

On Wednesday, February 20, Sholom prepared to board his ship. Hans handed him a small package. "A farewell gift for you."

The young emigrant opened the package and saw a box filled with cigarettes. He laughed. "What shall I do with them? I don't smoke."

"They're not for you to smoke. On the boat they'll be better than money. Hide them. You'll know what to do when the time comes."

"Thanks. I think this gift of yours is a little *meshugana* but you've been a good friend so I'll follow your advice."

Sholom saw huge steamships in the port, looking like tall metal buildings. He looked at his ticket to find his ship and the time it was scheduled to leave. With trepidation, he boarded the *Wieland,* one of the monsters. Then he carefully removed his hidden ticket and gave it to the collector.

The *Wieland,* a large steamer of the North German Lloyd Line, with huge smokestacks and several decks, like all transatlantic steamships, carried luxury passengers in first- and second-class cabins. The hold of the ship provided space for a profitable human cargo. The great migration to America was packed into its six holds with each passenger paying from twenty-five to thirty dollars. Sholom's passage took most of the eighty rubles saved for the trip to America. The ship was scheduled to arrive in New York City on March 9, after a trip of seventeen days.

The young emigrant stood in a long line, waiting for the ship's doctor to examine him. The company wanted to be sure the immigration authorities in New York would not reject people and return them to Hamburg at the company's expense. The doctor probed his body. "You're strong as an ox. Good luck in America."

As Sholom walked down the steep stairs that led into steerage, he looked up at the first- and second-class passengers in their aristocratic clothes going up to the luxury cabins above. But down in steerage, he saw incredible crowding. Every bit of the dimly-lit space was occupied with barely enough space for a path. The passengers had spread their bedding and pillows out over the floor to claim their territory and protect it against any challenger. Not only did they sleep here, but they also zealously guarded the space vacated by a relative or companion who waited in long lines to use one of the ship's toilets. No one risked a loss of territory.

Sholom knew from letters previously sent back home that days in steerage would be difficult because of diarrhea and nausea, which would soon be commonplace. If necessary, he could survive. But still, he scouted around for something better.

Surveying the area, he came up with a plan. The sailor on watch, a little man with a walrus moustache, stood at the top of one of the staircases leading to the upper deck and frequently disappeared for short periods of time, probably going to the toilet or sneaking a smoke. Estimating the time and frequency of these absences, Sholom began careful excursions to the upper deck, exploring for a few minutes and then returning to steerage to avoid being seen.

Near the staircase on the upper deck was a lifeboat and, behind it, a small, dark space indented into the wall of the ship. Like a bird with a secluded nest, he carried his belongings to his little home and hid there to avoid detection. Although in some places there were only a few feet between the lifeboat and the wall of the ship, for the most part his nest was quite spacious. The barren space gave him a sense of comfort and security where he enjoyed the quiet of his newly acquired home. Having been raised in crowded quarters, a private room, however sparse, was an unusual treat. The room became a concealed perch from which to observe the ship's activities.

The next morning he woke up, put on his yarmulke, and prayed. Consulting his Hebrew calendar, he noted that it was the 4th day of the Hebrew month of *Adar* in the year 5644 which coincided with February 21, 1884, his birthday. Eating his breakfast of a piece of hard black bread and some water from his water bottle, he thought, *"How I miss Momma. No matter how difficult things were, she always had a little treat for me on my birthday."*

Hopefully, he looked into his bag and in a corner found a little piece of *mandelbrot*, a sweet almond cake. Laughing, he proclaimed, "Even when she is not here, Momma always finds a way to give me my birthday treat." Slowly nibbling at the cake, he made it last as long as possible, enjoying each morsel, savoring the nuts, sugar, and cinnamon. He thought back five years to when he had his Bar Mitzvah and became a man under Jewish law, and then said to himself, *"I guess that today, since the Russians can now draft me, I'm a man under their law. But I have nothing to look back to in Russia and don't know what's ahead of me in America."*

Sholom knew from letters sent back from America to friends and neighbors that once they were on board, greedy owners cheated steerage passengers on food allowances. The meals were not much more than the minimal three meals required by American law, frequently only a cup of thin soup and a chunk of stale bread containing maggots.

Like many of the passengers, he ate none of the ship's food, believing that it was not only unhealthy but also not kosher. Momma packed good kosher food: black bread, hard-boiled eggs, boiled potatoes, dried herring, and dried beef. Tasty, compact, and most important, it would not spoil. He ate cautiously from his hoard of food so that it would last until he reached his destination. He made careful forays out from his den into the ship to keep his metal water container full.

A few days later, a sailor, seeing Sholom come out of his hiding place, smiled. Then in a deep voice, he asked, "Hello kid, what's your name? I'm Walter Liebnecht."

The first time he saw this sailor, something about the small fellow created an image in the young emigrant's mind of a little boy with a false moustache, dressed in a sailor suit. Walter showed a liking for him and they quickly developed a friendship. It was great to have a friend to break the boredom of his solitary existence. But Sholom knew that it would take more than conversation to keep his new friend from sending him back to steerage if any other member of the crew discovered him.

The next morning, Walter complained, "God damn it. Five days out and my cigarettes are all gone. I'll have to wait almost two weeks for a smoke."

Suddenly realizing the purpose of Hans's gift, Sholom ran back to his den and dug out a cigarette. The sailor's hand shook as he accepted the gift, then he moved to an inconspicuous corner and lit up. As he puffed away, he proclaimed, "Thanks kid, you saved my life."

Sholom carefully doled out the remaining cigarettes to make sure they would last until the ship docked. Walter warmed to the young stowaway and warned him whenever there was a threat of discovery.

Ten days later, as the ship drew close to New York, Walter called Sholom out of hiding. "It would be a good idea for you to go back to steerage today." Seeing alarm on the young man's face, he added, "Don't worry. Nothing's wrong. Whenever we near New York, my bosses worry about the expense of carrying back passengers who fail to pass immigration. So they get generous and serve good, hot food. Their doctors check you over. There'll be showers and medicine to make sure that any problems they might have missed in Hamburg are sorted out before the immigration doctors examine the passengers."

Sholom looked down into the hold that he had avoided. His fears had come true. Vile smells pervaded the packed steerage. He knew that it must have taxed the strength of the passengers to survive their ordeal. Unhappily, he returned to the hold.

He joined a long line. First they went through a cold shower. Then somebody sprayed him with some awful smelling stuff to kill lice. Finally a doctor quickly looked Sholom over and fed him a few pills. Then he and the other passengers were allowed onto the main deck as the crew hosed down the stinking steerage quarters. Standing at the ship's rail, everyone peered out into the distance, then one of them caught sight of a distant shore.

Shouts went up. "We are in America! Now we are in a free land! No more Czarist pogroms!" Men hugged their families while women wept tears of joy and kissed their children. A man with tear-filled eyes announced, *"Tzu Amerika kom Ich.* I have come to America." Then turning to the direction of the country he had left, he uttered, *"A mochi auf der!* A curse on the Czar and all the Russians! Now that you have driven us Jews out after we have helped you prosper, may you suffer the same fate as Spain!"

Sholom, like his fellow passengers, was happy to arrive at the new land, but sorry to leave his home, friends, and family. He trembled as he realized that he would soon be in the new land. Releasing his pent-up emotions, he joined in the cheering, "America, America, I'm here at last!" His journey had ended, his quest fulfilled. The tall buildings in the distance came closer. The ship docked at New York City on the southernmost tip of Manhattan Island. They would soon disembark.

"The rich don't have to worry about anything," said an old woman, pointing to a small boat that pulled up to the Wieland. "Those men are from immigration. They'll ask the first- and second-class passengers a few simple questions and then let 'em enter the country. But it's not as simple for us. They can send us back."

Sholom looked around at the anxious immigrants. Women, wearing their only dresses, coats, shoes, and bright babushkas, held infants or small children. Men and boys held paper suitcases containing all of their worldly goods. Many had started their journey with considerable household goods — bedding and clothing, pots and pans, menorahs and candlesticks — but little by little, their belongings disappeared, sold, lost, stolen, or abandoned until only a few items were left. So many eager faces ready to start a new life with so few worldly possessions!

Sholom remembered Walter's advice that the immigration authorities were tougher on the first groups whom they examined with precision and in minute detail to the point of being pedantic. Then they relaxed until the last group, when they resumed their vigil. So he waited until a sizeable number of immigrants had left the ship, then joined in a line feeding into barges and ferries, which carried as many as four hundred immigrants in each boat. He boarded a ferry, which moved slowly down the Hudson River to the dock in Battery Park, where they disembarked with their luggage in their arms. The steerage passengers were led into the large fortress-like building, walking to *Kessel Garten*, Castle Garden, where their fate would be decided.

Once inside the building, Sholom, like most of the others, froze with fear at the sight of uniformed officials, stirring memories of cruel Russian police. Soon they were shuffled into a big, round hall in the center of the first floor of Castle Garden. The hall was filled with hundreds of people, ranging from screaming babies to old men and women.

The raucous noise was matched only by the chaos as immigrants impatiently waited while the authorities decided if they would be let into America. Many small rooms surrounded the hall. Here the doctors examined them for the three main problems that plagued the immigrants. First, they checked the eyes to uncover the dreaded trachoma. Next they looked at the scalp, which might disclose fulva. And finally, the chest examination, which could reveal the most dreaded disease of all, tuberculosis. The discovery of any of these would lead to their return to Europe.

Then the immigrants joined in long lines, while officials conducted interviews, asking them questions about their destinations and their American guarantors. Sholom surmised that he might have to wait up to six hours to be interviewed. He worried: *"Will they let me in? Now that I've finally arrived, I must get in."* He remembered stories of immigrants sent home. But he also heard of Jewish volunteers helping their own. As his anxiety increased, a miracle occurred.

A dark-haired woman came over to him. Smiling, she asked, *"Bist du a Yid?* Are you a Jew?"

Sholom nodded.

"I'm Emma Lazarus from the Hebrew Emigrant and Homeless Aid Society." She pointed to her badge. "As a *Sephardic* Jew I meet these new *Ashkenazi* arrivals. As your ancestors helped my family find refuge from Spain, I now welcome you. Fleeing Spain or Russia, it's all the same. You are coming home to the open arms of your fellow Jews. I'll help you through immigration.

"Most of our brethren come to America through this building where New York State processes their entry. As soon as the federal government has Ellis Island ready, we will move there. But for now, Castle Garden is the port of entry. Since they don't have enough Yiddish interpreters, they allow us to help out. And, of course, we'll help you. What's your name?" Emma's kindly voice startled him, as she repeated in Yiddish. *"Vos is dein nomen?"*

"Sholom Rabinowitz."

She continued in Yiddish, "Here in America, we Jews take an English name in addition to our Hebrew name. Samuel is a fine Jewish name. May I suggest that you take that name and become Samuel Rabinowitz?"

Even though he had been warned of this practice, both by letters from America and by Momma's parting advice, he was still shocked at changing his name. But Samuel, formerly Sholom, stifled any objections and agreed.

Emma Lazarus took the young immigrant to the officials. "This is Samuel Rabinowitz." Translating from English to Yiddish and back, she helped satisfy the officials. Emma looked over at the young man. "Show them your letter from Cousin Abe." Samuel presented the agent with the letter as Emma added, "This is his guaranty that he will not be a burden on the United States Government."

The agent stamped his papers and said. "You are admitted to the United States this seventh day of March, 1884." The date remained fixed in Samuel's mind.

Once the ordeal was over, Samuel breathed a sigh of relief. "Thanks be to God, I'm in America."

Emma took out a map of a part of New York City. "This map was made especially for immigrants to show them how to get around. All of the streets, for the three miles between the lower east side and Castle Garden, are identified in both English and Yiddish.

"Watch out for the hustlers and pickpockets that fill the park outside Castle Garden. The only place to stop is at a moneychanger whose stand is marked by a golden flute. I know him to be honest." She then drew a route up Broadway, over to Canal, then to Bowery, and finally up to Delancey. There she circled Samuel's destination. "This is the home of Abe Schneider."

The young immigrant responded, "Thank you. Thank you!"

Elated, he made his way through Castle Garden and headed toward Broadway. The park was filled with immigrants looking for family members or seeking a way to get to their final destination. A crowd of hustlers tried to sell them lodging, transportation, or jobs, and pickpockets sought to rob them. Samuel avoided everyone until he found the moneychanger that Emma Lazarus had recommended. He changed his remaining five Russian rubles for two American dollars and fifteen cents in coins. His hands shook as he placed the new American bills and shiny coins into his pocket. He felt a man jostle him and a few moments later realized his pocket had been picked. The dollar bills were gone.

Samuel clutched his precious map in one hand, his few remaining coins in the other, and walked through Battery Park to where the city began at Broadway. A free man alone in this strange city, he was in the Promised Land without any money. He faced the problem of survival in a land where he had great hopes but little knowledge.

The Goldeneh Medinah – The Golden Land

With shaking legs from his long ocean voyage and overwhelmed by the strangeness of his new country, Samuel wandered until he located Broadway. The bright sunshine lit up old stone buildings and new tall brick ones. He generated a renewed vigor as he walked down that street. Samuel felt hungry and walked over to a fruit peddler with a pushcart, whom he heard speaking in Yiddish. "How much for an apple?" he asked.

"Two cents," came the reply.

He purchased the apple using one of the strange American coins remaining and received three new coins as change. He reviewed the new coins as if he understood what they signified, wanting to show the vendor he was no fool.

Anxious to reach Cousin Abe, he trudged north up Broadway, then east on Canal, and once again north on Bowery. Unsure of his destination, he approached a policeman and showed him the map. Samuel peppered his Yiddish with the few words of English he had learned on the ship. "Please sir, *kenst du* show *mir* how I should get to mine cousin?"

The policeman looked at the crumpled map and then with a sympathetic expression, he looked over at Samuel.

"Delancey Street is just down a spell, me lad." Looking as if he knew that this new immigrant might not understand English, the officer pointed to the next street and added a Yiddish word tinged with his Irish brogue, *"Dorten, that way."*

Samuel located Delancey Street and saw a number of tall, grimy structures. He guessed that these were the apartment buildings that his cousin referred to as tenements. Densely packed buildings in a congested neighborhood were new to him. No trees or grass here. Just a world of brick and concrete. Each building had a number of its own. Checking these numbers, 118, 122, then 124, and finally 126, he located a yellow brick five-story walk up.

Recalling from a letter that Cousin Abe lived on the fourth floor, he entered the building. Soon his eyes adjusted to the dimly lit hallway, and he found the staircase, walking up the four flights. On each landing, he could smell food cooking and hear the sounds of families talking and children playing. In the dim light, he made out the landing before each apartment until he arrived at the fourth floor and knocked on a door.

"What do you want, mister?" asked the skinny little girl who opened the door.

"I'm looking for mine cousin, Abe Schneider."

"Poppa, somebody's here looking for you," the child called out.

A moment later, a slight, middle-aged man in an undershirt with suspenders hanging down and a newspaper in one hand came to the door. He had a pencil-thin moustache, and his hair was slicked back. He asked, "So, what do you want?"

"I'm looking for my cousin, Abe Schneider. I'm Sholom." He paused to remember his new name and added, "Samuel Rabinowitz. My family wrote about my coming."

"Come in! Come in! I'm Cousin Abe." He grabbed Samuel and gave him a firm hug. "Welcome to America!" Samuel entered the apartment into a living room, simply decorated with inexpensive furniture that had been arranged with loving care. On one side, he could see a small bedroom with a bed and a bureau. On the other side was the kitchen, complete with gas range, icebox, table and chairs.

A smile spread over Abe's face, as he called out, "Momma, children, come quickly! Our cousin has just arrived from the old country."

A short stocky woman and her three skinny little girls walked over, much like a mother hen followed by three chicks. They were all smiling.

Cousin Abe proclaimed, "This is my wife Rifka and my *maidlach*. Sarah is fourteen, Leah, eleven, and Mindel, seven."

They shyly looked at Samuel, but Rifka gave him a big kiss and ordered, "Don't just let him stand there. He's hungry. Come eat. Have a cup of tea." She dashed into the kitchen and quickly returned with tea and sandwiches.

"Sit down," said Abe, leading Samuel to a sofa, the centerpiece of the living room. "How are your Poppa and Momma and everyone at home?"

Samuel brought him up to date and then stopped to sip his tea and take a bite of his sandwich.

His cousin said, "I came to America almost ten years ago. It took me two years to send for Rifka and the two older girls. My *kleine maidel,* Mindel, was born in America. She became an American citizen by birth. Now we are all citizens and doing well. I have a good job as a cutter with Mr. Stern. Here, if you work hard, you will do well, too."

After Samuel finished his snack, Abe led him on a tour of the apartment. "We've two rooms and the kitchen. My Rifka decorated it like a mansion, with beautiful pictures on the walls and lovely tablecloths. There's a cold-water tap in the hall that we share with the three other families on this floor. The toilet is in the back yard. Each week we heat water on the gas range and take a bath in a washtub in the kitchen. You can sleep on a pullout cot next to the girls and eat with us. While it's not a palace, we get along well."

"I'd love to, but I have no money," said Samuel, telling Abe of the theft.

"Don't worry. As your guarantor, I better make sure you make a living. I'll get you a job. Then you can pay me for room and board. With you here, we won't have to take in a new boarder. Our old one just left to get married. We're lucky. Since I make a good living, we don't have to take in more than one boarder. I can afford the twelve dollars a month rent and the quarters for the gas meter."

A great yawn escaped Samuel's mouth.

"The excitement has caught up to you," declared Rifka.

"Why don't you take a short nap?" added Abe, who smiled and added, "Today I'm home a little early to pre-pare for Shabbes. You can come to shul with me, relax Sunday, and then Monday, you'll meet my boss."

Late that evening Samuel thought, *"What a pleasing welcome to this new land, a Shabbes dinner and a trip to a shul."* While the shul seemed strange on the outside, the services carried him home to Belkov. Momma could have cooked the Shabbes meal. Perhaps life in America might not be so strange. He leaned back on the soft sofa and imagined the family safely here.

Early Monday morning Abe took Samuel to his factory. They walked down dirty streets filled with smells of garbage from crowded tenement buildings until they came to an area of large loft buildings. They went into one and walked up five flights of stairs into a dark workshop. All around, Samuel could see men and women packed close to each other, working at machines. Although large fans moved the air around, the workers perspired freely even this early in the morning.

"This is not like working under the sun in the open countryside of Belkov," Abe explained as they made their way. "All of these people are paid by the piece, so they are busily cutting and sewing women's dresses and hardly notice their surroundings." He turned to a man in a dark suit and said, "Boss, this is my cousin. You think maybe you could give him a job?"

"Unless he's got needle trade skills, I've no place for him," said Mr. Stern, a big man with a small amount of hair and a little moustache.

"He doesn't, but give the kid a chance anyway," pressed Abe.

"Let's see what he can do. But I can only pay him two dollars a week, and I hope he's worth that."

That evening, Samuel came home with his shirt soaked with sweat and his feet sore. As he wrote home, he wondered how long it would take him to save enough to bring even one member of his family over.

> Dear family,
>
> I've arrived safely in America. New York is the greatest city in the world. Jews do better here than anywhere else. Everyone speaks Yiddish. The food is like home and the shul reminds me of Belkov. Here we leave our shtetl ways and become Americans. The streets are not lined with gold and it's not easy to make a living. But jobs are here if you want to work.
>
> Cousin Abe has an important job as a cutter. He pushed his boss to give me a job as an errand boy. I bring the bolts of cloth to the cutters. They roll them out on large tables, where they cut the cloth according to patterns. Then I take the cut pieces to women sitting at sewing machines, who sew them into dresses. I take the finished dresses to the pressers, who prepare them to be sold. I put the finished garments on pipe racks or in boxes. I push the pipe racks out of the loft into an Otis freight elevator. This elevator is like an enclosed little room. I pull metal cables that lower the elevator from the fifth floor to the ground floor, where I wheel the pipe racks onto Essex Street. I push the racks down the street to distributors, who sell the dresses to stores all over the country. I only do this if the distributors are within walking distance, anywhere from a block to a couple of miles.
>
> When the distributors are far away, I put the dresses into boxes, put a label with the name and address of the buyer on each box, and place them into a cart. I push the cart into the elevator, go down to ground level, and then load the boxes on a horse-drawn wagon, which delivers them.

I do lots of other things, too: sweep floors, clean up, run errands, and anything else the boss wants. All of this I do from seven in the morning until six at night every day except Shabbes.

Poppa told me he wanted to hear all about my life here. This way we can imagine that we are still together. All day I will think of you and of the stories I will write to you. Please tell me about Belkov and your daily life. Soon I will be able to send money home to help Hannah come to America. However, since expenses are more than in Belkov, it will take a long time to send enough money home to bring the family over. I'll keep my eyes open for better opportunities.

I love and miss you all and await the day when we will again live under the same roof,

Sholom

Samuel settled into his new routine of working long hours every day except Shabbes, when he rested after shul. Each week he saved the few coins that could be spared from his meager salary and sent them to Belkov. Not a bad life, but concern over his inability to send more money home gnawed at him.

Samuel's two dollars per week salary was barely enough to pay for his room and board. He had a penny or two left over for a daily lunch of bread and herring washed down by seltzer. Unlike the other immigrant groups, Jews drank little alcohol. Seltzer or soda pop was their drink because of the dietary law prohibiting the mixing of milk with meat. A swallow of cold soda could restore anyone from the heat of the factory.

He increased his savings from five to ten cents a week by begrudging himself any expenditure not absolutely necessary. There was no money to be spent on an extra soda, a penny candy, or even new stockings. Changing his savings into rubles at the rate of forty cents for each ruble, he quickly dispatched the money home hoping it would arrive safely. But it would be a long time before enough for Hannah's passage could be accumulated.

Samuel wrote home relating his experiences so as to prepare his family for their new life.

Dear Momma and Poppa,

Life here is not the same as in Belkov, but many things are not strange. After a hard week of work at the factory, it is on Shabbes that I regain my energy and become livelier. I enjoy the little shul on Arthur Street because it reminds me of home. Except for being built of brick instead of wood, it is like our synagogue. Even the insides are similar. Once the services begin, I close my eyes, hear the prayers, and imagine I am home with you.

After shul, I spend a pleasant day with Abe, Rifka, and the girls. Abe reads aloud from the Yiddish newspapers. You would find that the Yiddish they speak here is strange, as it has so many English words.

Sarah, the oldest daughter, explains her schoolwork to me. She taught me the English alphabet and how to read. Just yesterday she explained American ways, like the Fourth of July and how this is the birthday of my new country. Sometimes I see in her a fine lady with lovely manners that any man would seek as a bride. Then I look again and she is just a little girl playing with her doll. Perhaps she and Hannah would be friends.

Abe is a fine man and very good to me. He takes great pride in himself for he is not only a cutter but sometimes the boss uses him as a foreman. Mr. Stern probably hired me because of his influence. They really didn't need an errand boy. While Abe is tough with most people, he is very kind to his family and me. He complains about the bosses but never about Mr. Stern. He makes sure the workers do not loaf, and he is trying to form a union.

Cousin Rifka runs the house, manages the children, and is always busy bustling around. When Shabbes ends, she has the best meal of the week, usually cholent. I love the wonderful roast beef with potatoes and lima beans that has been slowly cooked in the baker's oven over Shabbes. It makes me miss the wonderful food Momma would prepare for us at home. Momma, how is your

*garden? How are the cows? I pray that you have enough
of what you need.*

*After a day of worship, rest, and conversation, I'm
prepared for a new workweek. I'm very lucky that the
Schneiders have become my family and their home has
become my home. But as hard as they try to make me
feel welcome, something is missing in my life, and that is
my family.*

Love,

Sholom

Samuel regularly consulted his Hebrew calendar to
coordinate it with the Christian or secular calendar that
regulated much of his life. He took his small paper book
with Hebrew calendar dates on one side and the corre-
sponding secular dates on the other and found the dates
of the holidays on the regular calendar. Because the
Hebrew calendar was a lunar one and the Christian one
solar, it was only the leap year month of Adar II that
allowed the Hebrew calendar to adjust itself to the move-
ments of the sun, so that all of the Jewish holidays fell in
the same season every year. So Passover was always in
spring. This year that holiday fell on April 10, 1884.

Samuel participated in the Schneiders' Passover *seder*
as part of their family. The food included chicken, *gefilte*
fish, and chicken soup with *matzah* balls. The grape wine
filled glass after glass as called for by the services.
Everyone sang. The ceremony reminded him so much of
home that it could have taken place in Belkov. At the end
everyone cried out, "Next year in Jerusalem!"

On a somber note Samuel added, "Just as Moses followed God's command to lead our people out of Egypt, I
believe that God is commanding me to bring my family
out of Russia."

On the Wednesday after Passover, as Samuel was eating his lunch, Abe called to him. "Come here! I want you
to meet my friend, Max Goldberg, the peddler who sells
to us."

The large cardboard suitcase packed with merchandise
dwarfed Max, a short, dapper man. Displaying his goods,

he declared, "I've got some new razors that are a bargain. And some toilet water that's cheap. Maybe some fancy new suspenders or pocket handkerchiefs?"

Samuel looked at Max and got an idea. He knew he had to leave his job, but was uncertain where to go to make more money. Thinking that this might be his opportunity, he interrupted, "Do you think that someone like me could become a peddler?"

"For a Jew without needle skills becoming a peddler is always a good choice," said Max. "You seem to be a friendly young man. My supplier, Yankel Cohen, sells to me on credit. Maybe he'll do the same for you. No capital is necessary. You don't need any more inventory than your pack can hold."

"When can I meet him?"

"Do it for the kid," said Abe.

"Monday," added Max.

Early the next Monday morning, Samuel accompanied Max to an old brick warehouse just off the South Street docks. Here merchants bought from nearby ships and sold to storekeepers and peddlers. The smells of the ocean battled the musty odors emanating from the building as they walked up to the third floor and entered a small loft where they met Yankel Cohen, a bald, overweight man some forty years old.

Seated around an old table having breakfast were a half-dozen peddlers. The older merchant invited Samuel to a counter covered with tea, bagels, onion rolls, lox, smoked fish, and many other foods. "Have a cup of tea, a bagel, and maybe a piece of herring." With a cup of tea and a bagel in hand, the young man followed Yankel around the loft.

The merchant proudly displayed his inventory. "Most bargains are shoddy goods, cheaply produced and sold for much less than comparable products in the fancy stores uptown. That is what my competitors sell. But I do better, selling closeout goods left over when styles change, damaged goods, unclaimed freight, goods from bankruptcies, merchandise refused by the purchaser, or any other bargain."

Yankel paused, picked up a rag, wiped clean a spot on a dirty window, and pointed out the ships in the harbor. "I buy from those or anywhere else and then sell to small shopkeepers or peddlers, who resell the merchandise in the street markets of the Lower East Side or out in the country. If the price is right, a good peddler can sell anything."

After the tour, the two went back to the front of the loft where the peddlers were congregated over their free breakfast. "Sometimes a peddler has a rough week, so when they come here, I try to fatten them up. It's good for business," confided Yankel, who winked and added, "Hungry men are harder to deal with, so I pamper them a little. Every morning there's a few here to buy new merchandise. Monday is their favorite day since those who peddle in the street markets of the Lower East Side usually sell out on Sunday and those who peddle in the country don't sell at all on that day because the law prohibits such sales. So they come home."

The merchant looked at Samuel and suddenly said, "Many people try to become peddlers without success. Both personality and a good head are a must." He paused and then declared, "You'll do well! I'll give you a chance! I'll provide you with goods on credit to sell in the market. Sell out, come back, pay me, live on your profits, and I'll give you new credit for more goods."

"Thanks. You won't be sorry," responded Samuel.

Samuel had an ear for language and in Belkov he had learned Russian and Ukrainian just by listening, in the market. With Walter and Hans, he learned to distinguish German from Yiddish. He admired Yankel's ease in both English and Yiddish. Because English was just another language, he knew that by carefully observing the merchant and others, he could improve his English beyond the little that he had learned on the Lower East Side.

Yankel took the new peddler to a man across the street who rented pushcarts out for twenty-five cents a day. Samuel looked at the wooden cart. It was actually a platform upon which goods were placed. The front end had two large wheels while the rear had two handles so that the wagon was mobile but could be set down on its two support bars.

The merchant taught Samuel how to select merchandise that would sell readily on Orchard Street, the main market of the Lower East Side. He furnished the youth with a small amount of bargain goods including imperfect English woolen scarves, tea in damaged boxes, and other general items such as towels, socks, and undershirts.

The next morning, Samuel began life as a peddler. Knowing Orchard Street only from shopping there, he arrived early but it was already crowded with other push-carts and there were no good spots left. Forced into a bad location on a side street, he learned quickly and arrived early enough after that to find a good place.

Samuel soon learned to distinguish between different parts of the street as to which were better for his wares. It was hard to sell general goods in the part of the street where food was sold. He avoided places where customers would have a difficult time seeing his cart over barrels and discovered how to find a good location among the mountains of shoes, stockings, pants, and other general merchandise.

Samuel soon adjusted to his clientele. When necessary, he reduced prices to sell out even though it might lessen his profit. After his first week, he sold his goods, returned to the loft and, with a pocketful of small coins, used most of these to pay his debt.

Yankel smiled at the youth. "I'm never sure if a new peddler will come back and pay me or disappear with the money he collected, but I knew you'd be back. You're going to make a great salesman."

They headed over to a large samovar for a cup of tea. Samuel spread cream cheese on a bagel, picked up a hard-boiled egg and joined the others. Although the peddlers were usually anxious to be on their way, they always had a little time to *kibbitz,* passing tidbits of gossip while they ate. A mishmash of Yiddish and English could be heard.

The peddlers were a cross section of humanity with the common need of making a living.

Sol Abrams, a short, bearded Jew in his middle twenties, was in America less than a year and spoke mainly Yiddish.

Next to him sat Irving Fineman, a thin, clean-shaven German Jew, who spoke little Yiddish but excellent English. Luigi Colomo, a dark Sicilian, and Sam Johnson, an African American, were fluent both in Yiddish and English. Most peddlers, Jew or Gentile, spoke both. Luigi also spoke Italian and he sold mainly in Italian neighborhoods.

The remaining peddler, Arturo Lopez, was a swarthy young man who spoke English with a strange accent. As he didn't understand Yiddish, Samuel assumed he was not Jewish until he heard Arturo say, "My people were expelled from Spain in the Fifteenth Century and moved to Turkey, but our memories remain. We Sephardic Jews speak Ladino, a beautiful Spanish dialect, which we write in a Hebrew script just as you do Yiddish. I would like to go to the Southwest where my Spanish could help me make a living. But with an elderly consumptive father, I can't afford it."

Sam Johnson, a giant whose dark complexion made him look like an African prince, asked, "Yankel, those cans of fish sold well last week. My folks need good food that's cheap. Do you have any special bargains for me?"

"After you finish eating, I'll show you a few that just came in."

"I do best out in the country. I'm heading out next week. Does anybody know a good place to buy merchandise in Philadelphia?" inquired Irving.

"Try Jake Goldschmidt at the Bon Ton," replied Yankel.

"Is there any place where you *can't* find a good Yiddishe merchant?" asked Luigi.

"I can line you up all the way out to Las Vegas, in the state of New Mexico, where my cousin Mordecai Cohen runs the Main Street Emporium, the best store in town."

They laughed, finished their food and conversation, bought merchandise, and headed out.

On the Fourth of July, one of the few non-Jewish holidays that Abe didn't have to work, he took Samuel and Sarah out to explore New York City. Leaving home early that morning, they headed south down Orchard Street and walked around the few pushcarts that were there on the holiday. Then they crossed Canal Street, turned east on Division, and passed Chatham Square.

Samuel, confused at the maze of streets, asked his host, "Are you sure we're not lost?"

"Look down that street. That wooded area contains one of the earliest Jewish cemeteries in America, established just a few years after the Jews settled in New York."

Samuel saw a clump of trees in a lot filled with weeds. As they entered the cemetery, squirrels were running and birds singing. The day was sunny and a warm breeze made the premises refreshing. As they sat under the shade of a nearby tree and ate their lunch of salami sandwiches and apples, they were transported to a more ancient world, with timeworn tombstones grown smooth with age. Although the worn stones were barely legible, Samuel could make out the remnants of Hebrew writing but could not decipher any names

"The Jews landed in New York in 1654, just a few miles south of where we sit," said Abe.

"How did they get here?" asked Sarah.

"They came from Spain where they had to convert to Catholicism to save their lives. They escaped to Holland, returned to their Jewish faith, and settled in Dutch colonies in Brazil. Here they prospered, built homes, and established synagogues.

"When the Portuguese captured these colonies, life was no longer safe for Jews as the Inquisition came with the conquerors. They would be regarded as *relapsos* or fallen Catholics since they had returned to their original Jewish faith in Holland. This could lead to their death. Fortunately they were allowed to leave Brazil."

"And that's when they came to America?" asked Sarah.

"First, a group of twenty-three Jews prepared to return to Holland. They took a Dutch ship from Recife, Brazil to Amsterdam. Unfortunately they were captured by pirates."

"Did they escape?" asked Sarah.

"Yes, but it wasn't easy. The French captured the pirate ship, but instead of taking them to Amsterdam, they dropped the Jews off at a closer port, New Amsterdam. And so on July 6, 1654, the first Jews to come to America came to the city that was to become New York."

Sarah began to clean up, gathering the loose papers and anything left over from their lunch. She placed the rubbish into a nearby garbage can.

"New Amsterdam's Governor, Peter Stuyvesant, was a Jew-hater and wanted them to leave. But the Jews weren't dummies. They appealed to the Dutch West India Company, the owner of the colony. The Company, with many Jewish stockholders, didn't share Stuyvesant's attitude. They overruled him and allowed the Jews to remain. Over the years, our people prospered and became an important part of this city."

After lunch, Abe, Sarah, and Samuel backtracked and walked north, up Fifth Avenue to Nineteenth Street to see the new *Shearith Israel* Synagogue. Two blocks away, Samuel saw a tall building down the street and said, "What is that palace? It looks like one of those buildings I saw on Broadway on my way from the ship to the Lower East Side."

They stopped in front of the columned building and walked up the stone steps, looking up the marble columns at the name in both Hebrew and English.

"This is the first shul established in the United States," said Abe. "Those same Dutch Jews founded the congregation over two hundred years ago. Now it is in its third home. Its name, *Shearith Israel,* means the remnants of Israel,"

Samuel looked up. "It must be over a hundred feet high with those huge columns. What a contrast to my little wooden shul in Belkov!"

"It cost over a hundred thousand dollars to build in 1860," said Abe.

"I can't imagine such a large amount of money," said Samuel, trying to visualize an immense stack of dollar bills.

That night a thought persisted in Samuel's mind: *"How fitting the name of Shearith Israel was for this little group of Jews, forced to flee Spain, Portugal, and Brazil so that they would be able to remain Jews. It is comforting to know that my Jewish predecessors established my roots in this new land. I and many other Jews, scattered across the world in the Diaspora, are today's remnants of Israel. I feel the same lack of belonging that each of them must have felt. Perhaps one day I will find myself settled with a family and at home as they have done."*

In the month since Samuel had begun peddling, many coins passed through his hands. But after the cost of merchandise and other business expenses, he found he was not much better off than before. He approached Yankel, "How will I ever get ahead? Everything is so competitive on Orchard Street that there are only a few pennies profit left. After paying my room and board, there's not much left to send home. How could I ever earn enough to bring my family over?"

"Samuel, all of the *boychicks* are like you — afraid to leave their American shtetl. They stay in the streets of the Lower East Side and compete with each other so fiercely that no one makes a decent living. But they're content because they do not have to leave the comfort of their ghetto. Don't be deceived by life on the Lower East Side just because it is like Belkov and is less strange than the outside world. You're not at home, milking cows and going to shul. In America you must become a man."

Yankel paused and looked at the unhappy youth. "New York City is only a stopping-off point between the Pale and the real America. To succeed, it is not possible to remain on the Lower East Side. If you peddle out in the country, though it may be strange and new, a better living is possible. Begin by selling goods to farmers in upstate New York, New Jersey, and Connecticut, where competition is not as severe, since there are fewer peddlers. You'll do well."

With a trace of fear in his eyes, Samuel implored, "Can I do it?"

Yankel laughed. "Shave your wispy beard and trim your hair, so that you will look more like a Yankee. I'll help you improve your English by no longer speaking to you in Yiddish. But even with Sarah's help at home, it won't be enough. Why don't you take a few English lessons? There's a young Jew from Vilna, Abe Cahan, a journalist, who makes his living by teaching peddlers to improve their English. He could help you."

Samuel readily took Yankel's advice. Abraham Cahan, who reminded him of his brother Isaac, intrigued him. An intellectual from a family of Vilna rabbis, Cahan had rejected his religious heritage and was involved in the Socialist movement.

After a few sessions, the young peddler decided he couldn't afford Cahan. He transferred to a free school on East Broadway Avenue, sponsored by the Young Men's Hebrew Association in cooperation with the Educational Alliance. With the help of the school, Sarah, and Yankel, his English improved rapidly.

After a month, Yankel complimented the young peddler on his improvement and encouraged him to continue. "Out in America, a person has got to talk like a Yankee. You're beginning to even look like a Yankee, maybe one with a Yiddish accent. Soon you'll be a real American."

The merchant taught Samuel how to sell to farmers instead of city dwellers. "A backpack should be filled with small inexpensive items that can readily be sold, such as needles, thread, handkerchiefs, combs, and knives. Some cheap candy to give to children is always included as well as a few thimbles to be used as gifts for the ladies. A bolt of cloth, usually gingham, madras, or some cheap curtain material should be placed on top of your pack with some pots and pans tied to the bottom. Finally, add some bargain items to your pack to stimulate sales in the country."

Samuel looked strange with a bolt of cloth peeking out from behind and pots and pans that were always clanging as he walked. He stooped under the weight of his brimming pack, which when fully loaded, could weigh more than a hundred pounds. In physical distance, he was just miles from the Lower East Side in the more prosperous areas across the river in New Jersey. But it was a different world, a new *goyishe* world. Slowly overcoming his fears, he grew used to such new places as Long Island and Connecticut.

Each time Samuel returned from a selling trip, Yankel sat him down, fed him, and gave him sage advice. "Save money by sleeping in fields or barns. Eat bread or crackers and hardboiled eggs from home. Trade goods for food so you don't have to use cash. Try to hitch a ride so you won't have to pay for a bus or train."

As they talked with the other peddlers, the merchant made comments. "Do you see that skinny peddler over there? Loves credit." He called out, "Say, Itzak, how much money do your customers owe you?"

"Three thousand dollars!" boasted the peddler.

"And how much of that did they pay you last week?"

"Six dollars, but wait till next week."

"Samuel, you must learn to hate credit. Sometimes it may become necessary, but don't be tempted to extend credit by dreams of large profits. A small markup for cash is better than a larger markup on credit that will never be collected."

A few days later, Samuel again confided his fears to Yankel.

The merchant responded, "The best way to know America is to learn its speech, tastes, and needs. For this you must go far out into the country and peddle. Only there can you hope to find a place for yourself, and the success that finding that place will bring you."

Samuel knew that what Yankel said was true, but he remained fearful about breaking away from the comforts of life on the Lower East Side. His most recent letter from home confirmed a need that forced him to overcome his fear.

Dear Sholom,
It's good to hear from you and to know that you are

settled and happy in your new job. We are pleased that
you are with Cousin Abe and his family and that they
are helping you adjust to America.

Life is becoming more difficult here. Nathan and
Isaac are gone. Hannah must leave as soon as possible.
Please send money. Please help.

Love from all of us.

Poppa

Samuel knew the family must be careful of what they
wrote in their letters. The Russians would punish them
if a letter were discovered that was regarded as hostile to
the government. *"But what has happened to my brothers?*
I guess that Isaac has left for Eretz Yisrael, but I've no
idea about what's happened to Nathan." Was a pogrom
imminent? Was that the danger to Hannah? *"I can no*
longer put it off! I must go even further out into the country
to make more money!"

Across the Great Country

When Samuel returned after *Yom Kippur* to restock, Yankel looked at the youth, who wore a pained expression, and asked, "What's bothering you?"

"I've another letter from home filled with worry over Hannah. She is becoming an attractive woman and they're afraid of what could happen in a pogrom if drunken peasants catch her. Since I've come to America, I've sent only five dollars and fifty cents back. Thirty dollars are needed for passage and I go crazy over how much to save and how much to send home as I eke out a dollar. All I think about is helping my family. If I send too much home, I can't pay you and buy more goods on credit. My best is not good enough."

"What are you going to do?" asked Yankel.

"I must leave soon to make more money, but I don't know where to go," replied Samuel, shrugging his shoulders.

"Do you remember wanting to get out of the street markets of the Lower East Side?" Yankel asked.

Samuel nodded.

"You have begun to peddle in the country, but you still have one foot in the Lower East Side. It's not enough to peddle in the countryside just out of the city. Your English has improved enough to be able to sell to Yankees. Let's go the rest of the way."

He sat Samuel down in a chair by his desk. "The settlers who came to this country displaced the Indians,

killed wild animals, broke virgin soil, and found new
opportunities. Peddlers came shortly after the settlers.
From the former English colonies on the Atlantic Coast all
the way to the Pacific, they overran the country, including
those lands conquered from Mexico. In the American
West, they found no aristocratic classes or established
religions to demand obedience."

Yankel smiled. "That was especially inviting to Jews, as
we were never far behind. As merchants, Sephardic Jews
moved from New York City along the coast to other
American seaports: Philadelphia, Newport, Charleston,
and Savannah. Soon, joined by other Jewish immigrants,
we moved westward over the great mountains and across
wide rivers, seeking places where someone had a need to
buy, sell, or trade. First we came as peddlers and then,
with a little luck, we opened small stores. As our people
went west, we lost our immigrant ways. Changing our
dress and speech, we changed the country and the country
changed us. We became American Jews and that will
happen to you, too."

"But where should I go?" asked Samuel.

"The peddlers here have become my family. Since
we're friends, I've become interested in your future. Your
sister must come to America as quickly as possible. Even
if I were able to assist you, it would still take a long time
to earn enough to bring Hannah over. With God's help,
you'll do better out West. Move past the established
merchants. Keep moving until you find your place."

"How will I know?"

"Believe me, you'll know." Yankel reached into a
drawer and pulled out some papers. "I have two gifts
for you. The first is a list of names of good, honest
merchants who will sell to you at fair prices." He handed
the young peddler the list together with a large folded
sheet of paper. "My second gift is this map of the United
States." He walked over to a nearby table, unfolded the
map and placed it on the surface. "This is a special map
since some tiny point on it holds your future. Only you
can locate that point."

Samuel grasped the papers in his hands. He stared at those two simple pieces of paper that would mean so much to him.

Early the following Monday, October 1, 1884, Samuel left New York City. He wrote to his parents, telling them of his decision and asking them to continue writing to him in care of Abe until he had a permanent address.

Saying goodbye to the Schneiders was difficult, as they had become his family. Abe's brusque ways hid a warm heart. Rifka did her best to replace Momma. The girls all loved him, especially Sarah, who had begun to view him in more adult ways. They took the news of his departure with sadness, but understood. To help him start off, Rifka and the girls made him an extra large package of all the foods he loved: roast chicken with potatoes, brisket, hard-boiled eggs, fresh fruit and vegetables, and a big piece of homemade cake.

"Listen Samuel, if things don't work out, you've always got a home here. Maybe even after a few years, you and Sarah...," said Abe, who abruptly broke off as his daughter blushed. He paused, "God watch over you."

Samuel kissed Rifka and the girls. Abe held him in a strong hug.

With a heavy heart, he walked over to Yankel's, up the stairs and into the loft for the last time.

"Thanks for all your help. Without it, I'd have made plenty of costly mistakes."

Samuel noticed how the merchant's eyes moistened as he sold goods to the young peddler at unusually low prices. He thought, *"Yankel's giving me* tzedakah, *charity, and doing it following Jewish law, without embarrassing the recipient."*

As Yankel walked Samuel down the stairs, he continued, "One last bit of advice: try to hitch a ride whenever you're near a big city. You may have to make a small gift to the driver, but it will save shoe leather. People in cities don't need you as much as those living far from stores. Remember that distance is the great enemy of the peddler. Too much

walking leaves too little time for peddling, and there will
be a great deal of walking."

As they went out of the building, Yankel pointed to a
pimply-faced youth on a loaded wagon waiting at the
curb. "To start you off, I've asked Hymie Bernstein to give
you a ride."

Samuel climbed up into the wagon and rode off,
enjoying the sunny fall weather. The hypnotic swaying of
the wagon, together with Hymie's tedious recitation about
life in his father's store in Scranton, Pennsylvania lulled
the young peddler to sleep. Dreaming he was on a ship
going to America, it seemed hours later when he woke
with a start as the wagon suddenly stopped.

Hymie pointed at the farm fields bright with fall colors
from the burgeoning crops. "We're coming into an area
of rich farms. Try your luck selling here."

Samuel jumped off, thanked Hymie, and headed
toward Philadelphia through the farms that supplied it
with fruit, vegetables, and dairy products. The first sight
of an American dairy farm, a hundred times the size of
his family's few acres, astounded the young peddler. The
farms looked more bountiful than in Russia. Large buildings glowed with fresh coats of whitewash.

He decided to try his luck here and approached a
prosperous looking man in clean overalls, saying, "Hi! I'm
a peddler with great merchandise. What can I sell you?"

"I'm Charley Johnson. This is my farm. I could use a
few pots and a couple of small tools if the price is right."
After some haggling, Johnson bought two pots and a
screwdriver.

"Sammy, if you'd like you can eat with the hired help
in the dining hall and bunk out in the barn."

As Samuel sat at the table, he was served a large platter
of ham and eggs together with a large glass of milk.
Nausea arose in him at the sight of the ham, as pork was
not kosher and should not be eaten. One did not drink
milk with meat. He looked over to his right at a fat farm
hand devouring his food. "How would you like some
more? I'm not too hungry."

"Great."

Samuel gave him the ham and milk, but he knew he had to overcome his revulsion against eating non-kosher food to survive. While peddling he became conscious of difficulties for an observant Jew, as the world outside the Lower East Side was not conducive to the ways of Orthodox Jews. Trying to observe *kashrus,* the Jewish dietary laws, without facing starvation, was impossible outside of the Lower East Side. Slowly he changed his ways. When invited for a meal, he ate the non-kosher food but drew the line at pork and shellfish. Although he loved milk, he never drank it with meat.

He ate the bread and eggs and drank several cups of coffee. When he had finished, he turned to the farm hand beside him. "This is a huge dairy farm."

"What would a Jew peddler know about a dairy farm?" The man chuckled.

The remark didn't offend the young peddler as so many peddlers were Jewish that people used the terms, peddler and Jew peddler interchangeably. Samuel joined in the jest. "How about a small bet? Your red bandanna against the pick of my pack that I can fill a bucket of milk quicker than you."

"O.k. I'll take your bet. It's just easy money."

They went out to the barn, selected stools, buckets, and cows.

Eager onlookers joshed the young peddler.

"Hey boy, where did you learn to milk a cow?"

"On Hester Street?"

"Now fella, don't hurt Bossie."

Samuel doubted they ever heard of anyone milking a cow while cajoling her to give more milk with Yiddish compliments as to her beauty. But even if no one else understood, Bossie did and she cooperated. Catcalls turned to looks of amazement as the young peddler won easily.

"Here's my bandanna," said the farm hand, handing it to the winner.

Samuel reached into his pack and pulled out a fine
new blue bandanna. "Here's something for you." He
handed it to his defeated foe.

Everyone cheered.

The next morning as he prepared to leave, the farm
hand came over. "Sammy, the boys and I think you're a
good fellow. If you're looking for a job, I'd be glad to
recommend you to the boss. We don't make a lot of
money, but it's a good place to live and there's plenty of
fine grub."

Samuel thanked the man, but declined. While proud
to be befriended by Gentiles, which could never happen in
Russia, this was not his goal. Hard for him as it had been
to imagine a place where Jews were treated the same as
everyone else, he found that America was a strange place
and would take time to understand.

The boys sent him on his way with a large basket filled
with fruit, vegetables, and cheese from the farm. The next
day Samuel had a feast as he sat under an apple tree
whose fall leaves were fading. He thought, *"Now there's
plenty, so I'll eat my fill. Life isn't so bad, and the first thing
on my mind is always food. But beneath my sense of comfort
remain my gnawing needs. First, I must help my family, and
then, find a place for myself."*

He traveled for five days selling goods in this prosperous territory. By October 10, his pack was nearly empty.
Close to Philadelphia, he recalled that Yankel had mentioned Jake Goldschmidt's Bon Ton as a place to restock.
He hitched a ride from a man named Bill Jones, whose
wagon was carrying produce to Philadelphia. They crossed
over the Delaware River and in the late morning were at
Penn's Landing in the colonial area.

"Bill," he asked as he looked at his list, "I'm looking
for 720 Market Street. That's where the Bon Ton General
Store is."

"That's less than a mile from here." Bill gave him
directions.

A half-hour later, he entered the Bon Ton, a narrow
store, dimly lit and bursting with merchandise, either on

shelves up to the ceiling or in large barrels. Under a naked bulb, he could see a tall, skinny man, mostly bald with tufts of hair springing out of both sides of his head, engrossed in reading a Yiddish newspaper on a long counter.

"I'm looking for Jake Goldschmidt," Samuel interrupted. "Yankel Cohen suggested I look him up. I'm Samuel Rabinowitz, a peddler."

The man pushed his reading glasses up on his forehead, and studied the peddler. "I'm Jake. Put down your pack, rest a little, and have a cup of tea. Tell me, how is Yankel?"

Samuel thought the storekeeper looked as if he would rather read than talk, but the two soon became friendly. The peddler brought Jake up-to-date regarding Yankel and then told him of his travels. He refilled his pack with reasonably priced goods, including stockings, handkerchiefs, combs, thread, needles, small pots, and a bolt of cheap curtain material, and placed it on his back, preparing to leave.

"Where are my manners? What kind of a Jew am I?" Jake cried out, "My head is so much in the clouds I forgot that tonight is Shabbes and you are a stranger. You must come home with me and have dinner. A Jew may do no less."

Not waiting for an answer, the storekeeper called to his teenage son, "Aaron, we've a guest. Show him around Philadelphia, but be sure to get back early. Remember we close at three today to prepare for Shabbes."

Aaron came out from the back of the store. "Hi! Put your pack down and follow me."

They walked down Market Street to the historical district. "These old buildings go back well over a century to the days before the Revolution," Aaron said as he described the Declaration of Independence and the Constitution in front of Independence Hall, an old brick colonial style building where these documents were written. Then they saw the homes of Ben Franklin and Betsy Ross as well as many other historical places. Soon it was time to return to the store.

They arrived at closing time and walked to the Goldschmidt home, a narrow townhouse some three stories tall. Jake's wife Ruth, a buxom woman with graying hair, greeted them. Waiting with her two younger children, she gave Samuel a room to prepare for Shabbes, where he changed into the spare clothes from his pack: clean socks, best shirt, and fresh pants. Then he took a little nap.

Ruth prepared a fine dinner of gefilte fish, chicken soup with matzah balls, and roast chicken. The odors made Samuel's mouth water. He devoured the food while Ruth kept adding more to his plate.

That evening and the next morning, Samuel went with Aaron and Jake to the *Mikveh Israel* Synagogue, the old Sephardic shul. For the first time he saw Sephardic rituals, which seemed strange to him. Shabbes ended with *Havdallah,* the service that returns Jews from the holiness of Sabbath to the secular workweek. Samuel returned with Jake to the store to take advantage of a ride arranged by the shopkeeper. Ruth insisted, "Take a package of leftovers. You should have a little Jewish food to remind you of home."

Before leaving, he wrote a letter to Belkov.

Dear Momma and Poppa,

I'm now leaving Philadelphia. The son of my host here took me on a trip to see the sights. This city has much American history, especially about the founding of the United States. But the most interesting place of all was an old Jewish cemetery.

I bet that you are wondering why two young men went to visit a graveyard. That's what I asked Aaron, my host, as he led me down Spruce Street to a small cemetery. "It's not death that is important but what those tombstones represent," he responded. "Thirty-three Jewish Revolutionary War veterans, who helped this country become free, are buried here. Mikveh Israel Cemetery is the most interesting place in Philadelphia. When more than a hundred and fifty years ago, Jews came from New York and settled here, they founded a congregation, but

had no building until much later. They first established
this burial ground since they could put off building a
synagogue but they couldn't postpone death."

What a strange young man! I must close now.
Hopefully my next letter will include some rubles. Buying
goods here to sell in the country took all my cash.

I'm missing all of you more and more as the time
passes. I just hope that we are also coming closer to being
together again.

   Love,
   Sholom

Samuel traveled through the rural areas of
Pennsylvania, northwest to Pittsburgh. The gray winter
replaced the green summer. Fallen leaves and fading
flowers marked the land. He found himself selling to a
variety of customers and sleeping in open fields and
barns. One customer, a thrifty Amish farmer, looked
much like a Chassidic Jew. Peering through his long
beard, he haggled with Samuel until he extracted the lowest possible price. A Polish coal miner, with dirty overalls
and a face blackened with soot, bought a pretty piece of
lace for his wife.

The young peddler arrived in Pittsburgh on October 17,
just before Shabbes and was hoping to go to shul. After
services, one of the congregants, Abe Levy, told him, "Go
on to Cincinnati. The further west you go, the better the
chance you have of making a living. I can recommend a
friend of mine, a steamship agent, who will provide you
with free board in exchange for working as a cook's
helper. The boat will take you down the Ohio River to
Cincinnati."

The boat, a large white paddle steamer, left the following Tuesday. The trip down the river was restful with
three days of light work, plenty of food, and time to read
the magazines and newspapers that Jake had given him.

In Cincinnati, Samuel reviewed Yankel's list and found
a local merchant, Max Kugler. He arrived at the store
only to find that Max had died, leaving his widowed
mother Hilda, a wizened, seventy-five-year-old dowager, to

run the store. Her eyes reflected a shrewdness that per-
meated her being as she announced, "It's a *mitzvah* to
help a poor Jewish peddler. Come home with us for a
Shabbes dinner and then to shul."

He accompanied the Kugler family to the Plum Street
Synagogue. As he sat in the great temple, he heard the
famed Rabbi Isaac Meyer Wise give a sermon about Jewish
ethics. Samuel had never seen a synagogue as splendid as
this one, like a palace seen only in pictures. Its red brick
exterior with oriental towers even surpassed New York's
Shearith Israel. But most unusual of all, men and women
sat together.

Having tea and sweets after the services, Hilda took
him aside. "Would you like to take a vacation from the
road and come to work for me for a few weeks? I'm
short-handed. Izzy, my son, is my main helper in the
store since Max died, but he fell just a few weeks ago and
broke his leg. He's an easygoing bachelor and not much
of a businessman, but he's my son and does his best. It'll
be two or three weeks until he's back. You look like an
honest man and a good Jew. Help us out. I'll pay you
more than a peddler could make on the road and you'll
live at our house and eat well."

This offer was too good to even consider rejecting. "I'd
be pleased to work for you."

At the Kugler house he slept in a bed with sheets,
blankets, and pillows, and ate good food at a table with
others. There was plenty to read around the house including an English language Jewish newspaper, *The American
Israelite*, published by Rabbi Wise. From this paper he
learned a great deal about Reform Judaism. At first the
differences shocked him, for it was a radical departure
from everything he had known in Belkov, but in America
many things were strange.

Even though his crutches limited him, Izzy showed
Samuel around. But after three weeks, he was on his feet
and back to work, so it soon became time for the peddler
to move on. Hilda paid him and then added a bonus of

five dollars. "Don't think I'm getting soft in the head. Izzy insisted I give you the extra money."

Those three weeks had enabled Samuel to send home almost five times as much as he would have in a normal month. Seriously considering how his good fortune could help his family, he wrote home:

Dear Poppa and Momma,

Because of my good luck, I am able to enclose five dollars. Although my boss, Hilda Kugler, is very careful with a dollar, her son Izzy is generous. Due to him I have extra money to send home. It is only right that my family should benefit.

After considering the matter for a long time, I believe you should use the money for another cow so that life will not be so difficult. While it would be nice to use this money for Hannah's passage, I know how hard life has been. This will not be an easy decision for you but as important as it is to raise the money for Hannah, you must survive and that is almost impossible with only two cows. Do whatever you believe is best.

You might be interested to learn that in America, especially in the West, most Jews do not keep all of our laws. They call themselves Reform. Their leader, Rabbi Wise, is here in Cincinnati. It was strange to hear a rabbi lecture on a subject such as Jewish ethics as he commented on the week's Torah portion.

The rabbi does not wear a yarmulke, the services are in English, and the congregation reads responsively. At first, it appeared very goyishe. But as it becomes more familiar, I feel more comfortable. To me, Orthodox Judaism was just part of being Jewish. Now I am adjusting to the fact that there are many types of Jewish life here.

America is a strange place where there are not only all kinds of Jews but also all kinds of Gentiles. The Christians in America do not hate us as they do in the shtetl. You will like it here. I look forward to being able to share all of these new experiences with you in person. Until then, please use the money for yourselves, and take care.

Love,
Sholom

Samuel peddled to friendly Yankee farmers in the rich farm areas of Indiana and Illinois. The smells and sights of recently harvested crops of corn and hay were signs of prosperity. It was time to locate some place to spend the winter, and since he thought Chicago might be that place, he sold most of his goods and headed north.

Arriving in Chicago on November 20, he saw a large city of over a half million people and more than ten thousand Jews, many recently arrived from Eastern Europe. He soon learned that the city was as competitive as New York, and realized he could not succeed against the low prices of Sears Roebuck or Montgomery Ward.

Looking for a market like New York City's Orchard Street to sell the few goods remaining in his pack, he located Maxwell Street, a thoroughfare choked with pushcarts. Once again in a Jewish street market, Samuel felt at ease. The foods, smells, and noises were all Jewish, even down to the sounds of live chickens protesting their ritual slaughter, just like in New York. Nothing here disturbed him – not the clamor of screechy voices, not the vile odors of dirt and garbage strewn around, nor the sounds of the trolley running down Halsted Street which intersected the market.

People bought and sold anything, every day except Shabbes. Sunday was the busiest day of all since most Gentile stores were closed. Many customers came to Maxwell Street since only the Jewish market was allowed to remain open on Sundays. Orthodox Jews did no business on Shabbes.

As Samuel sought a place to set down and sell his remaining merchandise, a dapper man with slick black hair and a moustache to match approached him. "Boychick, you look like you're new around here. My name's Charlie Davis and I'm just the guy that can help you. Don't worry. I'm a *Yiddle* like you. My name's really Chaim Dubrowsky, but in America you've got to be a Yankee. Come, have a cup of tea by me."

The man's appearance put off the young peddler. But with nothing else in sight, Samuel followed the older man down Maxwell Street until it intersected with Halsted, a busy thoroughfare lined with small stores. Above one store was a weather-beaten sign that proclaimed, *Charlie Davis Bargain Store.*

In a little back room, Charlie called out, "Yetta, make a cup tea for my new friend." He looked over at the peddler and asked, "Say boychik, what did you say your name was?"

The young man reintroduced himself.

"Yetta, meet Sammy. Now give the poor boychik a cup of tea."

Then he looked once again to his new guest. "Meet my kid sister."

Samuel turned to look at Yetta and was stunned. She was the most beautiful woman he had ever seen, tall with striking features. Her red hair was swept up into a stylish hairdo. She was a real American girl, unlike the Orthodox women on the Lower East Side, modest in dress and using no cosmetics. Yetta wore clothes and makeup that he had seen only in pictures from newspapers and magazines.

The fast talker brought him back to reality. "Boychik, you're really lucky to meet up with Charlie Davis. I'll make your fortune because I know all the right people. I get the best buys: clothes, food, and tools. Anything that anybody could want from manufacturers, distributors, or stuff that just didn't sell.

"The market master is a friend of mine and for a couple of bucks, I'll get you a great spot for your cart. Buy from me at cost and on credit and we'll split the profits. Hitch your wagon to Charlie Davis and you'll soon be rolling in money."

Samuel quickly learned that Charlie always assumed assent and never waited for a response.

"Now, we've got to fix you up with a place to live," announced the storekeeper. Looking over at his sister, he added, "Do you think we could put the boychik in that room off the kitchen?"

"But that's only a pantry and it's tiny."

Ignoring his sister, Charlie continued, "Sammy, we live on the first floor of a three story frame cottage only a few blocks from here. There's plenty of room for you."

The deal was closed. While Samuel found his new bedroom quite small, it was still better than wintering in open fields or barns. The next morning, he began selling in the Maxwell Street market. Here, newly arrived immigrant Jews shopped. More came each day from the train station just a mile and a half away. Everyone spoke Yiddish and kosher food was readily available.

Charlie Davis brought the young peddler to *B'nai Yaacov,* a little shul in a building that formerly housed a grocery store. It was one of many small Orthodox synagogues within easy walking distance.

Samuel became part of the early morning *minyan,* where prayers could be said before going to work. If he could get away at noon or in the early evening, he joined in other *minyanim,* participating in as many services as possible.

A few days later, Samuel overheard Charlie telling Yetta, "I've never seen anybody sell like that kid. He's so earnest that the yokels can't resist him. His only fault is that he is too honest to con anyone. Well, I'll help out there."

Samuel began to feel he had at last found his place in America. He sold more than at any time in the past because Charlie provided bargains. Although new expenses were always added before they split the profits, the young peddler still made more money than ever before. Samuel never challenged Charlie's actions, but he still refused to use any dishonest tricks. Soon he sent home twenty-five to fifty cents each week. It still bothered him to think about how long it would take to raise enough money for Hannah's passage. Hard as he tried, he had only been able to send nine dollars and seventy-five cents home, not counting his five-dollar bonus. But there was a future in Chicago.

Something else tied him more and more to his new-found city. He had fallen in love with Yetta. He knew she thought of herself as an American girl and called him a *greener,* a greenhorn. He realized that she could afford to be generous to him. Knowing little about love and less about sex, Samuel, easily infatuated, was totally captivated by her within a few weeks. His only past experiences with the opposite sex were with Gittel, his former neighbor and Sarah, his cousin. But these were so limited that they were not much more than the fantasies of a naive boy. Nothing in his past had prepared him for the present situation, but he knew he craved the companionship and love of a woman.

Yetta pressed him into service as her chaperon. After long days at the market, no matter how tired, he accompanied her to the cultural events at the Hebrew Literary Society, Jewish Educational Society, or any other event that might have appeared in Chicago's Yiddish newspaper, *The Israelitsche Press.* At home she encouraged him to read American magazines and newspapers. Even though she had more of an accent than he did, Yetta helped improve the young peddler's English by correcting his pronunciation and grammar.

Whenever Yetta caught Samuel alone, she titillated him with a whiff of her perfume, a slight pressure of her breast against his chest, or a goodnight kiss, calling him "her Romeo." He sensed that she was toying with him but ignored the fact, growing more and more serious about their future, dreaming in the daytime as well as at night.

His next letter home told his parents about his good fortune.

> *Dear Momma and Poppa,*
>
> *I've settled down in Chicago. I'm doing well, as I have a pushcart and peddle in the market. Now I can send money on a steady basis. Maybe by spring, Hannah will be able to come here.*
>
> *I am working and living with someone who provides me with goods to sell from a stand. We split the profits. I don't trust him but I don't complain. We do a good business and there might be a future here.*

My friend's sister lives with us and is very nice to me.
A fine Jewish woman, but too high class for a poor boy
like me. Hopefully I'll be here for a while. God willing,
more money will follow soon. I hope you are well, and I
think about you every day. When we sit down for dinner
on Shabbes, I often pretend it's Momma's challah on the
table and Poppa who's making kiddush.

Before concluding, he paused, wanting to suggest that
they now write to Chicago instead of sending their letters
to Cousin Abe, who would then forward them to him.
But something made him hesitate and he ended his letter,

> *Love,*
> *Sholom*

While Samuel had to adjust to such American holidays
as the Fourth of July, he was used to Christmas. It was an
important time because of increased purchases by Gentile
customers. Samuel had never peddled in a place where
Christmas sales were so heavy. Although it was getting
colder and the wind and snow made the outdoor market
unpleasant, the brisk business activity helped him ignore
the discomfort.

One December afternoon, Samuel had a bad cold and
came home early to take a nap. In the midst of a dream,
a noise woke him. Charlie and Yetta, home early and
unaware of his presence, spoke in loud voices over a cup
of tea that they were having in the kitchen.

"That boychik is the best thing that ever happened to
me," he overheard Charlie say. "He's a great salesman
and not too bright when it comes to dividing up the *gelt*.
We've got to keep him here."

"So vat do you vant from me?"

"Marry him. I might even be willing to set you up
with a little shop and sell you merchandise."

"Vell, that vould take care of Charlie, the great deal
maker, but vat's in it for me? He's a greener! I'm a
Yankee, an educated American girl."

"Listen Yetta, maybe to Samuel you're the All
American Beauty, but you're not getting any younger and
they're not standing in line for you. He's eating out of

your hand. I know you're just teasing, but he's a fool and thinks that you're really in love with him. What else could you want?"

"I'll tink about it. Maybe a dowry from you vould help. But all he talks about is his precious family and especially about bringing his sister Hannah over. Ve don't need any more mouts to feed."

"Don't worry about that. Once you're married, I'll make sure that no money leaves Chicago."

Enraged at Charlie's treachery and at the burst balloon of his fantasy over Yetta, Samuel decided to leave. Returning to his stall, he secreted enough money over the next month to carry him on the road for two to three weeks. He told himself he was only getting even.

Samuel wrote Cousin Abe and told him that he would soon be on the road again and to hold his parents' letters until a more permanent address was available. He spent as much time as possible at B'nai Yaacov, wanting to store these experiences in his mind to counter the loneliness on the road where future religious life would be uncertain.

Deciding to leave as soon as possible, he selected Monday, February 16, 1885, a quiet day, to close the stall early. Cramming his pack full of his best merchandise, he squeezed in his few extra clothes. He left without so much as a note to Charlie or Yetta, as he did not know how to say goodbye. Samuel despised his own cowardice but hated confrontations even more. He put on his pack, took a last look at Maxwell Street, and boarded the south-bound Halsted Street trolley, riding to the end of the line before continuing on foot.

On his first night away he felt lonesome as he slept in a field south of Chicago. Barely warm enough to sleep in the open as winter was still in the air, his bones were frozen with a winter chill. The young man thought he had not only found a place to make a living and to bring his family, but could even find love and a home for a family of his own. While unsure of the meaning of sex and marriage in his life, he was sure of his desire to have both. There were tears in his eyes as Samuel realized what a fool he had been to be deceived by Yetta. Despite the cold, the comfort of sleep soon enveloped him.

Samuel worked his way southwest, selling goods to farmers and restocking in such towns as Quincy, Illinois, St. Louis and Columbia, Missouri, until he reached Kansas City, Missouri, the Gateway to the West. Much as he wanted to remain there for Passover, he couldn't afford that luxury. Buying a box of matzahs and a few other Passover necessities from a Jewish merchant, Samuel headed out.

Wanting to find warmer weather, it was easy to decide to head south instead of north. Recalling Yankel's mention of a cousin in Las Vegas, New Mexico, he decided to set off following the Santa Fe Trail.

Samuel celebrated the first day of Passover on March 31 in central Kansas, in a farm field. Every day when he stopped for the evening, he said his prayers, set out a meal, made special by the matzahs and a few other holiday foods. Each day there was a special seder, and he tried to recite from memory all he could. Although he remembered all of the ritual, here in the wilderness of this new land it was different. He was not the same man as the youth who had arrived in America.

Wandering in the arid prairie as his ancestors had done in the Sinai desert, he cried out for the loss of the good life in Chicago. After departing, one's former home always improves in memory. A solitary existence made him better understand his ancestors' travails. On the last day of Passover, he finished the last piece of matzah and drank the last few drops of wine with a toast that next year should find him reunited with his family in a new home, even if that home were not Jerusalem.

Samuel meandered across Kansas almost to the Colorado border, where he stopped at a farmhouse. A tall, bony woman opened the door and snarled, "Well, what do you want?"

"Lady, I'm a peddler with lots of good bargains for you."

"I doubt that, but if you don't try to cheat me, I might buy somethin' from you."

A half-hour later, after she had purchased two yards of gingham and a pack of needles, Samuel made her a gift of a thimble. As the afternoon continued on, each purchase made them friendlier. Her voice softened. He became more relaxed.

"I'm Alice Boydon. As a young girl, I came out west from Maine with my parents. We settled this land and now I am the owner of a large farm."

After the peddler told her of his recent travels, she said, "Sam'l, why don't you just stay for a good meal. Dinner's on the stove and lan' sakes, there's more than enough to eat."

He didn't need much convincing. She ushered him into the dining room, sat him down at the table, and went into the kitchen. He could hear the clattering of pots.

"It'll take me only a few minutes to dish up the fixin's." The smells of frying chicken and baking bread wafted their way to his nose. He hadn't eaten a home-cooked meal since Philadelphia.

As she moved in and out of the room, he inquired, "When will your husband be coming in from the fields?"

"I'm a widow. Let me put some hot chicken on your plate." She served him a huge helping that he quickly devoured.

"Well, what about your children?"

"Never had any. Take some more mashed potatoes and another biscuit." She again filled his plate, which he devoured only slightly more slowly than the first time.

"How about the hired hands?"

"I live here by myself. Take some more food. Eat to your heart's content. You look like you could use a good meal. I like nothin' better than feedin' a man."

He ate until he was so full he could hardly breathe.

"You can't run this big farm all by yourself."

"My neighbors help me. I hire them and their chil-dren by the day. But I do most of the work myself." She paused and then continued, "I sure could use a man around the house. I'd take good care of him. Have a piece of apple pie. It's my special recipe. Want some more coffee? Do you have far to go?"

Mellow from all that he had eaten, he still managed a piece of pie and three cups of coffee. Samuel waxed lyrical. "I'm a peddler. There's no place that waits for me."

"What about your wife and children?"

"I've never married."

"What about your home?"

"I've no home. No bed but the fields. No roof but the sky."

He chuckled and she joined in with laughter.

"Well then, why don't you stay here tonight? I've plenty of room."

He felt reluctant about staying the night, but the idea of topping off a fine meal with a good night's sleep in a real bed was too much to resist.

"Sam'l, come into the living room and have some more coffee and another piece of pie."

They talked for an hour, when Alice announced, "Lan' sakes, its almost ten. I'll show you the guest room." She led him to a large bedroom. Samuel's eyes focused upon a big bed with a wonderful comforter on it.

The bed, with its soft mattress, down comforter, and fluffy pillows put the weary peddler into a wonderful slumber until a stirring in the room woke him. In the moonlight, he saw the widow approaching. Pausing, she pulled the nightgown over her head, exposing her scarecrow figure. First bony knees, then her skinny stomach, finally, as her naked body moved toward him, Samuel was paralyzed with fear.

Although it was not unusual for traveling men to have sex with their customers, Samuel was not prepared by his Orthodox background to deal with a situation like this. As the naked body moved toward the bed, he panicked, grabbed his clothes with one hand and his pack with the other, and clad only in his underwear, ran out into the night.

While running, he could hear her. "You tried to rape me! I'll call the sheriff on you! They'll hang you for trying to take advantage of a poor widow, who was just too kind and trustin'!" Then he heard a dreadful sob.

Fleeing the sound of her voice, he ran at great speed. At the point of exhaustion, he paused to catch his breath and spied a bridge over a little creek. Crossing over to the far end he located a secluded dark spot. It was a little cave. He crawled into it. Despite the moonlight, he was unable to see into its seemingly barren interior, but the stench of animal excrement assured him that he was not alone. Every sound he heard raised a fright in him. But it was his haven.

Could they be looking for him? Would he be found by a sheriff and end his life in jail? Even worse, could he be lynched? Distressed by his inability to comprehend the situation, he found that at times the New World was just too strange. Was this really the end of his mission in America? Might his family never even hear of him again?

Survival

CHAPTER SIX

*S*amuel felt a small animal climb over him. Then a reflection of the sun off the stream struck his eyes and woke him fully. Peeking out from his hiding place, he saw a family of small mice running away. From the position of the sun, he could tell that it was almost noon. He couldn't remember when he had finally fallen asleep. After a long, fearful night, he must have been overcome by exhaustion and eventually dozed off. He noticed that he was still in his underwear, and the events of the previous day came quickly back to him. Although time allowed him to overcome most of his panic, enough fear remained for him to quickly dress and leave.

With his pack on his back, he headed due west away from his last customer. As Samuel traveled towards Colorado, the land became more barren. Almost a desert, it provided meager crops. With greater distances between farms, summer heat and rough terrain, traveling became increasingly difficult. As Yankel had warned him, distance between customers could become the worst enemy of the peddler. Too much walking with too few sales depleted his capital.

He hitched a ride from a teamster heading over the New Mexico border to Fort Union. Arriving at dusk, he found the fort to be a strange place. There were no walls. It was a massive distribution center that must have covered well over a square mile, more like a small city than a fortress.

Samuel avoided the headquarters unit, since he did not know how friendly the officers would be to peddlers, and explored the less occupied areas, looking for a place to sleep. Walking past the barracks and hospital, he viewed the quartermaster's area with its storehouse. Finally, by the corral there was a haystack, where he bedded down for the night.

A rooster's crowing woke him. Ordinarily that sound was a pleasant reminder of home, but lately the nights had been fitful with worries over his money running out. He shook himself fully awake, quickly rearranged his disheveled clothes, put on his pack, and prepared to wash in a little stream that ran down from the mountain to a plain behind the fort.

As Samuel washed, he was struck by his reflection. His first thought was that he was looking at a fur trader instead of himself. The hair and scraggly beard of the shtetl Jew were replaced by the long hair and full beard of a frontiersman. A beaver hat had replaced his cap. The sun and wind had tanned his pale skin. He remembered Yankel's words about becoming a Yankee, but now, staring at his new image, he wasn't sure that the change was an improvement.

His travels seemed endless. Along the way, there had been temptations to settle down and stay. Despite the poverty of the Lower East Side, it could easily have become his home except for the pressing need to send money to his parents. Cincinnati provided more funds but the need for him had ended. Chicago was lost because of deception. Perhaps none of these was the magic spot on his map. But he knew something must happen soon if he was to survive.

Locating a secluded place behind the quartermaster's building, he set down his pack, faced east towards Jerusalem, and fulfilled his morning prayers. Trying to work out a plan for survival, from underneath his shirt he pulled out the cloth pouch that was tied around his neck. He opened it and dumped its contents onto the ground. His few coins, a silver dollar, two quarters, three dimes, five nickels, and fourteen pennies, fell out. Counting and recounting his treasure, he found it came out each time to two dollars and nineteen cents. Pouring the coins back into the pouch, he replaced it around his neck.

His backpack was so light that there could be little inside. Removing the contents, he found his most precious belongings, the religious objects contained in his blue velvet bag: yarmulke, tallis, and tefillin. They had no commercial value. These, together with his prayer book and little Jewish calendar, comprised his religious world. He would never part with these, even had there been any purchasers available.

Next came his few articles of clothes: another pair of socks, a change of underwear, a jacket, an extra pair of pants, and a shirt. Nothing of value here. Nor was there any in the little food left: a piece of stale bread, a little dried beef, and a shriveled apple, hardly enough for a meal.

Then with mounting fear approaching desperation, he lifted the bag and shook it. Detecting a tinkling sound, he turned the bag over and emptied its contents. Two objects fell to the ground. He couldn't locate them until a reflection in the morning sun bounced off a ring and a necklace. The sight of the jewelry carried Samuel back a month to a bleak Kansas farmhouse where a haggard looking farmwoman had answered his knock on the door.

"Lady, I'm a peddler. I've lots of bargains for you. Things you really need."

"I couldn't afford a thimble. But come on in and have a cup of Java. You look worse'n I do."

As he sat drinking a welcome cup of coffee and resting his weary feet, she introduced herself, "I'm Clarisa Thompson. My husband, three children, and I left Cleveland, Ohio to claim this land as homesteaders. My husband Henry broke the land until the land broke him. He took sick and passed on. If I can last another month, this land will be ours. The crops are ripening, but there's no money for food. We've come so close, but now that Henry's gone, I guess we'll just have to head back East."

The peddler looked sympathetically at the disconsolate widow. She couldn't have been older than thirty, but looked fifty. She looked emaciated, her face wrinkled.

"Peddler man, would you be interested in buyin' somethin'?"

Samuel began to shake his head no, but something made him pause. Maybe it would help if he just listened.

Disappearing for a minute, she came back with a cloth bag and emptied its contents on the kitchen table. A small silver necklace and a simple gold ring fell out.

"Henry gave me these when he was courtin' me. That's all that's left of our marriage. But we can't eat these. What we need is food. What would you give me for them? If I had five dollars, we could just about make it until we could sell our wheat."

Struck by her terrible distress, Samuel thought, *"What can I do? I've little enough for myself. I haven't been able to send money home for almost two months. Yet I can't ignore this woman's plight. What would Poppa do?"* He heard his father's voice quoting Hillel, the great Jewish sage. "If I am not for myself, who is for me? And if I am only for myself, what am I? If not now, when?"

Samuel looked over at the poor woman and said, "Excuse me for a moment." He unbuttoned the top of his shirt, removed his money pouch, poured its contents on the kitchen table, and carefully counted his money. There were six dollars and twenty cents. He replaced one dollar and twenty cents back into his pouch. Looking over at her, he decided, *"I must do it. It is a mitzvah."*

"I'll buy that ring and necklace." His hands shook as he gave her the five dollars.

Suddenly, a bugle call filled the air. It returned him from his daydream to the Fort on a hot July morning. Putting his belongings back into the pack, he jumped up with renewed vigor. Wherever there are soldiers, a good peddler can always sell a ring and a necklace. Saved from disaster, he had been rewarded by God for his good deed.

Samuel knew that it would be easy to sell the ring and necklace to soldiers, but he had not realized how much the jewelry was worth. He soon found out that demand among the soldiers had raised its value. The peddler increased his capital to over ten dollars. He walked into the post trader's small, dark store. "I'm Samuel Rabinowitz, a peddler, and I'm out of stock. Would you supply me with some merchandise to sell on the road?"

"My name's Carlson. Robert Carlson," responded the storekeeper. "I'll sell to you if you agree not to resell it to soldiers on the post. I don't need competition. I assume you're going to Las Vegas. Instead of going directly there, head north into the mountains towards Mora. It's a better market. That way you can go into Las Vegas with money in your pocket." Then he warned, "Take care. There are some tough *hombres* up that way."

The young peddler listened, but wasn't sure what an hombre was, much less a tough hombre.

Three days later, Samuel had traveled up the barren mountainside towards Mora and sold most of his goods to isolated farmers who lived along the way. He figured it was about time to head down a narrow trail that a Mexican farmer had pointed out to him as a shortcut to Las Vegas. Taking the trail, he walked until dusk, bedded down, and fell into a deep sleep. A whinny woke him. He saw a horse riding away with his pack on the back of the rider, who resembled the farmer who had given him directions.

Samuel ran after the bandit, screaming out, "Stop! Stop, you thief!" and then added every curse he knew. But it was to no avail as the horse was too fast. He was seized with despair as the pack held his money as well as his goods and cursed his stupidity for not putting his money into the pouch he had tied around his neck. The dream of walking into Las Vegas with money disappeared. Now he would be lucky just to get there alive. So began a weary trek of three days to Las Vegas.

Early Monday morning, July 20, 1885, Samuel walked into Las Vegas, New Mexico. Though only twenty years of age, he felt as if he had grown old since leaving Fort Union. Weary from walking in the summer heat, he needed a hospitable place to stop. While the distance from the fort to the town was only twenty-seven miles, the young peddler's detour up the barren mountain path had added agonizing miles to his journey. The loss of his money devastated him beyond his physical weariness.

His last hope was Mordecai Cohen, whose name had been mentioned by his cousin Yankel back in New York. It was the last name on his list of friendly merchants. He needed someone who would help out an impoverished Jewish beggar who had lost all, even his cherished religious articles. Desperate, the time spent on the barren rocky trail seemed endless to Samuel until his arrival at Las Vegas.

Shortly after entering the town, Samuel turned off into an area of new homes along broad streets, identified by a sign as East Las Vegas. These homes of brick, stone, or wood were two stories high, plus an attic. They were built in a manner that the Anglos copied from the crowded towns of England or back east, where land was scarce and homes were tall and narrow, in stark contrast to the flat Mexican adobe homes. He thought, *"This must be where the rich live. I hope in the midst of all this wealth, there'll be a place for me."*

He came to a congested Mexican neighborhood of small adobe homes that lined the narrow streets of this older area. Children played in front yards minded by busy mothers who ran between their children and their kitchens. Having eaten nothing since last night, the pungent odors of roasting chili peppers wafting from open doorways and windows set his empty stomach churning. Continuing on the road, Samuel asked an old man seated in front of a little house, "Say fella, how can I find Cohen's Main Street Emporium?"

"Well, if you follow this street you're on, National, over the Gallinas River, which divides East Las Vegas from West Las Vegas, you'll find yourself in Old Town. The name on the street signs changes to Bridge Street as it crosses over the river. You'll see a grassy plaza in the distance. The Main Street Emporium is right there. You can't miss it."

Once over the river, he saw a plush meadow which gave the town its name. He knew that a plaza was in the center of every town settled by the Spaniards. A Catholic Church, government buildings, and stores surrounded it. Here he hoped to find Mordecai Cohen.

Main Street ran alongside the plaza and the young peddler saw a large sign announcing *Cohen's Main Street Emporium.* So near to his goal, he was overcome by pangs of anxiety as he thought, *"I have no money left. What will happen to me if there is no Mordecai Cohen or if he is unwilling to help me?"* Trembling, he paused to wipe the sweat off his forehead before entering the store. Once inside, he viewed a large space packed with merchandise of every kind. Here were dry goods, groceries, furniture, and firearms and even a little lending library.

For a moment he forgot his mission until a dapper young man with a pencil-thin moustache, walked over and asked, "Help you, sir?"

"Can you tell me if Mordecai Cohen is here?"

"I'm Alfred Grossman, the sales manager. Mordecai Cohen's back in his office doing some paperwork. He's my brother-in-law."

"May I see him?" Seeing the sales manager hesitate, Samuel put on his most pitiful look, which gained him entry.

Entering a small office crowded with stock and papers, Samuel swayed before a heavyset, balding man. Exhaustion confused his words as his feverish mind reverted back to Belkov. First in Yiddish and then in English, he implored, *"Einschuldig mir.* Pardon me. *Bis du a Yid?* Are you a Jew? *Kenst du helfin mir?* Can you help me? I'm a friend of your cousin Yankel and I...."

In mid-sentence, he fainted.

BOOK TWO

Arrival in the West

A New Home

CHAPTER SEVEN

O pening his eyes, he saw a woman's face. Her gray hair and warm smile raised questions about her mortality. She could have been his mother or perhaps an angel. Had he died and gone to Heaven?

Cradling a bowl in one hand, she moved a spoon toward his mouth with the other. Accompanying her actions with soothing sounds, she carefully placed the soup between his dried lips. "Take some of my chicken soup and you'll soon be all right. Come now. Take some." He saw her anxious eyes search his face as she asked, "Where do you come from? Who is your family?" Samuel ignored her questions and surveyed her worried look as she continued to feed him like an infant. *"Ess, ess mine kind.* Eat, eat my child."

Confused, he smiled as if he were at home with Momma and Poppa.

That night the Cohens took Samuel into their home. It was a new two-story wooden house with a gabled roof in the area he had passed through in East Las Vegas. For the next two days he slept in a real bed, waking only to eat or when some dark dream frightened him. The pressures of travel had caught up to him.

"Take it easy," said Mordecai, smiling at his guest. "You are our guest. Pretend that you are on a holiday."

For the first time in his adult life, Samuel had nothing to do. During the next week, he devoured the books in the lending library that Albert brought him as well as

Mordecai's newspapers and magazines. He found Jewish papers like the ones back in Cincinnati and Chicago as well as American magazines like *Harper's Monthly* and soon became acquainted with Dickens, Scott, and Sherlock Holmes.

At every opportunity, Bertha, who Samuel learned was Mordecai's wife, pressed him with questions. "Tell us about Cousin Yankel? Where do you come from? Who is your family? How did you get to Las Vegas?"

As Samuel related more and more of his past, she asked for details. He reached under his shirt and drew out a cloth packet from around his neck. From the packet he withdrew a few letters and a photograph.

Bertha looked at the precious picture. "Who is the pretty young Jewish girl?"

Samuel smiled at the mention of Hannah. "My little sister. She was not yet fifteen when I left home. Although shy, she was the prettiest and brightest girl in Belkov."

Bertha pressed on. "But what does she look like now?"

"I haven't seen her in two years, but in his letters, Poppa says that she is growing into an attractive woman."

To stop Bertha from further embarrassing his guest, Mordecai changed the subject to his own past. "I came to America from Bavaria in 1866, barely twenty, much thinner, and with more hair. I worked my way west as a peddler. After selling in the little villages north of here, I finally settled in Las Vegas. For five years I saved money to open a little store, and even then, needed help from my family. They helped me return home and introduced me to Bertha, who was, and still is, a beauty, and arranged our marriage."

Although gray-streaked, Bertha's braided blonde hair was a lovely reminder of her youth. Even though her face was beginning to show wrinkles, Samuel could still see through her smile the features of an attractive woman. Her figure must have thickened after four children, but her beauty still shone through.

"Shortly after I returned from Bavaria, I sent for her youngest brother, Alfred, so that Bertha would not be lonesome in this strange new land."

His bride smiled. "Mordecai is a mensch. He rarely denies me anything."

As Samuel gazed at his benefactors, he remembered the wealthy burgomasters and their wives, whom he had seen promenading in Hamburg. His eyes moistened over the thought of how lucky they were to have each other. Voices outside the door interrupted his thoughts.

"My children are anxious to meet you," Bertha explained. "They are curious." As they marched in, she turned to the tallest. "This is our eldest, Max, who has just turned thirteen and celebrated his Bar Mitzvah." Samuel looked at a lively boy with bright red hair as Bertha introduced the next. "This is Hilda, our only daughter, just eight years old and the apple of Mordecai's eye. Everyone calls her by her Yiddish nickname, Sheina." Samuel noticed that she, alone among the Cohens, was petite. After her, Bertha introduced Michael. "This is my second son, who is six, and finally my baby, Ernest, is three."

Samuel thought that Michael looked as if he would enjoy enticing Ernest into mischief, although the baby looked as if he would not need much encouragement.

After the children left, Bertha resumed questioning Samuel. "Tell me more about your family."

"Like most Jews in Czarist Russia, they have a desperate need to leave the country. I came first so as to earn enough money to bring them over. Unfortunately, I was robbed near Mora and have been unable to send any money home."

"Here, take a dollar as a loan from me to send home to your parents," insisted Mordecai. "Jews must help other Jews in need. It's a mitzvah."

"Thanks." Samuel put the dollar bill into his wallet. "I even lost my cloth bag with all my precious religious articles to the robber."

"Excuse me for a minute," said Mordecai, who soon returned with a blue bag.

Samuel immediately recognized the bag. With tears of joy, he took and examined it. "Everything's here. Thanks be to God."

"A Mexican farmer came into the store and sought to sell me this bag. I knew he had stolen it from some poor soul and became enraged. But a thought quickly soothed me. I must ransom this precious bag and save it for its owner, if he is not dead. And thanks be to God, you are alive and the bag has been returned."

That night Samuel sent a letter home.

Dear Momma and Poppa,
I have had some very good luck.

He put his dollar into the letter and told them what the Cohens were doing for him and, as always, minimized his difficulties.

Mordecai has told me that before the Mexicans and Americans came, Indian tribes lived here. After the Mexicans came to this region, up the Chihuahua Trail, which came north from Mexico along the Rio Grande River, they chased out the Indians and took their lands. Then the Americans came west on the Santa Fe Trail. After much violence, they learned they could not replace the Mexicans or the Indians. So now they all live at peace with each other.

Things are going well and my future looks prosperous, as I will soon return to peddling and be able to send money home. Please write in care of the Cohens, as I hope to remain in this area. Being in this warm home reminds me of my own where I was so lucky to have been raised by you both. I look forward to you meeting these people who have also traveled great distances for a better life. Know that you are always in my thoughts.

Love,
Sholom

Max watched Samuel praying the next morning and asked, "Why don't you come to synagogue with me?"

"Las Vegas has a synagogue?"

"Yes. Temple Montefiore. It's up in a second floor loft over one of the Jewish-owned stores until its new building is finished. The dedication will be held next month, just in time for the High Holidays."

They walked to synagogue where Samuel met Rabbi Joseph Glick, a small man with a little beard, moustache, prominent nose, and penetrating blue eyes. The Rabbi welcomed Samuel to the Congregation. "It is always good to have another Jew here."

Samuel asked the rabbi where he was from.

"I'm from Lithuania, where I studied in a theological seminary, the Vilna Yeshiva. In America, I realized the difficulty of obtaining a pulpit as an Orthodox Rabbi, so I adapted to the Reform ritual. Orthodoxy is so much more detailed and complex in its demands that the change was not difficult."

"That was the only form of Judaism I knew until I came to America. How did you come to be here?" asked Samuel.

"Hearing that the Las Vegas Jewish community was seeking to establish a congregation, I left my family in the East and came here in 1884, seeking to be their Rabbi." Sipping his tea, he continued. "We held our first High Holiday services in a fraternal hall and then found a home in this loft. Reminding the Jewish community of their good fortune, I exhorted them to carry out their religious obligations by establishing a permanent home. You might say that I, as an ambitious man eager to obtain a pulpit, used every bit of eloquence and drive I had to unite the Jewish community to build our new home, Temple Montefiore."

"Were you able to bring your family here?" Samuel inquired.

"Being in the right place at the right time, I was hired by the synagogue board and entered into a one-year contract with a salary of one hundred dollars per month. I was able to send back East for my family."

As the Rabbi continued, Samuel observed his pride in the Las Vegas Jewish community. "Although the Temple is

Reform, I make an effort to accommodate everyone from the Orthodox to the non-Jewish spouses. We have a place for anyone who wants to be with us. The Jews here are mostly merchants from Germany. They have contributed to the growth of Las Vegas. There are maybe eighty Jews here. Our synagogue has one hundred members."

"How can you have a hundred members with only eighty Jews in town?" the peddler asked, surprised.

"It's always difficult to count Jews. We have members in several nearby small towns. A half dozen Jews reside up in the mountains as far away as Taos. Others are peddlers like you, whom we may see only once or twice a year, probably at the High Holidays. Even in town, there's a problem counting because some of the non-Jewish wives are very active in the Temple but have not converted. So anyway, when you get done, we've somewhere between eighty and a hundred Jews."

Samuel laughed at the Rabbi's creative explanation.

The young peddler soon became a welcome addition to the small congregation, as there was always a need for a group of ten men to form the minyan necessary for daily communal prayer. One morning as he looked around him, seeing Jews praying together, he marveled at the strange collection that made up the minyan. Besides the rabbi there was young Max, two local storekeepers, a skinny clerk, three peddlers, and even a wiry cowhand. This gave him the Jewish companionship that he so sorely missed on the road.

A few days later, after Samuel folded his tallis and placed it with his yarmulke and prayer book in his blue velvet bag, he looked up at the bima, the eternal light, and the ark, and thought, *"Each minyan is a minyan of love, for as much as I enjoyed those prayers out by myself, it's more blessed to be with other Jews praying to God. No longer am I the only Jew on Earth. I'm part of a minyan. I'm part of the Jewish people. Israel lives."*

Two weeks after arriving in Las Vegas, Samuel felt strong enough to return to work. Feeling guilty about being supported by his host, he volunteered to help out in

the store. Here he worked closely with Alfred, who was
warmhearted and helpful.

"I'm the sales manager," he boasted. "It's my job to
greet the customers as they enter and guide them to a
salesman."

Mordecai laughingly referred to him as his floorwalker.
"Alfred gives this place some class."

Samuel could tell that it gave the storekeeper pleasure
to favor his brother-in-law so as to please his wife.

Early the next morning, Samuel overheard Bertha talking to Mordecai. "I'm worried about my brother running
about with fast women. He's spending too much time
and money playing the dandy, buying everyone drinks.
I'm afraid Alfred will not only marry the wrong kind of
woman but will marry out of his faith. I've taken a survey
of the Jewish community and found at least ten bachelors
and only one eligible woman and she's just about
engaged. Can't you send my brother home to Bavaria for
a bride?"

"The expenses for the matchmaker, the courtship, and
the trip are too much for us to afford with all the expenses
for the house and the family. We'll have to find some
other way."

"Well then, Hannah might just be the answer. Samuel
showed me a picture of his family and she's a pretty little
thing. They're a fine Jewish family. It could be worth a try."

"You might be right."

Two weeks after Samuel began to work in the store,
Mordecai called him into his office. "I must discuss your
future. But first let me to tell you a little about this
community." Mordecai walked over to the window.
"Look out at the town. It's like a picture with prairies in
front and the mountains in the background. It's peopled
with Indians, *Nortenos,* and *Anglos.* The Nortenos do not
like to be called Mexicans as they have lived in Northern
New Mexico for so long that they believe that they have a
separate identity."

He returned to his chair, sat down and continued.
"This was the first New Mexican town that the settlers

came to on the Santa Fe Trail. Las Vegas was a sheep and cattle town where sheep herders and ranchers contested for grazing land until the farmers gained control of most of the good land.

"Now it's a railroad town with the Atchinson, Topeka and Santa Fe Railroad. Despite all of the problems that come with the railroad, its presence pacified this area, ending the threats from Indians and whites alike." He paused, and then continued. "Just think, one day we'll be the most important city in New Mexico with a population of over ten thousand. Our store is in the center of an area that serves customers east to Kansas, north to Colorado, and south down to Lincoln County."

Samuel wondered what Mordecai was driving at.

"We Jews are called Anglos here in the Southwest but nowhere else in the country. While the whites here treat us well, we know that many of them do not regard us as their equals. Most Jews do not share the prejudices of white Gentiles toward Nortenos. They are a family-oriented people, believe in God, and wish to improve their lot in life. Are they not like our people? Our old stories are in their bible and they name their children after our prophets and heroes.

"My young friend," Mordecai concluded, "this town is filled with opportunities for an ambitious fellow like you. I've provided many peddlers with goods on credit and I'll do the same for you. Most peddlers go south and east where the land is flat and the farmers prosperous. Few bother with the territory northwest of here, as it is in the difficult terrain of the Sangre de Cristo Mountains. Some of the valleys have good, fertile land. Look at Taos, where a new prosperity has come with the raising of sheep and grain. Las Vegas is the town where they market their crops and wool. These people, mostly sheep herders and small farmers, may be poor, but still, they need the goods you sell and the news you bring. That's where I worked when I first came here." He looked into Samuel's eyes. "With Las Vegas as your base, you could make a decent living and even send a few dollars home. Your only limi-

tation will be your feet and your back. It's hard to work
out there without a horse and wagon, but I could arrange
a lift from a teamster who travels up and back from Taos
almost every week. It would make traveling a little easier
for you. What do you think?"

Excited at new opportunities in a virgin territory,
Samuel readily agreed. "I appreciate your kindness to me.
Because of what Bertha and you have done, I now have a
place to call home with friends for a Shabbes dinner and a
shul to attend. I am no longer alone." He paused and
sighed. "If only I could be of more help to my family."

"Bertha and I would like to do something for you. We
will lend you twenty-five dollars. With what you have
already sent home, it should be enough to bring Hannah
here."

Samuel gasped. Tears filled his eyes as he found himself unable to speak. Impulsively, he grabbed his friend to
his chest with a hug and then, embarrassed, released him.
"You have done so much for me and now you are helping
my family. Thank you, thank you my good friend."

"Maybe Bertha is right. Hannah could be just the girl
for Alfred."

Both men laughed and shook hands.

That day, Samuel sent the money home with a letter.

> *Dear Momma and Poppa,*
>
> *God has helped me in the person of Mordecai Cohen
> and his wife Bertha. Not only have they befriended me in
> my time of need, but they have also lent me twenty-five
> American dollars, which should be about sixty-five
> Russian rubles. These I enclose. Hopefully, with the other
> money I've sent home, it will be enough for Hannah's pas-
> sage. My heart reels with the knowledge that we are this
> much closer to being together in this new country filled
> with opportunity. Please hug and kiss each other for me.*
>
> *Love,*
> *Sholom*

A second letter was enclosed in the same envelope,

> *Dearest Sister Hannah,*
>
> *I'm writing Cousin Abe to have him meet you at
> Castle Garden.*

*Please let him know the name of your ship and when
it is expected to arrive. When you get to New York, don't
talk to any strangers, Jew or Gentile, except for the good
people from the Hebrew Emigrant Aid Society. They'll
help you through immigration and to find Cousin Abe.
Rest up a few days, and then take the train to Chicago.
Change to the Atchinson, Topeka and Santa Fe, which
stops at Las Vegas.*

*The station is only a short distance from Cohen's
Main Street Emporium, where Mordecai and his brother-
in-law Alfred will be present in the event I am out
peddling. They and Bertha, Mordecai's wife and Alfred's
sister, are good friends of mine and will be the same to
you. God watch over you until your safe arrival.
Hannah, we will once again be a family here.*

Love,

Sholom

After he mailed the letters, his mind was more at ease
than it had been at any time since he arrived in America.
"Hannah should be here by spring."

Returning to peddling the next morning, Samuel
found travel on foot difficult over the rough, winding
mountain paths between small valley communities. Back
in his old routine, he soon toughened up to meet the
challenge, sleeping in fields or barns except for the rare
occasions when a kindly farm family took him into their
home. Even though cash was scarce, a peddler was so rare
in these parts that the purchasers brought out and used
the few coins that they had hidden away. The young
peddler did not have to travel far before his backpack
was empty and it soon became necessary to return to
Las Vegas to restock. Samuel repaid part of his debt out of
the profit he made, provided for his few personal needs,
and even sent a little more home.

In mid-August, he returned to the store and overheard
a Kaintuck prospector speaking to Mordecai. "I'm goin'
back East. I jus' cain't make it here. But I wants to settle
up with you before I goes. I don't like to run out on mah
debts. I guess I owes you 'bout thirty-three dollars."

"Thirty-two dollars and sixty cents to be exact," corrected the storekeeper.

"Well, all I's got left is mah little donkey, Manuel. I hates to part with her. She's the only family I got. But I cain't take her back East no how. Suppose I give her to you and then we'll call it even."

Samuel heard Mordecai mutter to himself in Yiddish, "What choice do I have? It's the *burro* or nothing. It'll be a mitzvah to let the old codger go home, believing he's cleared all of his debts. But the animal won't be worth its keep." He switched to English and with a smile said, "Old Timer, it's a deal. Fair and square. Good luck to you on your way home."

The old man, relieved, pointed out a little brown burro tied to the hitching post in front of the store. "That's her."

Immediately Samuel decided. *"If I'm ever going to make a decent living, I'll need more than a backpack, especially with winter coming. I can carry from seventy-five to a hundred pounds on my back but a burro can carry three times as much."* Making a desperate decision, he looked over at Mordecai. "I'd like to buy that donkey from you. Will you sell her to me?"

"God works in strange ways." The storekeeper smiled. "A moment ago, I was doing a mitzvah that would cost me money. Now it is a double mitzvah because it will help you make a living. It will even make up some of my loss. Of course, I'll sell her to you."

They walked over to the hitching post, where the burro was munching straw. Her long ears twitched as her gentle brown eyes looked up at the two men. With an impish tone, Mordecai announced, "Samuel, I would like to introduce you to Manuelita. You may call her Manny. You two are now business partners. She, like all burros, is the pack animal of the poor and can be turned loose at any time to eat anything including weeds. With loving care, she'll do her share. You can pay me for her over time. Let's say fifty cents a month for twenty months. That's all she's worth."

Overjoyed with the merchant's generosity, Samuel rubbed the small animal behind her ears and then ran his calloused hands down her back. Giving her a lump of sugar and watching her ears twitch with delight, he immediately fell in love with the little burro, who would soon help him make a living.

As Samuel began peddling with Manny, he found that they were able to quickly cover great distances. The burro became the peddler's *compadre,* his dear companion. His first concern was always for her welfare. She was watered and fed before Samuel took anything for himself, following the Talmudic injunction to first provide food and drink for one's beast of burden before turning to one's own needs. When Samuel looked into Manny's eyes, he was sure that the little animal returned his affection, as each understood the other's need for companionship.

Samuel returned to Las Vegas for the High Holidays a few days earlier than necessary, determined to be at the dedication of the new temple. On September 26th, the new synagogue building was sanctified with the Presbyterian Church Choir providing music from Old Testament hymns. The exterior of the shul looked like any other wooden building in Las Vegas except for the *Mogen Dovid,* the Star of David, above its entrance.

Sunday September 30th was *Rosh HaShanah,* the Jewish New Year. It celebrated the year 5647 on the Jewish calendar, which dated back to the creation of the earth. Ten days later, the sounds of the *shofar,* the ram's horn, on Yom Kippur, the Day of Atonement, ended the high holidays, the Days of Awe. When Samuel left Temple Montefiore with the sound of the *Ne'ila* prayer in his head, he was ready to return to peddling with renewed vigor. The next morning after breakfast with the Cohens, he left with Manny, both of them fully loaded.

Five days after Yom Kippur came the holiday of *Sukkos,* the holy days when Jews celebrate their wandering in the desert on their trip from Egypt to Eretz Yisrael. He thought to himself, *"how appropriate to be spending Sukkos living outdoors in the desert wilderness."*

On this solitary October evening under the stars, he
contemplated his past life. It was in the shtetl and on the
Lower East Side that Samuel had taken his Judaism for
granted. Everyone was Orthodox and participation came
naturally. Being a Jew had meant being Orthodox. But
life on the American frontier was a different world.
Diversity had crept in, both in forms of worship and secular life. In the past, he had simply thought of himself as a
Jew, but now he saw that there were all kinds of Jews.

From the time he left New York and went west, shuls
became fewer and further apart. His religion meant a
great deal as it was a cherished part of his life and provided solace in a lonely world. Most of his prayers were
recited out in the country in solitude. Only there did he
discover how much he missed communal services.

Making camp near a small spring, he gathered
mesquite and dead pinion branches and built a campfire.
Soon the pleasant odor of burning wood filled the air.
Manny grazed nearby with one ear standing erect while
the other drooped. Samuel busied himself with his
evening prayers, making a warm dinner, and preparing a
bed for the night. Relaxing before the fire, he rested his
head on his pack and read the old newspapers that
Mordecai had given him the week before.

Drowsy, he looked up at the mountains and the stars
dotting the sky and wondered about the future. Samuel
hoped that he had found his place in America, especially
now that his sister was on her way. He dreamed that
when she came, Hannah would marry Alfred. Then they
would be family to the Cohens. He hoped to bring
Momma and Poppa over soon and imagined they would
all live in a little frame house in East Las Vegas. But for
himself, something was lacking. He had no idea of what
his future would be. Would he always be alone in a solitary world? Would he ever have a home?

Mi Casa es Su Casa ~ My Home is Your Home

In late October, Samuel and Manny traveled further than ever before into the rugged mountains to the northwest of Las Vegas. His customers found these visits welcome distractions from the barrenness of their lives. Few peddlers ventured into these small farming and shepherding communities in the remote valleys. Despite the impending New Mexican winter, Samuel was always able to find a sheltered spot to settle into for the night.

Although less than seventy miles from Las Vegas as the crow flies, the young peddler meandered more than a hundred miles in the ten days after he left Mordecai's store. He visited any place where goods could be sold. His customers, starved for the goods he carried, made purchases faster than he had expected. His bolt of madras cloth and few pots and pans sold out quickly. Although cash was scarce, customers could always rustle up a hidden coin or two saved for a purpose such as this. In addition, he traded for some Indian jewelry and small pelts, knowing that Mordecai would buy these from him.

Journeying over the mountains with their snow-topped peaks, Samuel walked through a pass and began his descent down a winding path leading to a small settle-

ment. Except where covered by snow or trees, the mountains mirrored the drab brown of the desert. The sun
made the cliff faces shine. It was cold in the mountains
and warm in the valley. He walked down among the
groves of huge ponderosa pines. He then passed through
the clusters of smaller junipers and pinion trees that lined
the path leading to a valley of small farms.

Samuel did not dare glance away from the treacherous
path with its rock outcroppings for more than a few
seconds. One false step could lead to a sprained leg or
broken bone and disaster for an itinerant peddler.
Walking long distances over rocky trails with sharp rocks
and prickly thorns penetrating his heavy boots made his
feet numb. His eyes smarted and his throat was parched
from wind blown sand.

As he approached the valley, dry air rising from the
desert distorted his perception of La Rosa, a typical New
Mexican *pueblo*. Samuel made out a system of irrigation
ditches that ran out from the little Rio La Rosa, a tributary
of the Rio Grande. He knew that irrigation came through
the *madre acequia,* the mother ditch out from the river
into a network of small acequias, which in turn, distrib-
uted water into the fields. Sluice gates, which were
opened for short periods of time, allowed the fields to be
flooded. As the surplus water streamed back to the river,
he saw farmers, whose land did not adjoin the irrigation
ditches, carry off buckets of the precious fluid to their
fields. This water, coupled with plentiful sunshine, helped
produce good crops. Without it, there was an ever-
present threat of the desert reclaiming the land the farmers
had taken from it.

As he drew closer, Samuel saw farms with fields of
greens and reds reflecting the remains of the recently harvested crops of corn, beans, and chili peppers. The fields
contrasted with the meager sagebrush and scraggly pinion
trees of the desert. Coming still closer, he made out a
dozen squat adobe homes that constituted the pueblo of
La Rosa. It was sheltered by a *bosque,* a small wooded
grove of cottonwood trees with a few willows and some

overgrown mesquite along a narrow winding path that followed the Rio La Rosa, whose water nourished their growth.

Although nothing was unusual about this little village, Samuel was struck by something special. Perhaps his weariness created a longing. He enjoyed the time he spent with his customers, but his desire for the warmth generated by human companionship remained unfulfilled as there was never enough time to create a meaningful relationship. He would visit his new customers, perhaps even share a meal, but too soon it was time to move on. The peddler led a much lonelier life in the mountains than he had back in Belkov, New York, or even Las Vegas.

As Samuel looked down at this little community, a strange feeling overcame him. This was not just another town. It was something else. His mind searched for the right word to describe what he felt. As his English vocabulary proved inadequate, he sought a Yiddish word. Then it came to him, the word *bashert,* predestined. Somehow this town would play an important part in his future.

Approaching the nearest house, Samuel saw a farmer standing on his portico and looking out at him. The peddler was struck by the appearance of the older man and the contrast to his own looks. The farmer, slender and over six feet tall, had an aristocratic bearing that made him appear much taller than Samuel's stocky five foot eight, which appeared even shorter because of his stoop. Both were tan, but Samuel's color came only from the sun. The aquiline nose and well-trimmed beard and moustache on the angular face of the farmer contrasted with Samuel's prominent nose and scruffy growth on his broad face. The farmer's clothing, all of a simple piece, included a white cotton shirt and pants and dust-colored sandals. On the other hand, the peddler's plaid shirt did not match his brown woolen pants, black jacket, and dark leather boots.

The thirsty peddler and his tired burro arrived at the house. Samuel's throat was raspy from the sand he had swallowed, so he mumbled a request for water. At first it appeared that his host did not understand, so the peddler set down his pack and while mimicking a man drinking, asked, "Could you spare some water for me and my burro?"

"Yes, water. One moment, please," replied the farmer, who disappeared into the house.

Weary from the hours he had walked under the blazing sun, and from the barrenness of his life, the peddler sat down on a small bench on the portico. He leaned back against the wall of the house, placing his hands at his sides. Closing his eyes, he slipped off into a daydream, enjoying the wonderfully relaxed state that comes only to the totally exhausted.

His travels across vast distances since leaving Belkov kept running through his mind. He retraced his trip across Europe, the Atlantic Ocean, and finally the North American Continent. Everything had been green until the brown of the desert. Nothing in his experience had prepared him for the New Mexican desert and its oppressive sun. Even his closed eyes could not block out the glare. Its bleakness accentuated the barrenness of his solitary life. He longed for a reprieve not only from the sun but also from the loneliness of endless mountains and sparse desert.

Words abruptly ended Samuel's daydream. *"Si agua, Senor.* Here is your water," said the farmer, emerging from the house with a tin cup and a bucket. "Water for you and your burro. I speak English but I am more at home in Spanish."

Although thirsty, the peddler gave Manny the bucket of water before drinking himself. He let her free to forage in the bosque, only then concentrating on quenching his own thirst. Samuel sat down and sipped the cool water slowly, savoring each drop. He set down the empty cup, drew out his bandanna, and wiped the sweat from his forehead. "Thanks. My name is Samuel Rabinowitz."

"Senor Samuel, I am Reuben Carvello. *Mi casa es su casa.* My home is your home. Please come in."

In appreciation of the kind welcome, the peddler gave the farmer a warm smile. Not everyone responded this way in a land where a stranger could threaten one's safety. This truly might be the special place he felt it to be.

"Please come into my humble home and rest for a few minutes," Reuben added.

Samuel entered the house. Then he paused to allow his eyes to adjust to the dim interior. What he saw was a pleasant surprise. Most farm homes had one-room interiors, but here the ingenuity of the occupants in dividing the room into two parts made the home look spacious. The placing of the meager furniture made it appear not only adequate, but also attractive. The kitchen contained a table and four chairs. At the opposite end of the room were two beds and two rough-hewn chairs, a combined living room and bedroom. All in all, it had a warm look.

Moving across the room, he noticed a young woman with her back to him, preparing food in front of a large brick fireplace. Samuel saw a large log running above the entire length of the fireplace with several nails hammered partway into it. Hung upon these nails were some modest utensils: a large spoon, a spatula, a large fork, a ladle, and a few others that he did not recognize. Tempting odors of roasting chili peppers filled the room. The fireplace added the aroma of burning pinion logs

"Esther, please come meet our guest." Turning to the peddler, he said, "This is my daughter."

As she turned to face Samuel, their eyes met. Both blushed. Believing that she could read his mind, he lowered his eyes, then peeked up a bit and saw that she had also turned her eyes away. He could see her lustrous black hair, large brown eyes, petite mouth, and small nose upon a tan face.

"Senor Samuel, please join us for dinner," said Reuben

"Thank you for your hospitality but I must be heading back to Las Vegas."

"Nonsense! You look famished and my daughter is a fine cook."

Rarely reluctant to accept the hospitality of strangers, and hungry as Samuel was, Esther complicated the invitation. He was unsure how to deal with his emotions since

the sight of her warm eyes, slender waist, and ample
bosom created within him a sensation of sexual desire.
Overcoming his reticence, Samuel decided to accept the
offer in order to be with her. He looked over at Reuben.
"I'd be pleased to join you. It's been a while since I've had
a good home-cooked meal. But please excuse me a
moment to wash up."

Stepping outside, he gave Manny fresh water and some
hay. She nuzzled him with her thanks. Samuel washed
his face, combed his hair, faced east toward Jerusalem,
and recited his afternoon prayer before returning to the
house for dinner.

When Samuel reentered the house, Reuben had seated
himself at the head of the plank table and invited his
guest to take a chair. The peddler looked down, nervously
avoiding Esther's eyes. He stared intensely at the *frijoles*
and *tortillas* on his plate. Then, sneaking a glance, he
noticed her head turned away, intensely involved with
her cooking.

"Esther, give Senor Samuel a large piece of meat. He
looks like a hungry man and your cooking will be just
what he needs."

Samuel watched Esther move to his plate, preparing to
serve him, and then said, "No thank you."

"But my young friend, you are hungry," said Reuben,
"Why do you not wish the meat? I assure you my daughter
is a fine cook."

"I don't doubt it, and don't wish to be ungrateful or
rude, but I do not eat pork."

Esther smiled. "Nor do we. This is lamb."

Samuel accepted the meat, cut it into small pieces and
ate the first bite with pleasure. "This is the first meat I've
eaten since I left Las Vegas. It is delicious."

"Why do you not eat pork?" asked Reuben.

"Eating that meat is forbidden by my religion as a Jew."

"Our family has a long custom of not liking pork. We
never raised pigs," said Esther.

Their leisurely conversation continued during the meal.

After the meal, Reuben invited Samuel to join him on

the portico. The spring night was brisk but pleasant. They watched the stars. The moon was a clear, crystal slice of light. The two, content with a fine meal and refreshed by a cool breeze, sat quietly. Soon Esther joined them.

Reuben broke the silence. "Tell me, Senor Samuel, where do you come from? You do not speak as we do."

The peddler told them about Belkov and of his travels in this new country since he left home. He spoke of his mission to bring his family to America and how he had sent money to fetch Hannah. He asked, "Tell me about you two. Have you always lived here in La Rosa?"

Reuben paused. He looked up as if he had never before heard that question. He pondered and then answered, "Senor Samuel, our family has not always lived in this little town. Pueblo Indians founded La Rosa, building homes close together for protection against attacks by Apaches, settling where the trail that comes from the mountain pass meets the trail that follows the Rio La Rosa. Here they had water for their crops and the bosques of cottonwood and other trees provided shade and wood. Today the Indians are gone and the pueblo is little more than a collection of a dozen adobe homes of farmers on an intersection of two trails. Esther and I came here from Ciudad Blanca a few years after my wife Miriam died. It was then that I bought this small farm."

"Father, tell me about our family," Esther broke in. "You never talk to me about them."

Reuben stopped, apparently stricken by the intensity of his daughter's emotion. He looked as if a realization had just dawned upon him. Then he responded. "It is only because Samuel is here that I have the courage to speak of the past. For all these years, I have been unable to tell you of our family because every time I start, I think of your mother, Miriam. The pain of losing her is still too much and I cannot continue."

Esther sat forward in her chair and with a pained look asked, "Father, please, please try."

"Bear with me, my dear *Hita*, and I will do my best. Our family is descended from the Spaniards, who settled

New Spain. They were mostly men because few women would come to such a wild place. Marrying Indian women, their offspring became the New Mexican northerners or Nortenos. They wanted only to be of Spanish descent and so denied their Indian heritage."

"But father, what you're telling us is merely history. Everyone knows that. What I wish to know is the history of our family."

"*Estherlita,* my love, please have patience. I am just warming to my subject. It is hard for me to talk of *our* family.

"These people settled in northern New Mexico and call themselves Nortenos, distinguishing themselves from others of Spanish origin, rejecting the idea that they were Mexicans. After the Americans began their domination of this region, the Nortenos maintained their independence with an identity of their own. They were always distinct from the Spaniards and the Indians, although they incorporated by marriage many of each. Our family was part of that group."

Samuel watched Esther's smile of anticipation, as her father approached the subject she had for so long sought to hear.

"For many generations, our family lived in Ciudad Blanca, a small city some twenty-five miles northwest of here. We lived on a large *hacienda,* where I was born and worked until my parents died. As a child born into a Norteno family, I grew up with all of the customs of our people. Our family pretended to be good Catholics, but in private, we were always hostile to the Church. In our family, there were many things that one did not discuss with strangers, but because this seems to be the only way I am able to communicate with my daughter, I must take the risk and trust you, Samuel." He looked around the room, appearing fearful that someone might overhear. "But since you are a Jew and must keep other secrets, I trust that ours will be safe with you."

Samuel felt something strange draw him to this family.

"There has long been a story told in our family," continued Reuben, "that we came from Spain but were not Spanish. But the matter was always treated in a secretive fashion. Unfortunately, many stories of my family were not told to me, as they regarded me as too unreliable to be entrusted with family secrets. I had two older brothers, Aaron, the eldest, followed by Jacobo. Aaron inherited the farm and owned it until his death. The eldest always inherited the land, because dividing the estate would force everyone into poverty. Life from farming is difficult unless a farm is large. Both of my brothers are long dead, but I have nieces and nephews in Ciudad Blanca, most of whom I have not seen since I came to La Rosa. From time to time, I learn of family events. Aaron had no sons, so his eldest daughter, Rachel, has inherited the farm. Today she and her husband, Arturo Mendoza, run it.

"After my father's death, the family purchased a farm for Jacobo. When I left Ciudad Blanca for La Rosa, the family helped me buy this small farm. I make a meager living growing the foods we use, raising a few sheep, selling or trading our small surplus of wool, and doing a little carpentry on my neighbors' homes and barns. For our other needs, I am handy. I can butcher in the way of our family, repair acequias, make adobe bricks, and do most of the trades required here."

"Why have you never told me these things, my father?" interrupted Esther. Her face showed her distress.

"Hita, my darling," he paused, a pained look spreading over his face. "I just could not do it before and don't know why I am telling you now. Perhaps it is because I am talking to you through a stranger. It is too difficult to sit and talk to you about your mother and our families. For me, life was wonderful with Miriam. Her death was a tragedy I just could not bear. I tried to blot out the memories because of the pain. Everything in Ciudad Blanca reminded me of her. I could not deal with the loss of my beloved." His face reflected his agony as he struggled to get his words out. "With a small child, it was irresponsible to just pine away. The family insisted that I come out of my grief. When I told them I could not go on living in

Ciudad Blanca, they looked around, located this farm, and helped me to resettle here.

"Life was easier away from Ciudad Blanca and its memories, but it was just too painful to even talk about my loss until today." He looked over at his daughter. "Please, forgive me, Ita, my darling. I never meant to keep knowledge of our family from you."

Holding back tears, Esther responded, "Even after listening, I still don't know how to deal with this. I've always been a dutiful daughter, but my unhappiness over your failure to tell me of our family is beyond my control. I have a right to know and hate feeling so alone."

"You are right," Reuben acknowledged. "Hiding the past from you has not been fair. I will do my best to tell you now. I do not know much more of the ancient history of our family, but we go back for many generations in Spain. Our family was more intellectual than most. Both boys and girls learned to read and write, while most folks here ignored education. We had a fine library, although it was rare for a family to own many books."

He paused, then continued with a pained look on his face. "As a young man, I learned to read and write in Spanish. Since there were few *norteamericanos* in our area, English was not necessary. But I learned that language anyway. Over the years, the wealth of our family diminished with the difficulties of farming. Many valuable family possessions were sold, including most of our books. Little remains of the past. Except for pride, our family is as poor as the rest.

"I knew that the farm would be left to my eldest brother, so I did not care about the future. Although I was not so responsible as a youth, I was a talented artisan, and could do almost anything with my hands and could make enough money for my needs."

He looked up at his guest as he continued. "Except for a half dozen families, we never mingled with others. Most of our free time was spent with the Caches, Mendozas, Lopes, Suerates, Huertados, and Reals, like a large family with most marriages arranged within the group. Mine with Miriam brought me close to her family, the Caches."

He paused and looked off into the air as if viewing the past. "I remember when Aaron took me aside and told me the family wished to arrange a marriage between Miriam and myself. At first, it was humorous, as I knew of her only as a young girl, eight years younger than I. That afternoon, I walked over to her house and hid among the trees. It seemed like hours before she came out. I saw her with new eyes, no longer a scrawny girl, but the most beautiful woman I had ever seen. Her eyes shone with excitement. Smitten, I was in love and that love never ended. It continues to this day."

Reuben paused. "When I married Miriam, I gave up the ways of a single youth and settled down. I loved her more than anything else in life except for you, Esther. You look so much like your mother. I see her in your eyes, in your walk, and in everything you do. You are a constant reminder of that dear woman."

Esther lowered her head into her hands to hide her tears.

"After we were married, she told me more about our families. The Carvello family secrets had not been previously related to me, as I was the youngest of the children. They had been handed down to the more responsible members of the family. Miriam was entrusted with many of the secrets of the Carvellos, as well as those of the Caches, but unfortunately, she died before telling me much of our history.

"I have a mixture of memories from Miriam and my grandparents. Some came from old stories and others are just a collection of things that confuse me. I frequently dream about a past that I'm never sure really existed. It frightens me, so I try to ignore my dreams. I don't think our family's standoffish attitude was due to any claim of Spanish blood, for we never had the Castilian arrogance. My ancestors were stiff-necked and proud but never arrogant. I sometimes enjoy a glass of wine but I do not sit and drink with the villagers.

"But, Senor Samuel," he said, looking into the peddler's eyes, "what is strangest of all is that I despise bullfighting. Imagine, a Norteno who despises bullfighting."
He paused to join in with the laughter of Esther and
Samuel. "The idea of grown men attempting to show
their bravery by baiting those dumb beasts is repugnant to
me. Treating bullfighters as brave and noble is the height
of stupidity. I suppose that if one cannot accept bullfighting and the ridiculous philosophy built around it, he cannot be a true Spaniard. But I always had doubts as to my
ancestry. We have always been different."

Esther, who had been curled up in the chair quietly
listening to her father, spoke out, "What you say may be
true, Father. But as I was just a two-year-old when we left
Ciudad Blanca, I remember nothing. I've never spoken to
you in anger, but it was cruel of you not to have kept in
touch with our relatives and friends in Ciudad Blanca.
I do so wish to have family and friends."

She sat up rigid in her chair, feet on the floor, her
small hands clenched in her lap. "I don't believe myself
to be different from the rest. Because you look down on
the villagers, I have no social life. I am caught between a
past that you have cut off and a present that barely exists
among the poor farm families of La Rosa. I love you dearly
but resent what you have done to me." She hung her
head, staring into her lap.

"Hita, I am sorry that as a widower left to raise a small
child, I was not able to do better. Your mother, a wonderful woman, was a great help to me, after our marriage,
she saw to it that I became a different person. I was
twenty-five, and she a mere seventeen, but even at that
young age, she had more good sense in dealing with people than I. She changed me and I enjoyed that change.
While I kept a steady job, we were able to save money and
plan for a home and a family. You were to have been the
delight of our lives as you still are in my eyes. But as you
came into this world your mother departed."

He paused, as if it was painful to continue. "When
she died in childbirth, I lost the will to continue.

Everyone was kind and helpful but I just could not deal with my despair. I fled and took you with me to La Rosa, running away from everything. There were too many memories of life with Miriam back in Ciudad Blanca. Trying to bury the memories might have been a mistake. Hopefully, I can make it up to you." With tears in his eyes, he added, "Had your mother lived, your life would have been much more fulfilling."

The two looked at each other without a word. Samuel, ill at ease, excused himself to check on his burro. After freshening Manny's water and giving her a nightcap of some hay, he took time for his evening prayers. Overcoming his discomfort, he returned to his hosts.

On his way in, he heard Reuben say, "Don't condemn me, my daughter, for not knowing how to deal with a situation that overwhelmed me. I did the best I could. Perhaps it wasn't good enough. If so, I am sorry."

She paused for a long moment, then stood, walked over to her father, and embraced him. "I'm sorry, too. Sorry that I doubted you and became angry."

Samuel looked over at his hosts, the lovely young woman chiding her father for his failure to tell her of their past. Was this really his predestined place? Was this truly bashert?

A New Way of Life

CHAPTER NINE

S amuel's peddling flourished as he returned with new merchandise. He came back to La Rosa every week, staying with Reuben and Esther. The Carvellos lived a quiet, routine life until the presence of their new friend led to change. Not only did they provide him with shelter against the elements, but also their home became his home. As Reuben would accept no money, Samuel always brought special gifts back from Las Vegas to add convenience and, sometimes, beauty to their home and to repay them for their hospitality.

One afternoon in late November as Reuben and Samuel talked on the veranda, Esther came out with a tray of coffee. As the three relaxed, sipping the hot beverages, Reuben asked, "Now that Hannah may soon be here, have you given any thought to your future?"

"I've never considered anything beyond bringing Momma and Poppa over. In the two months I've been peddling here, I've paid off some of my debt for merchandise to Mordecai as well as some of the money he lent me to bring Hannah to America. I still owe him for Manny, but that amount goes down each month. With a few dollars saved for supplies and emergencies and some money sent home, I guess life is going as well as can be expected."

Something in this innocuous conversation triggered his repressed dreams. Perhaps contemplating Hannah's coming, the success of his peddling, and the pleasant life with the Cohens and Carvellos made this quiet afternoon an opportune time for Samuel to air his hopes.

"I've traveled thousands of miles since leaving New York two years ago. I'm tired of walking and would like to spend less time traveling to and from Las Vegas." He smiled and added, "That would allow me to spend more pleasant evenings here. Someday I'd like to accumulate a little stock. But I would have to acquire a wagon and a place to store some goods to really build my business. Then I could travel greater distances without having to return so often to Las Vegas. Now, with so little carrying space, the best I can do is to buy or trade for some Indian jewelry and a few small pelts. But there are large furs and Indian woolens available, if there were room to carry them. Since I don't sell on credit, trading would fit in well. Cash is scarce out here, but folks always have something to exchange. My business would grow since trade consists of two transactions, a sale and a purchase, with a profit on each. Without a wagon or a storage place, it's impossible. But as long as I am talking about my dreams, maybe someday I might have a wagon and a storage building. Then with a little luck, I might open a little store and settle down. My customers could come to me, instead of me going to them one at a time."

Samuel paused, realizing that he had let his dreams take the place of reality. "But forget it. These are only daydreams on a pleasant afternoon. In reality, the best I'll be able to do is reduce my debts, spend a little money on myself, and send a few dollars home. Who knows when I'll be able to send enough money home to bring Momma and Poppa over?" Samuel's musings ended as suddenly as they had surfaced and he went back to sipping his coffee in silence.

The next morning at breakfast, Reuben said, "Senor Samuel, if it would not offend you, I might be of some help. I have never thought of it before we talked yesterday, but there is a building out back that has been used for storage where you could keep your extra goods. Also, there's an old broken-down wagon that could be repaired."

They walked behind the house where, with some effort, Reuben opened the shed door. There inside,

Samuel saw the abandoned wagon. It was the decrepit remains of its original self, but to the peddler's eyes, it was the most beautiful vehicle he had ever seen.

That day Reuben began rebuilding the wagon. In his frayed *serape* and wide brimmed *sombrero,* he worked from early morning until late at night. Even for as skilled a carpenter as he was, the task took a week of steady work.

When it was finished, Reuben and Samuel wheeled the wagon out of the storage building. At her first sight of it, Manny brayed in protest, giving vent to her displeasure with the new contraption. But Samuel's patient cajoling won her over and soon she pulled it comfortably.

In early December, Samuel took the wagon out for its first run. As Manny pulled the wagon up to Cohen's Main Street Emporium, Mordecai and Alfred came out to view the patched-up vehicle. The merchant, excited because he had a letter from Russia for his friend, anticipated that Alfred would make a jest at the peddler's expense over his new vehicle. Mordecai cut him short, handing Samuel the letter. "Say, here's some mail. I see you're moving up in the world. Look at that fancy wagon, just like the one I had when I was peddling out in the country." Then turning to Alfred, he ordered, "Take good care of Mr. Rabinowitz. Give him enough credit to fill that wagon. He's rapidly becoming one of our best customers."

Samuel beamed as he headed back that afternoon to La Rosa with a wagon filled to capacity. Although anxious to read the letter, he waited until he reached a rest stop where he opened and read it.

> *Dear Sholom,*
>
> *Thanks be to God. We received your letter with the money and I purchased my steamship ticket. Things are getting worse in Belkov and your money came just in time. It is taking longer and becoming harder to leave Russia, especially since Nathan left. But if everything goes as planned, I should be in Las Vegas in about three months, just before Passover. We cannot thank the*

Cohens enough for their help. It seems like such a miracle to me that I will, with God's help, soon be looking into the face of my oldest brother again. Momma and Poppa send their love.

> *Your sister,*
> *Hannah.*

Relieved that the money had arrived safely, Samuel was thrilled, as he had achieved his first goal. Putting these happy thoughts of Hannah aside, he still wanted more answers about why Nathan had left home. However, he breathed a sigh of relief. Soon he would see his sister.

At La Rosa, Reuben and Esther helped unload the burgeoning wagon. They stored the excess merchandise in the newly repaired shed, leaving the wagon stocked for the next peddling trip.

That evening Samuel wrote home.

> *Dear Momma and Poppa,*
> *Thanks be to God, Hannah is on her way. We seem to be a step closer to coming together again as a family. Things are going well here, first with Mordecai's help and now Reuben's.*

Then he explained about how the Carvellos had befriended him and how Reuben helped him by providing the wagon and the shed.

> *I'm blessed to have such good friends. Until I met the Carvellos, I never had any close Gentile friends. In Belkov and in my travels in America, I've had plenty of Gentile customers, but I never really got to know any of them. At most I shared a meal and spent a night with them. For the first time in my life, I have really come to understand that in America, all peoples are the same. It took me a long time to learn that lesson. And now I have.*
> *I hope to soon be able to send enough money for you to come here. What I am lacking in my ever-changing life is the warmth and stability of my family and the home I know we can create together.*

> *Love,*
> *Sholom*

Returning from peddling a week later, Samuel saw
Esther standing in front of the house, waving to him. She
called out, "I've made a great sale. Some farmers going to
de Navarro's store in Ciudad Blanca stopped in and asked
for you. They said that they had heard many good things
about you and wanted to find out for themselves.

"Father was turning them away when I came up and
told them, 'If you'd like to see Samuel's goods, I'll show
them to you.' Displaying your merchandise and telling
them the prices, I sold them over ten dollars' worth." She
held up a handful of bills and coins.

Excited over Esther's making the sale, the young
peddler hugged her, exclaiming, "You're wonderful!" She
blushed as he continued, "You must share my good fortune and keep half of the profits."

"Senor Samuel," said Reuben, "I am pleased that my
Esther was bold enough to undertake the sale, but we
cannot take money from you, our friend."

Esther nodded her agreement and added, "But please
send some extra money home to help bring your parents
here."

Samuel said, "I will, but it's not fair for you to take
nothing. You did the selling." Then an exciting thought
struck him. "We must become partners!"

Esther and Reuben stared at him as if they thought he
had gone mad.

"Why not? Carvello and Rabinowitz."

The two continued to gaze at him, as if now they were
sure he had lost his wits.

"Listen! We can turn the shed into a store. I'll run it
when not out selling. At other times, Esther can be the
storekeeper. She just showed us what a great job she can
do. Look, it's your shed and my supplies. We'll all help
out as partners."

Looking dazed at the sudden turn of events and uncertain as to what they should do, the father and daughter
finally acquiesced.

And so on a bright sunny day, December 17, 1886,
they raised a sign reading *Carvello and Rabinowitz*

General Merchandise over a shed in the New Mexican desert, and a new enterprise was born.

After the partnership began, none of them worked as hard as Reuben. For years, he had done only what was needed to get by: maintain his home, tend his few acres, feed his farm animals, and do an occasional carpentry job. Now with a goal in life, he was driven. Early each day he could be found working on the old storage building with his two young helpers, Juan and Jaime, the sons of his next door neighbors, Raphael and Maria Lopez. The boys dug out clay from a pit near the river and mixed sand, straw, and manure into it. Then they carried the mixture in a wheelbarrow up to a sunny area where Reuben removed the cement and shaped it into adobe bricks. He put these into a wooden frame and placed them in the hot sun to bake. When baked solid, the bricks were broken free from the mold and the excess clay trimmed away. The helpers piled the finished bricks near the shed, where they were put into thick adobe walls that would insulate the growing building from the heat of summer and the cold of winter.

Putting a roof over the new addition called for Reuben and his two helpers to go up into the high mountains, where the tall pines grew. They sought out solid timber to be *vigas*, the supporting members of the roof. After cutting down the trees, they carted them back in a mule-drawn cart that Reuben had borrowed from his neighbor, Raphael Lopez. Then they trimmed the timbers and placed them as the rafters into notched slots at the top of the adobe walls. They cross-covered the vigas with *latillas*, stripped pine or aspen branches. Then they used pieces of bark and cedar wood to fill the spaces. Finally, with an adobe-like plaster made principally of mud, they sealed the crevices. Reuben and his helpers slowly expanded the shed until it became a fair-sized store by the end of December.

When Samuel was off on his next trip in early January, Reuben surprised him by building onto the rear of the store a fairly large room with a place for a desk and chair

as well as a bed. This became an office and living quarters
for Samuel. Reuben even made the furniture: a bed, two
chairs, and a desk. When the peddler returned a week
later, he was overwhelmed. For the first time since he
came to America, he had a home of his own.

One morning in late January 1887, Samuel returned
from Las Vegas and Esther and Reuben noticed him standing at the doorway of the new addition with a hammer
and nails. Curious, they walked over to him. He put
down his hammer and looked at them. Proudly he pointed to a small metallic container, which he had just finished nailing to the doorframe. "This is a *mezuzah*. It
marks a Jewish home. Every Jew puts one on the doorpost
of his home. It contains a parchment scroll inside its
metal casing with special words from the Torah. The
Hebrew letter on the front is a *shin*, the first letter of the
first word of the Hebrew prayer which begins, *"Shema
Yisrael, Adonai Elohaynu, Adonai Echod;"* Hear O Israel, the
Lord is our God, the Lord is One. These words are the
watchwords of my faith. Now that I have a home with
you, my wanderings are over."

"Senor Samuel, helping to make a home for you has
created more of a home for Esther and me," added
Reuben. "La Rosa has become closer to my heart because
we are here together."

As that night was Shabbes, Esther had prepared a fine
meal of chicken soup together with roast chicken. She
had learned about Jewish cooking from recipes Bertha had
sent her. Candles were lit and after Samuel said his
prayers, he added, "In this new land, it is difficult, if not
impossible, for a Jewish peddler to observe Shabbes, for he
has to respect the Sabbath of his Christian neighbors.
This means not working two days in each week. When I
was only peddling, I always did my best to finish off my
work within five long days. But since the store opened,
Saturday became the most important selling day of the
week. I no longer have any choice but to work. I appreciate your efforts to provide me with the best Shabbes possible. In the same way, I've sought to keep kosher in a

world without Jewish butchers, but that was impossible. I have watched Reuben slaughter animals — as he describes it, 'butchering in the way of his family' — and it is almost the same as Jewish ritual butchering. Eating meat from animals butchered by Reuben is like eating kosher meat."

After dinner, they sat and relaxed. As always, Friday night was special. The three talked late into the night about the materials Samuel brought back from his journey on the road. These were usually old newspapers or magazines or a book borrowed from the store's lending library.

As Samuel educated himself, he taught the Carvellos. First Esther had taken her turn at reading aloud. Then Reuben joined in. Samuel usually had something to read like *The New Colossus*, a poem by Emma Lazarus, a newspaper story about pogroms in Russia and Romania, *Huckleberry Finn*, a new book by Mark Twain, or *Treasure Island* by Robert Louis Stevenson. Esther was enthralled and delighted as a new world opened for her.

Less than a week after he settled into his new home, Samuel was sitting at his desk when he felt something brush up against his leg. It was a little gray-striped kitten, which had apparently just left her mother. The kitten purred and rubbed against him and then allowed Samuel to pick her up. Barely a handful, her pretty yellow eyes looked into his. Her message was that she sought a home.

"I guess you've adopted me," acknowledged Samuel.

He went into the kitchen of the house and came back with food and water. She hungrily ate and drank and when at last she was satisfied, she found a corner on the desk and curled up to sleep.

Samuel looked fondly at her. "We must have a name for you." He rubbed his finger over the marking on her forehead. "You have a little crown and act like a queen. Your name shall be Malka, for in Hebrew that means queen."

From that day on, they were inseparable. The kitten traveled with Samuel in the wagon and slept by his side. One night when he was out on the road, the young peddler set up camp as usual, feeding Manny and Malka, building a fire, and completing his evening prayers. As he sat down after a warm meal to read the paper, Malka cuddled in his lap.

Samuel soon became comfortable and fell asleep. Suddenly awakened by a cat meowing and biting his neck, he impatiently brushed her away. Alerted by Malka's bites and Manny's braying, he opened his eyes and saw flames. The fire had spread to his blanket and was close to his pack. Jumping up, he pulled the pack out of the way and smothered the flaming blanket in the sand. No real harm was done thanks to the persistence of Malka and Manny. Had they not been there, Samuel might have lost his life. Manny received special care and extra food, while Malka accepted his pats with regal dignity.

A few days later, Samuel told Reuben, "Look, you and Esther are my partners, yet you refuse to come with me to Las Vegas to purchase goods. I've been trying for some time to get you to go to there. Now I must insist you come, for if anything were to happen to me, you and Esther must be able to handle that part of the business by yourselves."

"I'm an old man and hate to travel. Do it without me," replied Reuben.

"You are not old," answered Esther, "but have just made yourself old by hiding, to mourn my mother's death. Hiding away in La Rosa for so long, you really believe that you're not able to travel. In fairness to me, end this charade, for without you, as an unmarried Norteno woman, I cannot go to Las Vegas."

Finally, Reuben consented.

On February 4, 1887, the three rode into Las Vegas. Reuben expressed surprise. "I have't been here for many years and was not prepared for the changes to the town. I can't believe the size of Cohen's Main Street Emporium, with such a magnificent stock of goods. I have never seen so many fancy dresses and expensive saddles."

Esther laughed. "We could never sell those. Our customers would not make enough in a year to buy such fancy goods."

But they selected many inexpensive items that Samuel had never before considered selling. Esther and Reuben's suggestions added a new perspective for Samuel.

When Samuel introduced them, Mordecai looked at Esther and gave her a fatherly hug. "You must call me Uncle, for Mordecai is the uncle of Esther." Seeing her quizzical look, the storekeeper continued, "We Jews have a festival called *Purim,* which is described in our holy scriptures and celebrates Queen Esther's saving the Jewish people. Well, her uncle is Mordecai."

"We Nortenos have a feast of Saint Esther, where a young woman saves her people," added Esther. "Perhaps the two are related."

"With your name you have come to the right tribe. Your ancestors must have felt a kinship with the Jewish people in choosing your name."

Reuben paused and added, "You know I never thought much about it. Esther's name is common in our family. We use a great many biblical names, mostly from the Old Testament."

"Come to Las Vegas at Purim, which is next month. You should see what a Jewish festival is like," said Mordecai.

While picking out new merchandise, Esther called out to her father, "Look, *trompitas.* Norteno children like these. Shall we take some back to the store to sell?"

Samuel picked up the toy and carefully examined it. "But these are *dreidels.*" Again, he looked carefully at it. "It is strange. We Jews have a four-sided top as opposed to this one with six sides. How does one play with it?"

"The trompita is spun," Esther replied. "The side that is up indicates whether the player shall take out or put into the pot."

Samuel looked over in amazement. "That is the same game we play on *Channukah* with a four-sided wooden toy with Hebrew letters which we call a dreidel."

Mordecai, overhearing the conversation, said, "Since I have been in the Southwest, I have noticed many similarities between our people and the Nortenos. Perhaps it is a coincidence or maybe those stories we hear about some of them having descended from Jews are true."

Reuben and Esther, perplexed, looked at each other as Reuben said, "Who knows what has happened in the past?"

It was growing late. The three packed up and prepared to leave.

Mordecai looked at them and said, "Esther and Reuben, I'm pleased to meet you after all I have heard. You're good people and a family for my friend. Because of this, you are also my friends."

As they rode home, Samuel recounted his blessings to himself. "*Life is going so well that it frightens me. I can only pray to God that it continues.*"

Evil Afoot

CHAPTER TEN

*T*he sunset behind the San Juan Mountains cast a lonely shadow over the little pueblo of La Rosa, New Mexico as its orange hue faded and darkness drew in on this cool February evening. There was a squawking of birds, suddenly so disturbed that they flew up from their perches in the pinion trees, uttering a warning which violated the stillness of evening.

Hearing their cries of distress, Esther stepped out onto the portico of the small general store and sought out its source. In the distance, obscured by twilight, she saw a dust cloud that signaled horses galloping down along the trail from Ciudad Blanca. She called out over her shoulder. "Father, the last two customers are leaving. Should we close the store?"

After a moment, Reuben's soft voice drifted out to her. "Yes, my darling Ita. I will be ready to go home as soon as I finish sweeping."

The sound of hoof beats caught her attention. She looked back towards the trail and saw horses coming closer, riding hard down the pass through the pines, junipers, and pinions that covered the mountainside. She noticed the horses with their fancy leather saddles, and knew that the horses bore *desperados,* not farmers. A bolt of fear paralyzed her when she saw faces masked by bandannas and foreheads obscured by broad-brimmed sombreros. As they came close, she froze at the sight of drawn revolvers.

Reuben came up alongside. "What can these riders want?"

The horsemen came to an abrupt halt at the top of a small rise. Esther heard a voice through the quiet air as the men circled their leader, the one with the largest horse, the biggest sombrero, and the most splendid serape. He pointed down at the little store. "Hey hombres, this is it, the Jew's store. Senor de Navarro says to smash their windows! Shoot! Break everything! We do what *el Patron* wants us to do. *Verdad?*"

A shout rose from the riders as they charged furiously down the hill, firing in the air. "Christ-killers! Jew-devils!"

The two customers were terrified. One, a tall scare-crow-like figure, nervously mounted his horse and the other, a short, squat man standing by his wagon, jumped up, and they both fled.

Struck with disbelief, Esther stood her ground. She held her head high, and with her hands on her hips and fire in her eyes, she faced the approaching riders. Reuben dropped his broom and ran towards the house. Esther could not believe that he had abandoned her.

The *caballeros* dismounted in front of the store and swaggered onto the portico. One shoved Esther aside as he entered the store. "Out of the way you stupid woman!"

Much smaller than her oppressor, Esther stumbled and fell to the ground. Shocked, she placed her scraped hands under her body, regained her balance and rose to her feet. She watched the devastation with tears in her eyes.

A second desperado pushed over the counter and the display case, scattering tobacco and candy. The leader laughed and ordered, "Leave nothing for the dirty Jews."

Another desperado pulled down the shelves. Jars of preserved fruit smashed to the floor, their contents spilling out onto bolts of bright gingham. "This all right, *patron?*"

A thug in a white sombrero swept his arm over a shelf, hurling flour, thimbles, sugar, needles, salt, and soap all about. Another knocked over barrels of oats and corn, and they disgorged their contents. Laughing as their dem-olition contest continued, the desperados dumped potatoes, apples, and onions from the buckets in front of the store onto the ground.

Overcoming her initial panic, Esther cried out, "My God, what can I do? What can I do? Stop! Stop! Please, you must not wreck our store!"

They ignored her plea and the devastation continued. Mounting rage overcame Esther's fear. Unable to restrain herself any longer, she grabbed the leader of the thugs and scratched his face in a vain attempt to halt the destruction. He had little difficulty in pushing her away. She fell to the floor amidst the wreckage and broken glass.

The leader ordered his men back to their horses. "Let's leave, but first," he paused to pick up a rock, "let's finish off the Christ killers' store!" His missile shattered the first of the two windows, leaving slivers of glass. A shower of rocks followed, pulverizing the second window into thousands of sparkling crystals.

Anger welled up inside Esther as she ignored the cuts her face had received from flying glass. She called out, "You devils! Get out of here!" and waved her fist as tears flowed down her cheeks.

Armed with an ancient hunting rifle, Reuben came out of the house. Like a Spanish nobleman, he aimed and fired. The recoil of the gun rocked him back on his heels as the musket ball traveled over the heads of the horsemen.

Esther covered her eyes with her hands, unable to bear seeing any harm befall her father. A moment later, looking out to see if she could help, she saw a desperado lift his revolver and take aim at Reuben.

But, before he could fire, the leader shoved his arm aside. Holding up his hand, he brought his men to a halt. *"Tonto!* Idiot! I said no killing. We've done our work. Now, let's *vamoose!"*

A final volley of bullets completed the devastation. As quickly as they had appeared, the riders vanished into the darkness of night.

The freshly whitewashed building was pockmarked with bullet holes, giving it a sinister look. The windows, devoid of glass, gaped. The bullet-riddled sign, proclaiming *Carvello and Rabinowitz - General Merchandise,* lay face down in the dust.

Esther's fears subsided as she cried out, "We're alive! We're alive! Somehow we've not been killed. What's happened to us must have been a visitation from the devil! He and his minions are now on their way back to Hell!"

Reuben came over. "Hita, my darling child, your face is bleeding. I am sorry I could not find my gun sooner."

"Don't worry father, I've only a few scratches. But my heart aches for poor Samuel. Is he ever to find peace and contentment? I hoped he could find it here, after all his travels. But is that still possible?" Soothed by Reuben's comforting embrace, Esther regained control of her trembling body. "Thank God we're not hurt. Now let's clean up this mess."

They set to work, sweeping up smashed glass and gathering damaged merchandise. Esther put all the goods that could be salvaged back on the uprighted shelves. Within a few hours Reuben restored the sign to its proper place and boarded up the open spaces that had been windows.

Esther moved quickly, concerned that the store be put back together before Samuel returned. "I can't bear to have Samuel see the destruction of his work. Everything in the store was so precious and new."

That night, hours after the raid, they heard the rattling of Samuel's wagon. He climbed down, and in the moonlight saw Esther's bandaged face and Reuben with his ancient rifle. "What happened?"

"I was closing up," answered Reuben, "when six masked riders descended upon us and began shouting terrible things about your people. They smashed the windows, pulled down the shelves, knocked over the counter, and tossed merchandise all about. Like a tornado, they wrecked everything and left."

"No one was hurt," Esther assured Samuel. "I've only got a few small cuts. These bandages make it look worse than it is. Father shot off his gun to scare them away. It will be all right."

Samuel saw her brown eyes seek out his. He looked at her pretty face and her long black hair.

Shaken, he sat down, lowered his head into his hands, and wept. Samuel struggled to regain his composure. "Please forgive me. Memories of Russian pogroms float through my mind. I never allowed myself to imagine that anything so terrible could occur in America, not in 1887."

"You must not forget that this is a primitive region," said Reuben. "Since the Spanish left, both the Mexican and American governments ignored us as too far away and too unimportant. American soldiers came only a few years ago. And it was only last month that the Federal Government sent us a Marshal. But he is only one man and is twenty-five miles away in Ciudad Blanca. Even though this is rough country, this violence will never happen to us again. My rifle will always be at my side."

"I'm not afraid for myself. My concern is over the two of you being hurt because you're partners with a Jew," said Samuel, with a pained look. "You both mean so much to me. Maybe it's a mistake on your part. My friends, my dear friends, I couldn't continue to live if I've brought harm to either of you. Thanks be to God, you're not hurt."

"They had no intention of harming us," declared Esther. "Their leader said that de Navarro gave orders not to kill us. He must not succeed in using hatred of Jews as an excuse to drive out competition. The damage can be repaired. I've swept up the debris and put back the stock. Father put the shelves back up and boarded the windows. After a while, we'll be able to replace everything that's been ruined. It will be difficult but we can do it. We must do it!

"Please Samuel, don't be afraid for us. Don't give up! This is different from pogroms and other dangers your family faces at home. America may not be perfect but it's far better than Russia. Here your family will have a chance. Remember, they are depending on you. We must concentrate on rebuilding, to help you send for them."

Morning sunshine poured into Father Sullivan's study. The priest sat at his rough plank desk, slowly thumbing through his tattered bible, praying for inspiration for some powerful new subject for his Sunday sermon. He sighed and decided to dredge up his old standby, the parable about the Good Samaritan.

Suddenly, the door burst open. Louisa, his housekeeper, filled the doorway, breathing heavily. Her face, red with exertion and excitement, amplified her sharp features.

"Father, *oh Dios mio...*"

The priest rose quickly, "Calm yourself, Louisa. Breathe easy." He guided her gently to his desk. "Come sit in my chair and gather your wits."

Louisa dropped into the hard chair. Between gasps of air she delivered the news of the attack on the little store in La Rosa. Under the guise of duty she told him everything. "*Padre,* de Navarro's men have just come back from La Rosa, boasting about their trip to the Jew merchants, Carvello and Rabinowitz. You know that new store the peddler and his friends set up about two months ago? De Navarro's men broke up the Christ-killers' store real good, even smashing the windows." Adding details as if she had personally participated in the raid, Louisa smirked as if expecting a compliment for a job well done in delivering the news.

The priest's face flushed with rage, not merely at the news, but more at her delight in delivering it. Usually the fifty-year-old cleric would have preferred to read without being disturbed. He would simply ignore her gossip, but this time it was not possible. He could not help but be concerned with the barbarity of the attack. "No one deserves such a raid. What has the poor peddler done? Who has he hurt? I have heard that he is a fair and generous man. Much more so than many Catholics in this parish. 'Tis probably the reason they vandalized his store. I am ashamed at your joy at this horrid act."

Surprised, the housekeeper stepped back.

Rising, he walked toward Louisa, his face reddened with anger. "And what of Salvadore de Navarro? His vile acts do not make him the agent of God, or of the Catholic Church. If anything, he represents evil. I have fought him without success since he began exploiting our people years ago."

"But, Padre," she protested, slinking out of the room, "that's not how they see it in the town."

"God give me strength!" exclaimed the priest. "How stupid can people be? Who in this town could believe that man after what he has done to them? This reminds me of Ireland at the time of the great potato famine. De Navarro is just another oppressor doing to poor Mexicans what the English did to my people long ago."

He paused and sat back down in his chair. *"There is no time left to think about it. I must not allow that villain to become a hero by acting out his hatred of Jews, sanctioned by this Spanish Church. If he destroys Rabinowitz, who will be able to stand up against him?"*

The clock struck ten. He had lost track of the hour. Time for Mass. Hurriedly he composed himself, put on a white vestment, tied his cincture, and proceeded into the church. Holding a large cross, he led a procession from the main door, followed by two altar boys. Then walking up the stairs, he placed the cross in its holder and went to the altar.

Father Sullivan found it difficult to concentrate on his rituals. He began with the traditional Latin prayer that announced his going unto the altar of God to begin the Mass. *"Et introib ad altare Dei."* After finishing the *Kyrie,* he crossed himself and turned to face his flock. He noticed the faded drawings of the Stations of the Cross on the walls, as well as the eager faces of his congregants. As he walked toward the old wooden pulpit, he realized that there were more important things to say than had been planned.

He looked out at his congregation. Recognizing the forty or so people who attended that morning, having baptized or married virtually all of them, he watched his audience restlessly straightening up in their seats and looking up at the altar.

Abandoning his prepared text, Father Sullivan began. "Let me remind you of last Easter Sunday's sermon. I don't wish to repeat that sermon." Again, pausing to look

out at the parishioners, he saw their reactions, first looking at him, then turning their gazes away as they adjusted
themselves in their pews. He didn't mind making them
uncomfortable.

As if in a dream, Father Sullivan remembered how as a
small boy, with an elderly priest taking his hand, he had
left a shabby house — then empty — never to return, his
family and home gone. After a moment of silence, Father
Sullivan snapped back to the present, trembling with the
realization that his stand could lead to censure.

Conscious of the long Church tradition of blaming the
Jews for the crucifixion of Christ, the priest determined
that it was now necessary to end that vile doctrine in his
parish. It had been harmless in a region without Jews, but
now, it might be claiming victims. More important to
him, it was being used as an excuse by de Navarro.

"The scriptures speak of Christ being crucified by
Roman soldiers. Except for those soldiers, everyone there
was Jewish. Christ himself was a Jew. I would have you
know that there were no Mexicans or Irish in Jerusalem at
the time Jesus was crucified."

Having captured the imagination of his flock by pro-
jecting them back into Biblical times, he forged ahead.
"The crucifixion of Christ was clearly the act of Roman
soldiers under Roman law. It was not the Jews who
ordered this punishment, even though they had rejected
Jesus as their Messiah. When our Savior died, He took
the sins of Man upon Himself. The Lord would never
excuse violence against innocent persons under the guise
of blaming the Jews."

He paused, again looking out at his congregation.
"We have amongst us, dear friends, some who would
approve of the vicious attack upon a little store that took
place at La Rosa a few days ago. This was done in the
name of Jew-hatred, as if condoned by our God. But the
Lord commands that we love one another. He has
instructed us to oppose violence. He will not tolerate
these actions occurring again!"

Looking out at the stunned faces, he slowly turned his back to the parishioners to finish the Mass. Hearing gasps from his audience, he hoped that they might accept his view of de Navarro's violence. Although speaking frequently of the suffering of Jesus, he had never talked to them of this type of violent religious hatred.

The congregation began to whisper. He knew that by tomorrow the town would be filled with talk. Except for his condemnation of violence, his comments were a radical departure from the position of his Church. But this stand must be taken if there was to be any chance of saving the people of Ciudad Blanca from de Navarro.

Hoping that his homily had had its desired effect, Father Sullivan speculated that those who reveled in the actions of de Navarro's thugs might now have second thoughts. Could the Church's position on violence offset its assertion of Jewish blame for the death of Christ? Could they be pondering whether to accept his version of the death of Christ, rather than the Jew-hating version they had been raised with? Could they be asking themselves, *"Was Father right in chastising us? Were de Navarro's acts evil?"*

Early the next morning the priest was walking from his church back to the rectory when a voice called out, "Howdy, Padre." A tough-looking Anglo, with a low-slung revolver peeking out from under his vest, continued, "Pardon me. I should of introduced myself. I'm Pete Williams, the new Federal Marshal, appointed last month and just been here a few days."

Only then did Father Sullivan see the badge, half hidden by the young man's coat.

"The whole town's been buzzin' 'bout what's happened out in La Rosa. Shucks, I didn't even know there was a general store there. Just heard 'bout your sermon late yesterday. It sounded like powerful stuff and I wanna let you know I agree with you. Couldn't do nothin' to catch those culprits. They slithered back into their holes like snakes."

Williams continued his speech, emphasizing with the movement of his hands. "I heard them boastin'. News gets around real fast in this town. So I go out to de Navarro's store and asks the big man himself about it. Well, he takes me over to the tavern, where they was all drinkin' and braggin'. When I come in, a silence falls over the place like it was a wake. Couldn't see too much. It was as dark as a bear's cave and stunk of stale beer and cigar smoke. It took my eyes a mighty long time just to be able to see the folks in the room. To a man they tell the same story, claimin' everybody drank and played cards all night."

He looked the priest in the eyes. "Now Padre, ain't nobody gonna testify to the truth. Shucks, no one in town was even gonna swear to hearin' them boastin' so there was nothin' I could do. I know they was lyin' but without evidence an arrest won't stand up. But I'll tell you one thing. People like de Navarro get carried away with themselves. The next time I'll be there and he won't get away with it."

The priest folded his hands. "Thank you, Marshal. But it's not enough for me to merely deliver a sermon." Returning to his rectory, Father Sullivan mulled over these events for two days. Then on the third day, making sure that everyone saw him, he mounted his burro and set out for La Rosa.

Since the attack, Esther watched all approaching travelers with apprehension. A lone rider came down the pass. Her heart beat rapidly. Then she saw that the rider was wearing a black coat, a Roman collar, and had a fair complexion, and her tension receded. It could only be the Irish priest from Ciudad Blanca, a big man with his feet hanging close to the ground riding a little burro. She recalled that he had come this way in the past in his circuit riding duties to serve remote areas, such as La Rosa, that had neither a church nor a priest of its own.

The priest dismounted and entered the store. Walking past the boarded windows, he selected oats for his burro, pinto beans and potatoes for meals, and soap powder for cleaning, as well as many other items needed for the rectory.

Esther scurried about, filling his order. She blushed with excitement as Samuel and Reuben loaded the order on the waiting burro. The priest paid, carefully counting out many small coins from a pouch he carried under his cassock. Then he turned to the three, saying, 'Tis my belief that de Navarro's attack on your store was not caused by his hatred of Jews. That villain despises anyone who stands in his way. Surely he is consumed by his desire to take land away from the poor farmers. While he probably hates Jews, he would exploit that hatred or any- thing else to maintain power over his helpless customers and keep out any competition. But if he is not stopped, our town will be destroyed."

"Father Sullivan," said Samuel, "we were so involved with building our business that we were not aware of him. I can't thank you enough for coming here. The three of us will repair the damage and continue on. De Navarro doesn't represent everyone around here."

"There is something that must be done," said the priest. "Visit me as soon as possible. Because this is a land of justice, this evil deed must not go unpunished. I have opposed de Navarro by myself without success. You have a reputation as a good man. Just as God sent me here to you, He has sent you here to help me." Then he mounted his burro and moved off for home.

Esther, watching him depart, said, "That trail not only car- ries the followers of the Devil, but also the messenger of God."

Overwhelmed with gratitude for their newfound bene- factor, Esther and Rueben silently watched the priest and his heavily-laden donkey ride off.

In the shtetl where Samuel lived before he came to America, he knew no Christians except customers. Relations with the Gentile world were dangerous. Only in America did the outside world seem less threatening. Now with the Carvellos, Samuel had established a little store. His destiny was now intertwined with theirs. But the attack shook his belief that he could survive in this non-Jewish world of the New Mexican frontier. Could he, as a Jew fleeing Czarist Russia, find a home in America?

BOOK THREE
The Plot to Save Ciudad Blanca

Envy

CHAPTER ELEVEN

*S*panish settlements in the Sixteenth Century required the construction of a *presidio,* a fort, whose gates could be closed to secure a frontier outpost against hostile Indians. The walled structure enclosed *conquistadores,* soldiers seeking fame and fortune. They were quartered with Indian servants and horses. Single men lived in the barracks, while officers with families resided in small houses. The finest house belonged to the captain who, as the presiding officer in the garrison, was usually a Spaniard with a claim to nobility. As such, he was granted the best accommodations available.

Once a settlement was established, a jail was added for enemy captives or disobedient soldiers, and a Catholic church was built, with an enclave for converted natives. Horses were quartered in a large stable near the barracks. Nearby, but just outside the wall, corrals provided space to exercise and pasture the horses.

Over time, Mexican soldiers replaced the Spanish conquistadores. They purported to be pure Castilian, but their broad noses and flat faces spoke of their Indian ancestry. As soon as the troops settled in, a community grew up around the presidio. Wives, children, domestics, friendly Indians, merchants, farmers, and civilian employees relied on the fort for protection and employment. The presidio expanded from a garrison to a civilian town, surrounded by farms and ranches and became the center of commerce with its plaza at the core.

Such a community was Ciudad Blanca. By 1887, it had grown into a city of two thousand — not a state capital like Santa Fe or a large city like Las Vegas or Albuquerque, but merely an old Spanish town built around a plaza with its presidio, church, and stores. As the largest town in New Mexico north of Santa Fe and Las Vegas, and the center of commerce for fifty miles in every direction but south, the people of Ciudad Blanca fancied their town as a great city.

Ciudad Blanca's plaza compound contained a large rectangular Spanish fort, whose major building, the military headquarters, faced the plaza. The other buildings extended away from the presidio. The headquarters now held the courthouse and a few territorial and local governmental offices dealing with paying taxes, recording deeds, enforcing laws, and other mundane but necessary activities. The old military jail became a prison for civilian offenders accused of crimes from drunkenness to murder.

The Church of St. Xavier, a dull yellow adobe structure with twin towers and a large cross over its entrance, dominated the north side of the plaza. One of the towers contained a bell whose peal broadcast tidings of church events to the town. Next to the church stood the rectory, where Father Patrick Sullivan lived; its color and shape were copied from the church. There was also a small frame structure, which had housed the original church, built when the Spanish priests first came to convert the Indians over two hundred years earlier.

Stores around the square replaced the open marketplace, where farmers and artisans in times past once came to sell their wares. The market, originally the sole source of commerce in the town, was now a mere relic of its former glory as only a few farmers and artisans came on Saturday morning. Once in a while, a peddler wandered in. If he became too conspicuous, the local merchants drove him off with threats of violence or acts of intimidation.

The new stores that replaced the market included a tavern, which served as a restaurant, hotel, and barbershop featuring hot baths in large open tubs. In addition

there was a livery stable, with horses located in the presidio compound and a large general store, belonging to
Salvadore de Navarro.

De Navarro boasted of his Spanish ancestry. In truth,
he may have had a Spanish-born ancestor, probably a
soldier sent from Spain, but like most Nortenos, he was of
mixed Indian and Spanish blood. With the rise in his
economic status, de Navarro became more pretentious,
ultimately claiming to be of pure Castilian descent, insisting that all employees and customers refer to him as
Senor de Navarro. A squat man with squinty eyes, de
Navarro sat on the portico in front of his store. From his
vantage point as the ruler of all he surveyed, the merchant
could overlook the plaza and the buildings surrounding it.

On Sunday afternoon, February 11, 1887, an old
wagon harnessed to a small burro drove up in front of
the parish house. Two men climbed out. The older one
carried a basket. The younger one, a *gringo,* tied up the
burro and busied himself giving her food and water.
De Navarro watched as they entered the rectory. His
attention was drawn away from the strangers by the
yapping of Pepe.

Looking down, he saw the little brown dog, whose
ancestry was as doubtful as that of his owner. The only
creature that de Navarro ever treated with kindness, the
dog shared his master's dinner, bed, and mean tempera-
ment. As de Navarro nibbled at his spicy sausages, he bit
off and threw chunks to Pepe, which the little dog greedily
devoured.

De Navarro washed down a sausage with cool fruit
juice, while continuing to watch the activities in the square.
Constant surveillance was important to him as the owner
of the only store in town. He knew the danger of allowing
a rival to settle in. His motto was, *"Never let anyone get a
foothold. Destroy them before they destroy you."*

Down in Lincoln, in the southern part of the territory,
the owner of the general store recently faced competition
from a new store, and a five-day war, ruinous to both
owners, took place. He did not want to have to fight a

gringo, a hired *Americano* like Billy the Kid. His desperados feared dealing with such a gunfighter even though they might outnumber him.

The storekeeper intimidated potential opposition into leaving, resorting to violence when necessary but never directly involving himself. He always hired desperados to do his dirty work. Just last week his henchmen returned from their successful trip to La Rosa. After their violence and destruction, his latest competitor should have closed up shop and fled, having been in business less than two months. He would hear no more of Carvello and Rabinowitz.

De Navarro drifted in and out of his daydreams. Reverting to his youth, he recalled his father telling him of his heritage. "Remember, my family is of pure Castilian blood. It's true that I made this unfortunate marriage to your mother, an Indian. But you are descended from the finest nobility of Spain. I have lost our heritage but you, the hope of my life, will regain it for me."

Then he recalled how as a young man he courted Esmeralda Vasquez, an attractive young woman. Dressed in his finest white suit, a flower in his buttonhole and scented with perfume, he approached the home of his beloved and knocked on the door.

A beautiful young woman with a rose in her hair and a flowing white dress answered the door.

"Esmeralda, I bring you a little puppy as my betrothal gift." He thrust the tiny mutt towards her.

Stunned, she refused. "Salvador, I cannot marry you." She turned her eyes from him. "My family has decided I must marry Senor Alphonse Guterriez."

"You can't marry that stingy miser," de Navarro's face took on a pained expression. "He's an old man. Your family is just selling you for the money. You don't love him."

"He made many gifts to my mother and offered a large dowry. There is nothing I can do. I must obey my parents." With a tear in her eye, she concluded, "Good-bye, my love."

Dejected, he turned away. He tore the rose from his lapel and was about to throw the puppy to the ground, but told himself, *"This is all I have left to remind me of Esmeralda."*

He smiled down at his little pet and then recalled that after his loss, the only worthwhile goal in his life was to accumulate wealth and acquire land and become a person of importance. He would have the pick of the daughters of the finest families in the city.

"Senor de Navarro," a voice interrupted. Pedro Lopez, a shriveled little man, quivered as he asked, "May I speak to you for a minute, Patron?"

"What do you want?" de Navarro responded as his pet snarled at the man. "Be quick. I do not have time for you." And then to the dog, "Be quiet, my little Pepe."

"Thank you, Senor. Your clerk told me I have no more credit. I need seed. The crops must be put in soon, and I must bring food home for my family."

"But Pedro, you owe me a great deal of money. Each year it becomes more. You will never be able to repay me."

"Senor de Navarro, every time my crop comes in, I pay you. But, somehow, I always fall more in your debt."

"You stupid Indians do not know how to manage. No, you will get no more from me! I have only gone this far because we Spaniards try to help you poor fools. Now it is over." He bit off another piece of sausage and threw it to Pepe.

"Please Senor, my family will starve." Pedro's voice cracked as his emaciated body trembled.

"That is no concern of mine. There are too many of you here now." De Navarro paused and looked at the pathetic little man, reading defeat in his eyes. He would submit to any conditions set.

"I'm soft hearted," he continued. "We Castilians take our obligations to the poor too seriously. I will let you turn your land over to me to pay your debt. You will stay on to work for me. I'll provide you with seed and credit of one hundred dollars against your future wages."

"But the land has been in my family for many years. Without it, I will have nothing to pass on to my children." Lopez paused as his voice broke. "I have no choice. I

must accept your generous offer, otherwise, my family
will starve."

De Navarro chuckled and said to himself. *"Now I have
another fool who is so far in my debt that I will own his
land. Soon I will be the greatest landowner in Ciudad Blanca.
I will have more land than any of the old families."* He called
to his clerk. "Luis, come here."

"Si, Senor de Navarro."

"Pedro will be turning over his land to me. Cancel his
bill and give him seed and one hundred dollars credit."
He paused and then added, "By the way, Luis, I have been
going over our books and noticed that some of our customers from the area near La Rosa are no longer coming
here. I thought with Carvello and Rabinowitz gone, they
would have returned."

"But Senor de Navarro, Carvello and Rabinowitz have
not gone."

"What! How can that be?" Hearing no answer, he
ordered, "Bring me back another sausage for Pepe. Then
go back to work, Luis. That's why I'm paying you."

Then to himself he continued, *"Those damned Jewish
peddlers are stealing my business. My plan to rid myself of
that curse must have gone wrong. It was a week ago when
my banditos returned. By this time they should have left. I
don't understand. It's always worked before. It must be that
drunken priest that ruined my plan. I despise that Irish fool.
He is the only person stupid enough to oppose me."*

De Navarro remembered the priest's homily and could
not understand how he could defend the Jews. *"In my
lifetime, I have never heard of such a thing. At every opportunity our Church condemned the Jews as Christ-killers. This
could only come from the Church bringing in a gringo priest.
Things like that never happened where there was a Spanish
priest."*

It suddenly occurred to de Navarro that his acts
against Carvello and Rabinowitz might have misfired.
Could it have inspired Father Sullivan's sermon? Could

he have unwittingly created an ally for the priest, the lone voice of opposition? A new plan must be devised. Carvello and Rabinowitz must be driven out, killed if necessary!

Potatoes and Politics

CHAPTER TWELVE

Early Sunday morning, February 11, 1887, just one week after the raid on the store, Samuel and Reuben left La Rosa for Ciudad Blanca. Esther, who stayed behind to mind the store, had packed a hamper of their best food and wine to repay their debt to Father Sullivan. During the four-hour ride, the two spoke of what the priest's invitation meant.

"It is awkward for me, as a Jew from Russia, to be in a meeting with a Christian priest. I don't know how to behave," stated Samuel.

"I understand that feeling, and must warn you, be wary of this man," Reuben advised. "Although I am a Catholic, it must be said that the priests in this area have not always been our friends."

"Back in Belkov, priests frequently led the pogroms, where the peasants attacked the Jews. I need no warning as I'm already much too suspicious."

"Perhaps he thinks that because you are a Jew, you are rich and will contribute to his church."

Samuel laughed.

At the plaza, they rode past the general store, noticing a short, dark man sitting on the portico, nibbling sausages and tossing pieces to a small dog. They pulled up in front of St. Xavier, a small stucco building. Samuel tied up Manny by a water trough and worked the handle of the water pump so that there would be fresh water. Once Manny had satisfied her thirst, Samuel slid on her feedbag filled with fresh grain. Reuben removed the hamper from the wagon and together they went around to the small parish house.

A tall, shrewish looking woman answered the door. "I'm Father Sullivan's housekeeper. Please wait in the reception and I will inform Father Sullivan of your arrival."

She returned in a few minutes and took them into the study where the large, stocky priest had just finished Mass and was reading.

He looked up from his book. "Welcome my friends. I'm pleased that you were able to come."

Reuben responded, "We came to express our gratitude for your help." He held out the basket towards the priest. "This is a token of our appreciation."

"Thank you," echoed Samuel, shifting from one foot to the other.

The priest took the offering into his hands. Smiling at the men, he said "So much food, I could not possibly eat it all by myself. Won't you please stay a bit and join me in a meal."

Rueben glanced over at Samuel, who dropped his eyes. Rueben knew that he would have to be the one to decide whether they would stay or go. He smiled back at the priest. "It is for you, for what you did for us, a gift of gratitude, but we would be pleased to join you."

"Ah, a shared gift is more blessed. And, to be sure, I am as hungry for your company and for news of the world beyond my tiny parish as I am for food."

As Samuel and Reuben seated themselves at a small table in the large, pleasant room, the priest walked over to a large window that looked out at the desert. "Sometimes, as I view the rock formations and the mountains, I again see the ruins of an ancient Irish castle near my home and the towering cliffs of Ireland where the land meets the sea." He turned and faced the two. "Ireland has a climate where the relentless rain creates a plush green carpet, so unlike this one of scorched brown." He paused and sighed deeply. "I must have transgressed some divine law to trade my moist emerald home for this barren desert. It makes me miss even the damp Irish winters."

"Well," asked Reuben, "if that is so, why did you come here?"

"Alas, we're not always given a choice of where we will spend our lives," answered the priest as he walked back to the table and filled his glass with wine. He offered the wine to his guests, who accepted gladly. Taking a sack from the basket, he gave them each a piece of fruit. "My story is a long one that takes much time in the telling and I beg your indulgence in the listening."

The two guests pushed their chairs away from the table and settled in to listen.

"I fled Ireland, driven out by despair and tyranny, much as the Jews fled their oppressors. The Irish, like the Jews and the Nortenos, are a patient, long suffering people." Then he looked over at Rueben. "Look at your friend Samuel. There was no place for him in Russia. I don't think I'd be here except for the failure of the potato crop and the hanging of my father."

Rueben's eyes grew large with amazement.

Samuel sucked in a large breath and shifted nervously in his hard wooden chair as his curiosity overcame his reticence.

"Despite our poverty, we were quite content to remain in Ireland. As difficult as life was, everyone adjusted, until famine threatened our very existence. When our choice was to leave or die, we left."

The priest sat down and refilled his glass. He offered more wine to his guests, who declined. He took a sip of wine. "Before I tell you why I have asked you here, I would have you know a bit about me and where I come from. 'Tis why I came to your store after de Navarro raided it. But, be patient while I tell you my story for I tend to ramble a bit," said Father Sullivan, taking a sip of wine.

"Go ahead, we've plenty of time," said Reuben.

"I began life's journey in Ireland as did many other priests." He chuckled as he added, "The priesthood was my way out of that devastated land." Standing up, he stared into the air as if looking back into the past. Sorrow darkened his face. "Beginning in 1845, the potato famine brought a terrible disaster on my family as well as on all of Ireland. Our population was decimated by starvation from more than eight million to less than three million in a few years. Our alternative, as for many others, was to emigrate or die."

Uttering a deep sigh, he paused and then continued. "The disaster began after our Irish and English landlords imported an easily-raised potato from the United States, which could be grown on one-fourth of the land and feed three-fourths of the farm folk. But, alas, the perfect potato had one flaw. It contained a tiny microscopic fungus that multiplied rapidly in the damp climate of Ireland. Our potatoes turned black, stunk, and could not be eaten. 'Twas ironic, the famine need not have caused starvation."

He paused, took a sip of wine and then continued. "We had enough other food to fulfill all our needs, growing wheat, oats, and barley and raising cattle, pigs, and poultry. All of these our landlords took from us and sold overseas." He uttered a sardonic laugh. "Nothing embittered us more than our landlord exporting our food while we who had grown it starved." His hand shook and his face reddened as if tears were about to flow.

Rueben stared with renewed intensity as Samuel looked away, afraid to make eye contact.

"Like most landowners, ours lived well in England off the rents from tenants. He regarded his holdings simply as a source of income from which to extract as much money as possible. To him, Ireland was a damp, disagreeable place, neither comfortable nor safe enough for one to live in. He did not care that once we were evicted, we had no way to survive. Like all of the landlords, he chose not see Ireland's tragedy because he had no interest."

As Father Sullivan paused to change positions in his chair, Samuel, who no longer averted his eyes from the priest, asked, "Have you kept these thoughts within yourself for all these years?"

The priest, ignoring Samuel's question, continued. "They sought to rid themselves of tenant farmers so as to enclose the fields and raise sheep and cattle for greater profits, just as the British had done in England. The famine helped them accomplish this since tenant farmers, unable to pay their rent, were evicted without trouble. They abandoned their farms and sought refuge in the cities. But this did not solve the problem of hunger. Evicted tenants walked and begged, begged and walked. First they moved to charity and then if that failed, they starved to death. Those fortunate enough to survive went to all parts of the world but especially here, to the United States." He looked over at his guests. "To us, America was not the *goldeneh medinah* of the Jews but simply our last hope for survival."

Samuel nodded in understanding.

"Is that why you came here?" asked Reuben as he reached for a cake to have with his coffee.

"Let me tell you the worst. I last saw my father when the English hanged him. There I was, nine-year-old Patrick Francis Sullivan, the youngest of six. We lived in the Town of Cork in the County of Cork in a one room, windowless stone cottage with plastered walls and a thatched roof. There was little furniture: a bed for my parents, a few chairs, and a table. We children slept on straw in the attic loft. In winter, we burned peat cut from the moors. Although the fire made the house smoky, 'twas warm and comfortable in those damp winters. But even with so little, we had more than many and were quite content until there was nothing to eat."

"That sounds even worse than life in Russia," murmured Samuel.

"I would have you know that my father was panic-stricken as he saw his family starve. With a few close friends, he broke into a storage building in the port, where food was waiting to be shipped to England. They stole a cartload of grain. My father and his friends were not very good thieves." The priest paused to take another sip of wine, sighed, and then continued, "So many times, we Irish seem condemned to committing futile acts which harm us but never completely destroy us."

"We Jews have never had that luxury," commented Samuel. "Too often our mistakes have led to our destruction."

"British soldiers captured my father before he made it home. His Majesty's government declared him to be a dangerous rebel and not just a poor soul trying to keep his family alive. They hung him. I was too young to ever be sure if my father was a rebel or not. 'Twas little difference between the two, but to a small lad watching the hanging, I preferred to believe my father to be a rebel, for then he could go to his death with his pride intact."

The priest rose from his chair, took off his black coat, removed his clerical collar, and wiped his forehead with his handkerchief. Then he walked to the window. "At the end, my mother refused to eat, insisting we eat her few morsels of food. She and two of my brothers and a sister starved. Three of us survived. I have a sister living in Liverpool and a brother in Australia."

Father Sullivan moved abruptly away from the window. His face darkened as if tears were about to come. "I have asked God for forgiveness. I hate no one, but I hate the tyranny of man. I hate it in the British. And I hate it here, in the actions of de Navarro."

"But what happened to you?" asked Reuben.

Samuel felt less tense. His fists opened and his face muscles relaxed as he waited for an answer.

"The Church took me in," Father Sullivan returned to the table, picked up a small pastry, and refilled his glass. "In time I became a priest to escape the terrible realities of Irish life. I am unable to say that I felt a calling. I knew only that my life was in the hands of the Church. First I went to the Jesuit school in Dublin for a year and then to a Franciscan seminary in Spain to prepare me for a Spanish-speaking parish."

"How did you get here?" pursued Reuben.

"Many of us came to the United States but only those few trained in Spain became priests in this area dominated by the Spanish clergy. Most Irish priests here are diocesan but a few of us are members of Franciscan or Dominican

orders." He smiled at his guests and added, "A poor Irish
lad like me could never expect to rise high in the Church,
so I was assigned by the Franciscan order to this parish.
I have spent most of my adult life here as its priest."

"Padre, I do not wish to be rude," interrupted Reuben,
"but with all of your feelings about Ireland, how could
you support the Church against your own people? When
I was a young man, I mixed with a wild group that vehe-
mently hated the Catholic Church, criticizing it for standing with the oppressors against the poor, betraying its
flock not only here, but throughout the world."

"Every priest has a problem of obedience when he
disagrees with his superiors. The Irish parish priests lived,
worked, and starved with the poor."

"But," Reuben persisted, "is it not true that the parish
priests were silenced by their Church?"

Father Sullivan looked at Rueben. "Sadly, I cannot but
agree with you. When the split between the hierarchy and
the parish priests increased, Pope Pius IX chastised the
Irish priests and ordered them to abstain from politics.
Unwilling to oppose their Pope, they withdrew from open
opposition to quiet support of their parishioners. But 'tis
not fair to place the faults of the hierarchy on the Irish
priests. For as long as they could, our priests openly
opposed the Church's support of the English. Only after
the hierarchy overrode them did they surrender and sub-
ordinate their Irish loyalties to Rome."

Samuel watched, captivated by the discussion.

"Unable to oppose their British rulers and the Church
hierarchy, most young priests avoided the conflict and waited
for an appropriate time to speak up. Others risked censure
by secretly cooperating with the radicals. Few regarded
their views as disloyal, believing that the Mother Church
had erred and should be helped to correct her views. But
we knew we were not like other Catholics. Our Celtic
Christian background made a difference to us as the Celtic
heritage tolerated more discussion and dissent than did the
Roman. The older priests were dominated by the hierarchy
but the younger ones referred to the British occupation of
Ireland as the worst of all colonial occupations."

Samuel listened eagerly. A new world was opening to him.

"When the Spanish came to this hemisphere, they killed two million Indians whom they were unable to enslave. On the other hand, the British in India entered into compacts with local potentates, who declared loyalty to the Queen. They adapted the outward trappings of British education, law, and customs while continuing to maintain their own culture. But British policy in Ireland was similar to Spanish colonial policies, yet even worse, for the Spanish engaged in no hypocrisies as the English did. The British pretended to merely rule over the Irish, when in fact, they sought to decimate them. The English policy in Ireland was really Spanish policy in an English disguise."

Father Sullivan looked at Reuben. "This is the first time since I left Ireland that I have talked this way to anyone. I may sound bitter. Were I not an Irishman but an Englishman, I might see it differently. To me, all oppression is vile."

"Perhaps I have misjudged you," acknowledged Reuben. "I must agree with you."

Father Sullivan, a big man, appeared to have shrunk after his emotional catharsis. "I have rambled enough. My story may be interesting, but the telling of it has returned the pain of the past to me. My dreams of Ireland haunt me. I can no longer look the other way at injustice. It is always wrong. I cannot accept the cruelty of the Spanish to the Indians any more than from the English to the Irish. As a result of my father's murder, something in me is always angry against oppression. *I cannot remain silent against de Navarro! It is my plan to oppose him and you two must become part of that plan!*"

Shocked, Samuel and Reuben froze.

"'Tis why I've asked you here and why de Navarro is so important. He places the farmers in debt, steals their land, and then turns them into peons. I have a plan to end his oppression that requires your help."

Suddenly Samuel understood the point of the priest's story. Others had suffered from oppression besides Jews.

Father Sullivan was one of these. His trip to La Rosa had been for a purpose. "But what can we do?" he asked.

"Yes," echoed Reuben. "What can we do?"

"De Navarro's attack on your store was not simply because of his hatred of Jews," said the priest. "Greed and power were his principal motives. It is doubly evil to employ bigotry for one's selfish gain. Sometimes I wonder if my concerns about de Navarro's injustices against you were motivated by my beliefs against his anti-Jewish feelings or my concern over his exploitation of Ciudad Blanca. I may have had less concern with his hatred of Jews than a man of God should.

"But to return to why I asked you here. De Navarro owns the only general store in Ciudad Blanca. Come join me. You can see it from here." The priest walked over to the window and pointed across the square to the general store with its proprietor sitting out on the front portico. "He is probably planning your demise. Until you opened your store, there was no other place to go. You became a rival and he could not tolerate that. De Navarro extends easy credit to the poor farmers who are his customers. Trapped with no alternative, they sink deeper into debt. Without competition, he is able to raise his prices to outrageous levels."

"How well Yankel knew when he told me of the dangers of credit," muttered Samuel.

"Finally, when their debts reach a level that is impossible to repay, de Navarro forces them to deed their lands to him. Then he allows them to remain on almost as if they were slaves." He concluded. "You two became a threat to him since those farmers not yet trapped in his net could buy from you. So he must destroy you."

"But Padre," replied Reuben, "we've done nothing."

"Yes," concurred a concerned Samuel. "Father Sullivan, you are the one with courage."

"Not so. The fact that you did not flee was an act of bravery." He looked back and forth between his guests' eyes. "Had I come to a deserted building, we would not be here. For as long as anyone can remember, the farmers here have lived in poverty. It was this very poverty that de Navarro exploited. Last year the opportunity of a lifetime came along but instead of helping out the farmers, it was absorbed by the greed of one man."

"What you are talking about?" asked Reuben.

Samuel, overcome with curiosity, rose from his chair. "Yes, what do you mean?"

"Let me come directly to my request of you and be more specific. From the time the Americans took this area from Mexico until shortly after the end of the Civil War, the United States government gave little attention to this region. The land was opened to waves of Yankee settlers, who complained to the government about Indian attacks. So forts were built and soldiers were sent here to put down the Indians. These forts remained with a fair number of troops."

"But what has that to do with us?" queried Reuben.

"I'm getting to that," answered the priest. "About fifty miles northwest of here, in an area where Apaches live, is Fort Madison. From the time the Fort was built until last year, it was supplied from back east through Fort Union. Under recent changes from Washington, the fort was allowed to contract locally for supplies. A contract for corn was opened to bid last year. The only person around here who could deliver the required amounts was de Navarro. He obtained this lucrative contract that should have brought prosperity to everyone in Ciudad Blanca. Instead of helping the people out, de Navarro used the contract to place the farmers further under his control, forcing them to sell corn to him at a price so low that they only went deeper into debt."

The priest paused to let his words sink in. "This year bids were to be made in the fall, well before the time for planting. I had given up the idea of anyone competing with de Navarro. Once again, my opposition was futile. But the hand of God intervened. Bids were postponed until this spring based on Washington reviewing the bidding procedures. When de Navarro's raid failed to chase you away, I knew that He had sent you."

"What can we do?" asked Reuben.

"Yes, tell us what?" echoed Samuel.

Father Sullivan rose from his chair and walked towards Samuel, looking directly into his eyes. "Do you not understand that God has sent you here to defeat that devil? He inspires these events to make us all men of courage." He paused for a sip of wine. *"Now listen carefully to me! I wish you to take the contract for the corn away from de Navarro!"*

Stunned, the two guests sank back into their chairs, disbelief written across their faces. Samuel stood up and prepared to speak when the priest cut him off. "This contract could make everyone in and around Ciudad Blanca prosperous. You must take it away from de Navarro and use it for the good of the farmers. Knowing your reputation, I have no doubt that you will treat them fairly."

"And how do you propose to do that – with divine intervention?" said Samuel.

"Divine intervention is always a possibility. God sent you here. But first, let us see what we can do by ourselves. I spoke in confidence to Reverend Miller, the chaplain at the fort, who has obtained the necessary information from the Quartermaster. We must win the contract, but it will not be easy. First, it is necessary for us to fill out all of the documents required to make a bid. Then we must be selected as the lowest bidder. And finally, we have to fulfill the contract. Time is short as bids must be filed at the fort within three weeks and awards will be made two weeks later. We must be ready to have the farmers plant adequate crops within a month after we win the award."

"Impossible!" declared Samuel.

Father Sullivan ignored him. "In order to obtain enough grain, we require the cooperation of a sufficient number of farmers, who must be supported until they grow and deliver the corn. This means it is up to us to provide seed and supplies." With a voice that dropped to a whisper, he added, "And finally, we need a guarantor, someone who is financially solvent."

"I think we're now ready for divine intervention," declared Samuel. "There's no possible way we can do it."

Father Sullivan laughed, relieving the tension. "It is a good thing that Moses did not have you with him or the Jews might still be in Egypt. When his courage failed, the Lord strengthened him. He will do the same for you. Just give him a chance."

"We have no alternative," Samuel admitted.

Reuben nodded in agreement.

"Will you be able to provide seed and food for the farmers for four months until the crops are harvested and paid for?" the priest inquired.

"That's impossible. It's difficult for us to even comprehend a plan of this size," said Samuel. "I'm little more than a peddler. We make a living and from time to time I send a few dollars home to bring my parents over. Thanks to Esther and Reuben, we've opened a small store. Nothing like de Navarro, or Mordecai Cohen in Las Vegas." Suddenly Samuel stopped as a thought struck him. "That's it! I'll ask Mordecai to help us. He might give us the necessary credit to make the plan work."

"Senor Samuel, please be careful," said Reuben. "You may lose everything you have worked for since you came to America and may not be able to bring your parents over."

"Don't worry, my good friends," assured the priest. "God will not desert those He has sent on a mission. Let us see how many of the farmers desire to join, but we must not let anyone hear of our plan before we win the contract. Otherwise there will be foul play from de Navarro. If it all works out, the farmers will get a fair price and you should make a fine profit, more than enough to bring your parents over. But, best of all, we will have broken that villain's hold over this community."

Reuben broke his stunned silence. "I am an old man, concerned only with what this could mean. I must protect Esther, but I must do the right thing."

"We agree to your plan," said Samuel. "There's no way we can refuse, with our obligation to you."

Then, looking at the solemn white-haired priest, he said, "You remind me more of a suffering Jew than of a Catholic priest. You are my ally and I must be there for you. You seem sapped after your exhausting conversation, which must have released feelings that have been held back for many years." He paused. "But I'm as frightened as I've ever been. Never before have I made these kinds of decisions. Now one must be made that will not only affect my life but that of my family."

Samuel looked around as the three men sat speechless. He knew that each was dumbfounded with his own sense of dread, thinking of the risks. They were huddling together for comfort, knowing that each was committing himself to something that could adversely affect his future. The undertaking seemed impossible. Yet it could be done! Indeed, it must be done! It was worth the risk!

Slowly and thoughtfully, Samuel and Reuben rose from their chairs and readied to leave. Chastened by the weight of their undertaking, they shook hands, and the visitors silently departed.

The Fast of St. Esther – The Festival of Purim

CHAPTER THIRTEEN

*A*fter returning to La Rosa, Samuel told Esther what had occurred. She asked, "If we fail, how will you be able to send for your parents? How will you provide for Hannah? You're risking everything you have worked so hard for."

Reuben remained silent, looking down at his hands in his lap.

Samuel found it difficult to look at Esther as he thought about her question. *"I couldn't continue on if she failed to respect me."* Then he answered her, "Somehow this is all bashert, predestined. If God allowed me to be placed in this situation, it must be for some purpose. I can't run away. But still I'm frightened."

He stood up and looked into Esther's eyes. "Ever since I came to America, my only concern was to bring my family here, as if my very existence was only to satisfy that goal. I can't ignore the fact that this is now my home. I've been befriended by you two as well as by Father Sullivan and would like to remain here, but that will be impossible if I don't stand up. It's no longer enough for me merely to survive. I'm not a brave man and I don't seek fights, but I can't run away. I must take a stand and trust in God that whatever happens, I can still bring Momma and Poppa to America."

Esther and Reuben nodded their agreement.

Samuel spent the next day calculating and recalculating. Leaving his desk, he went into the store as Reuben was closing up. They entered the house and seated themselves at the table where Esther had a dinner of *tortillas* with beans waiting.

As they ate, she commented, "Samuel, I've never seen you so quiet."

"I estimate that it would take two thousand dollars to finance the project. Checking my cash, I confirmed what I already knew. I can't raise much more than a hundred dollars and must ask for Mordecai Cohen's help."

"Perhaps this project is a mistake. Is it leading you to despair?" asked Rueben.

"Well, I have never worked harder, estimating costs and looking at risks." Samuel stood up and looked at the two. "I'm fearful for all of us. You're my partners. It's your decision as well as mine. We'll be risking everything. If we lose, there will be nothing left. Is that fair to the two of you?"

"My only concern is for my daughter. She is all that I have."

"Father, what is most important is that we do the right thing. When the desperados attacked, they came with a challenge and our life changed. If we cringe and run away, de Navarro wins. I'm not willing to do that. Nor are you. It's as simple as that. I share your fears. But what else can we do when a bully attacks? Had it not been for Father Sullivan, we would have had no alternative and done nothing. Now we must either fight or run away."

The silence was evidence to their agreement.

"Well, the decision is made," said Samuel. "Now let's go see Mordecai. We can't do anything without his help."

On Thursday March 10, 1887 they rode to Las Vegas. The sun made it a pleasant drive. The date coincided with Purim, the holiday that Mordecai Cohen had invited them to share with his family.

As they entered the store, Samuel said, "Reuben, Esther, you must come along with me to see Mordecai. After all, these decisions are yours as well as mine."

"Senor Samuel," said Reuben, "I believe that for us to accompany you would be a grave mistake. Senor Cohen does not know us and might be uncomfortable with us there. You would not want to offend him if he turns you down, and that would be easier without us present."

Reluctantly, Samuel agreed. Leaving his friends to select merchandise, he called out, "Mordecai, I must see you for a few minutes."

"*Gut Yontiff,* Good Holiday, Samuel. Wait until I finish with this customer. Then I'll have plenty of time to *schmooze.*"

A few minutes later, he entered the merchant's office. While it was disorganized with papers strewn all over, Mordecai seemed to know where everything was. "Just a minute, Samuel." He located a bill and called Alfred in and told him how to price some new merchandise. Then he raised his spectacles to his forehead and looked over at his guest.

Samuel told him about the meeting with Father Sullivan.

Mordecai cried out, "Are you *mishugana?* Why are you so concerned with the impossible plans of that crazy priest?"

Samuel was animated as he told how Father Sullivan came to see him after de Navarro's attack on the store.

"Hmm, I remember that Jew-hating bastard, that mamser, de Navarro," asserted Mordecai. "I've never told anyone this story before because it was too embarrassing. When I first started peddling, I sold near Ciudad Blanca. The farmers welcomed me even after de Navarro used Jew hatred to try to get them to boycott me.

"Then one evening, after I had set up camp, fed my mule, and was cooking dinner, four of de Navarro's men rode up. They shot my mule, burnt my wagon and beat me to within an inch of my life. I survived only because a friendly farmer found me and took me into his home where he and his wife cared for me. When I had healed enough to be able to travel, I walked back to Las Vegas.

Frightened half to death, I'd have left if only there had been some place to go. But there wasn't. So I wrote home for money to start a little store here. I'm not thrilled about the odds on your deal. But let me think it through."

Mordecai sat back in his chair and appeared to be doing some mental calculations, as his facial expression grew tense. "You make my life difficult, but I've a debt to repay to de Navarro, too. I'll give it a try. You'll get two thousand dollars of credit. I won't take your personal guarantee. If you fail, I'll not only lose the money because you'll never be able to repay the loan, but I'll also lose your friendship. If the deal succeeds, I'll take ten percent of the profits in addition to the repayment of the loan. If it doesn't work, I'll write it off. Let's not call it a loan, but rather an investment. I'd rather be your partner than your banker."

"Thanks for everything."

"It's only good business. This way, if the deal goes bad, I'll lose only the money and not a good customer. Now that our business is complete, let's get back to Esther and Reuben."

They walked into the store. "It's time to go to my home for dinner," Mordecai told his guests. "My Bertha is waiting for us. Then we shall go to Temple Montefiore for Purim services."

Samuel whispered to Esther and Reuben, "It looks like everything will be alright. I'll tell you more later."

At the Cohen home, Bertha met them at the door. She grasped Esther to her ample bosom. "I've heard so much about you. I feel I've known you for years."

Esther blushed at the unexpected show of affection. Delighted, she hugged Bertha back. Impatient, the three youngest children in their costumes paced back and forth, squealing with excitement and anxious to leave for the synagogue. Mordecai turned to his daughter, a miniature Queen Esther wearing a cardboard crown and a tinseled gown. Then pointing at Esther, he said to his daughter, "This is our real Queen Esther from La Rosa."

Sheina's eyes grew large with wonder.

Mordecai turned to his eldest son Max, the only one of the children not in a costume. "My Bar Mitzvah boy is helping Rabbi Glick with the reading of the Book of Esther." It was with apparent pride that the gangly youth wore his bar mitzvah suit to dignify his position as the Rabbi's assistant.

Turning to Michael, a little boy with a regal robe, a cardboard crown, and a large wooden staff, Mordecai announced, "He is King Ahasuerus, the husband of Queen Esther." Finally, he looked down and smiled at the littlest boy who was snuggling up against him, dressed as an old man with a long, gray beard and wearing a plain white robe. "This is Aaron, our youngest. He is portraying my namesake, Mordecai. We'll have a wonderful time tonight."

Bertha took Esther into the kitchen. "As you are now watching over Samuel, I have a few more of his favorite recipes to show you."

Laughter was heard from the kitchen along with the sounds of dinner being prepared, pots clanging, and dishes moving about. Bertha invited everyone into the dining room where a sumptuous meal was spread out. Living up to her husband's boasts, she had prepared the finest Jewish dishes: chopped chicken liver, chicken soup with matzah balls, then roast chicken, wonderful roast potatoes, and some carrot *tzimes*. For dessert, she served a special three-corner pastry filled with fruit called *hamantaschen,* named after Haman, the villain of the Purim story. These were quickly devoured and washed down with black coffee.

The children left the house and led the way to their father's wagon. They climbed on top, singing and shaking their *graggers,* a special noisemaker consisting of a wooden rattle with a metal clacker attached to it, used only on Purim. Their excitement mounted on the drive to the temple as a caravan of wagons with other children converged upon the small frame building that housed Temple Montefiore. Everyone joined in the merriment. The sounds of elated children grew louder as they slowly filled the synagogue. The frenzy was amplified as the noise reverberated in the small hall, which occupied the first floor. The bare room had been magically transformed with blue and white paper decorations and cardboard stars of David and menorahs. There were little Queen Esthers, King Ahasueruses, bearded Mordecais and even a few Hamans.

"This is a time when Jews conduct themselves in the synagogue with a sense of humor that is almost ludicrous," said Samuel. "It is a carnival atmosphere. The purpose of Purim is to make sport of Haman. As an Amalekite, our traditional enemy, he is the villain who seeks to destroy the Jews and as such has come to symbolize all people who hate Jews.

"As the story is read out, the custom is to hiss when the name of the villain is mentioned. Each child has a gragger, which adds to the clamor, in addition to the hisses at every mention of Haman when the congregation seeks to drown out his name."

At Rabbi Glick's side, Max helped lead the congregation through the story of Purim: Esther is selected by King Ahasuerus of Persia as his queen. Fearing the King's displeasure, she hides the fact that she is a Jew until learning that her people are in danger. After fasting, she discloses her true identity to the King, saving her people from annihilation by Haman when the King allows the Jews to protect themselves.

As the tale unfolded, Esther Carvello became entranced and was drawn into the frenzy as if a child. She joined in the merrymaking as Queen Esther ran through her adventures and at one point whispered to Samuel, "I have heard similar stories from father and have always found something special about the Fast of Saint Esther. Like your Purim, this holiday celebrates the adventures of a woman masquerading to protect her people and sacrificing herself. But my father's version has little of the glamour of this Purim."

Esther began to feel that there was more than a coincidental relationship between the two holidays. *"I wonder if my Fast of Saint Esther might have come from Purim. The*

secrecy as to Queen Esther's Jewish identity and her self-
sacrifice to save her people ring true to the stories I was told."

The next morning, after Samuel and Reuben loaded
the wagon, Esther joined them. "My mind is still at the
Purim festival. I'm filled with memories of the Fast of
Saint Esther. Now with these additional adventures of
Queen Esther from this new Jewish holiday of Purim it is
even more exciting. The noise of the graggers, the screams
of the children, the excitement of the costumes, and the
wonderful food have all entranced me. I'm wondering if
there might be something more than a mere coincidence
between the two."

"We are anxious to find out what happened with
Senor Cohen," interrupted Reuben. "I have been impatient to hear."

The trip home passed quickly as Samuel shared his
conversation with Mordecai. Then Esther reviewed her
exciting evening. "This has been a lovely trip. The
Cohens are wonderful people. I have always thought of
Queen Esther as a far-off heroine, but now with de
Navarro trying to dominate the poor people of this area,
we are like the Jews waiting to be destroyed. Now de
Navarro is our Haman!"

The Guarantor

CHAPTER FOURTEEN

"Well, the hard part is done," said Samuel. "We have the credit necessary to supply the farmers until the government pays us." The trip to Ciudad Blanca on this late February day made Father Sullivan's coffee especially welcome. As the three sat in the priest's study with their cups on the small stained table in front of them, Samuel asked the question that had long troubled him. "Now let's get to the impossible: how can we obtain a guarantor? It was difficult enough to get someone to give us credit, but who has the kind of wealth necessary and would be willing to guarantee our promises under the contract? That's the condition we'll never satisfy."

"I do not understand," asked Reuben, "why the government insists upon a guarantor. We are taking all the risks."

"Well," answered the priest, "governments are in positions to do as they please. If we fail, they will go out and buy corn at a higher price and they want to be assured that the defaulting bidder will pay the difference. Anyway, I believe that we have a guarantor here in the form of help from the Mother Church. For with her help, nothing is impossible."

"Padre, with all due respect, you must have lost your sanity," said Reuben. "The Catholic Church is not about to become the guarantor of our contract."

"You are almost right. But I have not taken leave of my senses. When all of you went to Las Vegas, I knew Samuel would succeed, for I have great faith in him. Immediately after your departure, I left for Santa Fe. That city is the most important one in this part of our new country. It is the center of civic, business, and religious life in this territory, where the trade from Mexico comes up the Chihuahua trail and meets the Santa Fe Trail with the trade from the East. These trails end in the Plaza where they lead to the Cathedral, just as all roads lead to Rome. It was there that I went to see Archbishop Nunez.

"When the Yankees captured these lands from Mexico, the Archdiocese, our governing body run by an Archbishop, was shifted some fifteen hundred miles north from Durango, Mexico, to Santa Fe in the United States. So the St. Francis Xavier Roman Catholic Church of Ciudad Blanca transferred its religious obedience from Durango to Santa Fe, just as it had transferred its civil obedience from Mexico to the United States.

"As I rode into town, the Cathedral loomed before me. It is a magnificent stone edifice, whose steeple rises over the city at the north end of the plaza." Looking over at the peddler, he continued, "Samuel, you might be interested to note that over the main arch is inscribed the Hebrew word for God, *Adonai*.

"The Archbishop Emmanuel Nunez is a very distinguished man whose regal robe covers his ample frame, heavy from luxurious meals and plentiful wine. He is reputed to have come from a wealthy Castilian family. Nunez lives a life of luxury, as he has no vow of poverty. A gourmet, it is his custom to invite his guests to dinner before discussing any business. It was the finest meal I had eaten in many years. Capon, fish, roast mutton, delicious fruits, and especially wonderful wines and desserts. It seemed like hours of feasting on sumptuous food and drink. The food was so fine that I felt guilty since that meal alone might have saved the Irish from their famine."

Father Sullivan paused and joined with the others in laughter. "After telling the Archbishop of our project, I

made a plea for his support. I would have you know that
he abruptly dismissed me, telling me there was nothing
that the Church could do. I let him know in no uncertain
terms that I was not asking for the help of the Church, but
for his personal help. Either the wine or my mission must
have emboldened me, for I found that I had the courage
to speak out to this man who, as my superior, I respected
and even feared. This project has become the most important goal of my life. It is my debt to my dead father."

Samuel watched Father Sullivan's face take on a
somber look.

The priest paused to sip his coffee and continued. "I
told him I had heard tell that he was part of an extremely
wealthy Castilian family. I needed only his signature and
that could cause him no problem. I demanded and pleaded.
I must have been completely out of my mind. Nunez
summarily dismissed the idea that the Church or he had
any duty to my parishioners. For the first time in my life,
I became furious at the indifference of a superior. I could
not risk defeat. A great strength came over me, subduing
the habits of a lifetime of obedience. I had to win this
argument."

The priest looked at his guests, "I confronted him by
saying. 'For nearly forty years, since the time I was a boy,
I've belonged to the Church. I've seen the Mother Church
back the vile British landlords against the starving Irish. I
have seen it back corrupt Mexican leaders against the
peasants. But I am not going to watch my parishioners
crushed by an obscenity like Salvadore de Navarro! The
Church owes it to them, I owe it to them, and you, your
Excellency, owe it both to them and to me!'

"It may have been my courage or merely the wine
speaking. After a long silence, Nunez responded, 'Father,
you come close to impertinence, but you must be close to
the truth, to talk that way to me. We have spent many
years together in this archdiocese. You have always been
humble and obedient. But rebelling as you have done
today, the voice of God must be speaking through you. I
will help, but never again take such a tone to me. Father

Sullivan, somehow this has become a time for plain speaking that may never occur again. You will never rise in the Church, for you fail to understand church politics. The guarantee will not be a problem to me.

"'First of all, you and your *amigos* have invested your entire beings in the success of the project. Do not worry. You will not fail in your task. And then, even if it fails, do you think the United States government would proceed on the guarantee against me, a prince of the Roman Catholic Church? It is a mere scrap of paper with my autograph. My loyalty to you will better my position, as my parish priests will admire me for my support of one of them. There is no way I can lose on this matter.'"

"He relaxed, concluding with a smile. 'Besides this, it would give me personal pleasure to see your Jewish friend Rabinowitz win out over de Navarro. I have heard of your sermon denouncing our Church's blaming of the Jews for the crucifixion of Christ, so I do not have to worry about you making any embarrassing comments. I, too, have some old grudges to settle.'"

A Trip to the Fort

CHAPTER FIFTEEN

Once provisions for credit and the guarantee were completed, it was time for Samuel to work on winning the government contract. In order to do this he had to first contact Chaplain Miller and then the Quartermaster at Fort Madison. Using a peddling trip in the vicinity of the fort to disguise his true purpose, the peddler sought to keep news of their plan from reaching de Navarro. If that villain learned of their intentions, all he would have to do to defeat his opponents would be to lower his bid.

It took three days to travel to the Fort, and Samuel passed through a stretch of desert before coming to a mountain range where Yankee farmers had settled in fertile valleys. The desert was more desolate than any area he had ever passed through. Even the scraggly bush was sparse and the tumbleweed rolled in solitude. The sun made it even more wearying.

Then the Sangre de Cristo Mountains were upon him. At times he had to help Manny over the rough spots by encouraging her through narrow passes and down steep descents. The Apaches selected this region for their home as the rugged mountains and vast desert areas protected them. An easy place to defend, the site protected the tribe of warriors from their foes. It had been an unsafe area before settlement by Americans, but now with troops here and the Indian Wars about over, the threat of violence from Indians no longer existed.

Only Geronimo with a small band of warriors remained undefeated. Traveling between Mexico, Arizona, and New Mexico, his raids still struck terror into Mexicans and Americans alike. But this area was far enough away from the fighting to be safe.

Passing through Apache country reminded Samuel of his first contact with an Indian. One morning about two months before, as he came out of his room, he saw a half-starved Apache asking Esther, "Can I do work for something to eat?"

Frightened, she replied, "Sorry but there's nothing here for you to do."

The Indian began to leave when Samuel took over. "We can always find some work for a hungry man." Knowing that a long-standing enmity, caused by a history of violence, existed between Nortenos and Apaches, he became sensitive to Esther's fears. But his Jewish background had taught him never to turn a hungry man away without giving him something to eat. The Indian, too proud to beg, had offered to work. Samuel brought the Indian into the house and sat him down at the kitchen table to a large plate of leftover tortillas and beans. "Here, eat something, so you'll have strength to work."

The Indian trembled as he ate. Revitalized by the food, he looked over at his hosts. "My name is Running Deer. I speak English that I learned when I went to a missionary school as a young man."

In the days that followed, the Indian worked around the store sweeping the floor and the grounds with a broom and shoveling away the debris. He dusted the shelves and straightened the merchandise. As Esther grew to know him, her fears subsided and she made sure he had plenty of food. Samuel made it a point to sit and eat with Running Deer.

As the Indian became more at ease, he talked of his past life. "I fought with Geronimo and other Apaches south of Tucson. I was captured by American troops and placed with other prisoners in a boxcar on a train headed east for Florida where we were to be imprisoned in a government fort. I escaped and traveled to remote areas to avoid capture, trying to return to my tribe. I am eager to reach my people and must leave in a few days."

Esther packed enough food to last the journey and Samuel forced him to take two silver dollars. No one ever saw Running Deer again.

Although he posed no threat to them, Samuel knew that he was not immune to attack by a wild group of young Apache braves. He hoped they felt no hostility towards him. Although they were too poor to purchase anything, the Indians always had a stock of jewelry, hides, and blankets and were anxious to trade for the peddler's goods.

He traveled over the mountain range into the small valleys that nestled between the mountains. The Yankees clustered in small farms in these valleys with their narrow streams. Although they were always referred to as Yankees or Anglos, most farmers came from Kentucky. These newly settled folks would not travel to Ciudad Blanca, which they regarded as a Mexican town. With no competitors, Samuel found sales easy to make.

As he continued his journey, he considered his mission. The Federal Government was using trade to encourage development of the local economy. Each one of the string of small forts spread across the Territory of New Mexico was allowed to purchase its own supplies instead of going through a center such as Fort Union. This boosted the frontier economy as peddlers were allowed freer access to sell to soldiers. Fort Madison became a logical place for Samuel to be heading, even if not for the contract.

Arriving at the Fort, he found tan adobe buildings built around a parade ground in an area about a thousand by eight hundred feet. Samuel knew the garrison was there to escort wagons, protect settlers, and fight raiding Apaches out in the country. With no need to defend against Indian attacks, a wall was unnecessary.

From the parade ground, he sought the Chaplain's office. To the south, he saw buildings that he guessed were the officers' quarters and married officers' housing, as well as the administrative headquarters. To the north, the barracks housed the infantry and the cavalry. Then, to the west, were the quartermaster with his warehouse and the post trader's store. The entire complex fit well into the Mexican style of architecture used throughout the territory, looking more like a small village than a military outpost.

Finally he located the Chaplain's office in a remote corner of the administration building, a plain room without a clerical look. Here he found Reverend Miller and gave him the priest's letter of introduction.

The Chaplain, a slender, pinched-nosed New Englander, invited the peddler to have a cup of coffee and a piece of cake. "Father Sullivan explained your mission to me. It's a little unusual for an Irish Catholic priest and a Jewish peddler to be working together to protect Mexican farmers from exploitation by one of their own. But this country is changing and I guess that nothing should surprise me anymore."

Samuel smiled at what he believed was a compliment.

"When I see the poor Indians in their hopeless fight to preserve their way of life against the cruel policies of our government, I totally despair. Hopefully, there's a place for most everybody in this wonderful country, but I wonder how long it will take.

"And now we must deal with freed slaves. These newly liberated men are not like our free men of color back in Massachusetts. They are poor, maltreated former slaves, ill prepared for freedom. Those Buffalo soldiers, whom you see in our fort, joined the army beginning with their emancipation. They have been placed in segregated units, subjected to racial prejudices, and confined to special barracks near the stables. While it is wrong, it is still a great improvement over slavery. When I see the vile attitude toward our Buffalo soldiers, I wonder how long it will take for them to achieve equality. But still, with all of its problems, the army is the best way to bring these poor souls into our society."

"Are you so sure?" interrupted Samuel. "I left Russia to avoid the Army. For me it would be little above slavery.

I would be gone for twenty-five years and driven from my religion. How can these people be better off in the Army?"

"In America, as opposed to Czarist Russia," replied the minister, "the Army is where farm boys, laborers, immigrants, and freed slaves meet and get to know each other. Prejudices do not disappear but they lessen as everyone learns the necessity of relying upon each other for survival. The Buffalo soldiers still have a long way to go, but hopefully, they will overcome their difficulties. The Irish, the farm boys, and everybody else must learn to do the same." He paused to sip his coffee. "To get back to your mission, I know why you are here and that secrecy is important. I agree with Father Sullivan on the justice of what you are attempting to do. America has no place for despots."

He looked over at Samuel to emphasize his point. "I'll introduce you to Quartermaster John Jones. Keep your goal from him as it might be to his advantage to encourage competition with de Navarro to get the lowest bid. Start by expressing a desire to do some modest trading with individual soldiers. That will keep your presence here subtle." The Chaplain stood up and shook hands with Samuel. "Now let's get you over to meet the Quartermaster."

They left the office and walked through the deserted parade ground over to a large warehouse. They then went to a room in the building where Quartermaster Jones had his office. He was a stocky, bearded man, who looked more like a frontiersman than an army officer. Looking up from his ledgers, he invited the two men in.

"This is my friend, Samuel Rabinowitz, who wanted to meet you."

The peddler inquired, "I guess you sell to the soldiers."

"No," responded Jones. "Many confuse the Quartermaster Corps with those people who do sell to the soldiers. We merely provide supplies to the Army that are given to the men while others sell goods for their personal needs. For a long time, trade in an army post came under the sole control of sutlers, storekeepers with an exclusive right to sell within a post. Patronage appointments of these sutlers led to corruption and that position was abolished shortly after the Civil War."

"So what happened?" asked Samuel.

"Post traders were then appointed by the Secretary of War. But like sutlers, post traders left much to be desired as they offered a limited variety of goods at high prices. The growth of the Quartermaster lessens the reliance of the soldiers on outsiders but we can't provide for many of their personal needs, and the post trader is inadequate. That's why soldiers like peddlers. Peddlers find soldiers good customers since they pay in cash, have nothing to sell, and are eager to buy goods."

Samuel briefly told the Quartermaster of his little store in La Rosa and his desire to expand into this newly settled region. Then he asked, "How does one do business with the government?"

"Trading with the Army," answered Jones, "is a little more complex than trade with individuals on the post. I have a great deal of discretion for day-to-day purchases and would be pleased to deal with you if your prices are reasonable, your merchandise good, and you yourself are responsible. But for the larger orders, there's a lot of paperwork.

"All army contracts are under the Office of the Chief Quartermaster at Fort Union, but for all practical purposes, the bids for Fort Madison will come through me and should be delivered here. You may submit a bid for specific supplies."

Samuel answered, "That's too much for a small peddler like me but I might be interested in doing that at some future date. How would I go about it?"

"We're now contracting for corn to be delivered after the next harvest. We will be seeking to purchase eight thousand *fanegos* of corn. That's a local measure of weight carried over from the Spanish. It's approximately two and one half bushels for each fanego. The total would be about twenty thousand bushels."

Samuel felt the veins in his forehead throb with excitement.

"I have some written specifications for these bids," continued the Quartermaster. He reached into his desk, pulled out a packet of forms, and handed them and a copy of an ad to the peddler. "This is a proposal for army supplies we published in the local newspapers. It will give you the general rules under which we operate. All bids must be submitted by the tenth of March."

Samuel's hand shook as the Quartermaster handed him the remaining materials. "This is your bid form. You must fill it out and file three copies with me. Do not overlook the guarantee. The awards will be made to the lowest bidder on March 24th. This might be too short a time for you this year. But if you bid and win, then the proposal becomes a contract and the guarantee, a bond."

"I'm only a peddler and have never sold to anyone except farmers and artisans," said Samuel. "If you don't mind, I'd like to be considered for selling to Fort Madison. I'll read your materials and then maybe I could come back from time to time and see if we might be able to do some business. Thanks for your help."

Leaving with his precious packet of instructions and application to bid, Samuel was elated. He climbed into his wagon and couldn't wait to get his information back to Esther, Reuben, and Father Sullivan. As he stopped to camp, he worried, *"Are the priest's plans too ambitious? Are we courting disaster? What will happen if we fail?"*

The next day, Samuel returned to La Rosa, clutching his valuable forms. Entering the store, he saw a few customers.

Samuel waited in the house until the store cleared, then Esther and Rueben joined him.

"I've got the bid proposal forms and the instruction booklet. There's a long form that we have to fill out." He opened the small packet and spread its contents on the table. Then he picked up the newspaper ad and read off, "Proposals for Army Supplies."

He continued reading aloud when Reuben interrupted by asking, "Samuel, what does future appropriations mean?"

"I'm sure I don't know, but what about the word merchantable?"

Then Esther smiled and added, "How do you entertain a bid?"

"Well, maybe you tell it funny stories," said Samuel. "Enough of this. Let's look at the next form. He began to read the contract for corn. The phrase "Articles of Agreement" left all three of them with dazed expressions. Then when Samuel read off "Heirs, executors, administrators, and assigns," they were completely baffled. So he moved on to the next document, the bond, and read, beginning with "Know all men by these presents..."

A look of bewilderment came over their faces. The three partners sat around the table; their limited education, their life experiences, and their language backgrounds were all inadequate for the occasion.

Samuel said, "Perhaps my problem is that I think in Yiddish. Every time I read a question and see the strange words, I say to myself, *Vos meint dos?* What does it mean? I try to translate the words into Yiddish, but even then it doesn't make sense."

"My problem is similar," confessed Reuben. "I say to myself, *Que significa?* What does it mean? I translate the words into Spanish, but it doesn't make any more sense in Spanish than it did in English."

"If you two will listen to me," interrupted Esther, "you will take the forms to Father Sullivan. He is an educated man, who can both read and think in English. He will know what to do. Why don't the two of you go early tomorrow? I will watch the store."

At daybreak the next morning, Samuel and Reuben were off to see the priest. They arrived at St. Xavier before noon. After they knocked, the housekeeper opened the door and led them to his study. Father Sullivan told her, "Please see to it that we are not disturbed. Sit down gentlemen." They seated themselves in comfortable chairs in the study. "How can I help you?"

"Padre, we need your help," the visitors declared. "We can't understand any of these army forms."

A knock on the door interrupted them. It was Louisa with a tray of coffee and some cakes. "Please come in," said the priest, who then put a finger to his lips. He took the tray and then dismissed Louisa. Then in a low voice, he said, "Please, speak quietly. Secrecy is crucial, especially when my housekeeper is around. She is a fine woman, but loves to gossip. In a matter of hours everything would be back to de Navarro. If our secret is out, all is lost." As he poured the coffee, he added in a whisper, "Now gentlemen, sit down and tell me what is the matter?"

As Samuel spread the papers on the table, he quietly confided, "I don't understand these forms. They're just beyond me."

"I don't either," added Reuben.

Father Sullivan sat down and carefully examined the instruction booklet and the application. After reviewing them for several minutes, he looked up. "Don't worry, gentlemen, the fault is not yours. These forms aren't in English, they are in the language of all large institutions. But as a long-time member of another bureaucratic organization, I understand the language and can help."

Reuben and Samuel listened eagerly to every word.

"Basically, we must deliver twenty thousand bushels of corn. The corn must be dried and free of dirt, cobs, and all foreign substances. And it must be delivered in sacks of one hundred to one hundred and fifty pounds."

And so the priest sat down with the forms and with the help of Reuben and Samuel, carefully filled them out. He then reviewed, corrected, and fully prepared the papers for submission.

Then the priest winked, a broad smile filling his face as he reached for the bottle of sacramental wine in his cabinet. "Gentlemen, let us ask for God's blessing on our enterprise." Pouring three small glasses of wine, he said a few words in Latin.

Samuel added, *"L'chaim."* He thought, *"I hope to God that we are able to complete this task. Failure is too frightening to contemplate."*

BOOK FOUR
The Plan Must Not Fail

The First Victory

CHAPTER SIXTEEN

On March 4, Samuel returned to Fort Madison. He meandered between Ciudad Blanca and the Fort, visiting clusters of American settlers in fertile valleys and Mexican farmers in the more mountainous regions. Having learned his new customers' needs, he brought a more desirable line of merchandise. His new patrons, pleased to see him, made sales brisk.

Four days later the young peddler arrived at the Fort in early morning, the day before bids were due. He went first to see Jones to give him the pick of his wares. After that he sold most of the remaining goods to the soldiers.

He watched the Quartermaster Building until he saw one of de Navarro's men deliver an envelope, which had to be the merchant's bid. Once the messenger left, de Navarro would have no way to learn of Samuel's bid in time to react.

Later that afternoon, the peddler returned to the Quartermaster's office. "Mr. Jones, I'll be leaving in the morning for La Rosa and just wanted to say goodbye. Do you remember when I first came here? You were good enough to show me how to sell to the government."

"Sure Sammy!" Jones raised an eyebrow and, in a tone of mock surprise, suggested, "Are you preparing to make a bid?"

"I'm bidding on the corn, all 20,000 bushels. Here are my forms in perfect shape, all three copies signed and sealed, guarantee included."

Reaching out to accept the envelope containing the documents, Jones gasped, "Good luck to you, Mr. Rabinowitz."

Samuel left the building inflated with a feeling of success. All the way home he thought about how much more remained to be done. He then contemplated all the difficulties that might arise.

The two weeks between the submission of the bid and the date of the award passed so slowly as to be barely tolerable. It became the most important thing in their lives, all they talked and dreamed about. It occupied every waking moment for Father Sullivan, the Carvellos, and Samuel.

Finally, Samuel headed back to the Fort. Too impatient to meander, he arrived the night before results were to be given out. There he saw the Quartermaster.

Jones smiled. "Samuel, why so nervous?"

But this made him worry even more, as he awaited the posting of the award. His relative indifference when Father Sullivan first proposed the plan had now become a total commitment and, perhaps, even an obsession.

He bedded down in a haystack and tossed and turned all night. He woke well before dawn even though the award would not be posted until 9 A.M. Up before the bugler summoned the soldiers to their morning duties, Samuel dressed, made his morning prayers, and then headed to the Quartermaster building, where he arrived long before the time for the awards.

At last, at 9 A.M., Jones walked over to the bulletin board and began posting awards. Bidders crowded around to see the results. They peered intently as each item was posted. Shouts of excitement came from the winners and sighs of disappointment from the losers. Finally, when the results of the bids for corn were posted, Samuel let out a scream.

Suddenly an angry face stared at him. "You have stolen my contract, you dirty Jew. I'll get you, your friends, and that drunken Irish priest for what you have done to me. You'll regret the day you came to La Rosa."

As de Navarro stormed away, Samuel felt a terrifying chill run through his body, dampening the thrill that had come with victory.

All the way back to La Rosa, the peddler's mind moved between elation at winning and depression over the threat. Esther and Reuben stood on the veranda, eagerly awaiting his return. Concerned over how to tell them of the threat, Samuel smiled and waved so that they would first know of the victory.

He came down off the wagon into their open arms. "We've won! We've won!" said Samuel.

"Bravo!" shouted Reuben.

"It's a miracle," added Esther.

The three hugged each other and danced together.

"Come into the house," urged Reuben. "My daughter has made a marvelous dinner."

"Do you think God will mind? I've made you a Shabbes dinner to celebrate, and its only Thursday."

Samuel's smile contained a hint of theological approval.

After their festive meal, they sat on the portico. Samuel reviewed the day's proceedings and then told them of de Navarro's threat.

"We should have expected it, but I'm frightened," said Reuben.

"Father Sullivan will know how to deal with him," Esther suggested.

Early the next morning, Reuben and Samuel rode to Ciudad Blanca, with Esther remaining behind to run the store.

"Welcome," said Father Sullivan. "Please come into my study."

The peddler repeated the story of winning the bid. He paused and then told the priest of de Navarro's threat.

"I must congratulate you upon winning the bid." said Father Sullivan. Then, in a more somber tone, he continued. "Although we must thank God for our initial victory, we must fully understand that His testing of us is not over. De Navarro will use every vile trick he can think of to defeat us. If this town is to be saved, we must over-come his threats and maintain our victory until we deliver the corn. We must not fear the forces of evil for God is with us, but we must be ever vigilant."

That night they made detailed plans as to how to proceed. Near midnight, Father Sullivan summarized their discussion. "Samuel, as you've completed the arrangements with Mordecai Cohen for seed and supplies, and I have secured the guarantor, we must now implement the plan, for unless we produce the corn and deliver it, all will have been in vain.

"The most important thing for each of us to do is to find enough farmers. Reuben and Esther must contact those in and around La Rosa. Samuel must see those he peddles to in the outlying areas, and I will talk to my parishioners here in Ciudad Blanca."

Samuel and Reuben nodded in agreement.

"We must plan to harvest, prepare, and deliver the corn, but the farmers must not overextend themselves. While credit here is a necessity, too much credit could be destructive. They must have monies left over after the government pays for the corn to protect their future."

A week later in the priest's study, Father Sullivan asked Reuben and Samuel, "How have you done in signing up farmers?"

"Esther and I found twenty-three farmers who will join with us. We had made discrete inquiries and prepared a list of prospects well before our winning the bid so that we could move quickly. Each has been offered seed corn and other supplies while setting a goal of growing two hundred to two hundred and fifty bushels of corn. This will allow them to continue to grow most of their own food," said Reuben.

Samuel added, "I've nineteen farmers willing to join on a similar basis. The outlook for more is quite good."

Father Sullivan said, "'Tis an embarrassment for me to tell you of my problem. I should have had the easiest task of all of us, as I've known these farmers since I came here. I've baptized them, married them, and buried their loved ones. They are my parishioners. I had forty farmers committed, but some are leaving each day.

"Would you believe that I, who knows de Navarro best of all, have underestimated that fiend's pressures on his customers? All of their lives, they have been intimidated, afraid of what could happen if they opposed him and lost.

"I've sought information as to what he was up to. I've made inquiries around town and finally found a parishioner who is willing to talk to us after I promised him secrecy. He is Luis Francisco, the owner of the livery stable. I've sent for him."

A few minutes later Francisco, a portly man in his late thirties, was ushered into the room. "Gentlemen, please keep my presence secret for I do not wish to incur Senor de Navarro's wrath."

After they assured him of confidentially, Francisco, perspiration on his forehead, turned his head down to avoid looking at them. In English, heavily accented with Spanish pronunciation, he began, "De Navarro has ruled this town for so long that he believes he is unbeatable. Unfortunately, since he has always prevailed, most townspeople agree with him."

Then, looking up at Samuel and Reuben, he continued, "When you took some of his business at La Rosa, he merely resented you. But when he failed to force you to leave, it enraged him. Then when you obtained the contract for corn from the Fort, that was the last straw. He was livid. To him, it is now an insult that must be avenged."

He paused, wiped his sweaty forehead and thick moustache with his handkerchief, and continued. "Yesterday as I was having lunch at the tavern, he sat nearby with his little group of desperados around him. He ranted on about getting the Jews, Samuel, Reuben and Father Sullivan. For now, with what has occurred, all his enemies are Jews.

"He will do everything possible to keep you from fulfilling the contract. As the *rancheros* come to obtain credit from him, pressure is applied. If they are working with you, he calls in his credit. They are helpless, as they are unable to repay him. If all else fails, expect violence. He is obsessed with destroying the three of you." Francisco rose and readied himself to leave.

"Thank you for your help," said Father Sullivan.

Francisco left, looking around carefully to make sure he was not seen.

As if he were reading the young peddler's mind, Father Sullivan said, "I am and have always been a man of peace. I, too, fear the violence that de Navarro threatens. But it is too late to look back. He will try to destroy us. Pray to God for His protection. Already his vile threats are coming true. I am unable to keep many of the farmers involved in the project and we can't fulfill the contract without them. While we must increase our efforts by recruiting more farmers and reassuring those already committed, it won't be enough unless we stop de Navarro here in Ciudad Blanca. I fear what will happen to this poor city, everyone in it, and us if we fail. Pray to God for His protection. The plan must not fail! We must succeed!"

When they met a week later, Father Sullivan reported, "The dire predictions of Luis Francisco have come true. Half of the farmers I recruited have backed out, giving lame excuses. 'Tis clear that de Navarro has frightened them away. In this part of the world, they have been intimidated for more than three hundred years. The Spaniards taught the Mexicans how to oppress their own. De Navarro has created an image of himself as a Spanish *Grande,* a nobleman, who strikes fear in his inferiors by treating them with contempt. The worst part is that the farmers accept this."

"Even with our new recruits, I don't see how we can save the plan," said Samuel.

"The farmers must be convinced that they'll be protected from de Navarro's wrath," said Reuben. "But they have been let down too many times and find it difficult to believe they can win. We must reassure them by creating another place for them to buy. Perhaps Samuel can bring a wagonload of goods into town each week."

"I can't do it without dropping some other territory," responded Samuel. "When we expanded to Fort Madison, I stretched myself as far as possible. I just can't do anything more and keep my new territory."

"Let us retire. You shall be my guests here. We will sleep on it. God sometimes has a way of suggesting things in our dreams," said Father Sullivan.

As the three men parted with heavy hearts, Samuel knew they must save their plan. But how could it be done?

They came to breakfast showing the effects of a sleepless night. Each admitted to having tossed and turned, not able to drive the problem out of his mind.

Reuben began, "Padre, I don't pretend to be a preacher, but I believe that God has given man the tools to solve his problems. If de Navarro controls this town, he will frighten away any of the farmers who are willing to come in with us, and so the project will fail."

Father Sullivan interposed, "Samuel, is there no way for you to come and sell in Ciudad Blanca?"

"For the life of me, I don't know how," replied Samuel. "I just can't give up any of my territory, especially since we need it to keep the project going. I must bring in more new customers from the north."

"Since Miriam's death I have always thought of myself as an old man although I am only a little more than forty," said Reuben. "But when Samuel came into my life, for the first time I quit feeling sorry for myself. Suddenly I was doing more work. I have always done some farming, but I fixed the old wagon, remodeled the shed into a store, and built an addition. Maybe I can do more. Perhaps I could come to Ciudad Blanca. I must do whatever is necessary for the success of our project."

"I, too, feel helpless," added the priest. "I had a fretful night, and I will tell you of my strange dream of the old Bible story of the Israelites leaving Egypt. But the Pharaoh was de Navarro and the Israelites the farmers. The Pharaoh's overseers, who, strangely enough, looked like de Navarro's desperados, beat the Israelites. Moses, who looked remarkably like Reuben, struck down the overseers and led the farmers to St. Xavier. They did not go into the Church but continued past it to the old abandoned building that had been the original church. Here, Moses gave the men food. Then he led them toward the Holy Land, where they crossed over a dry *arroyo*. When the overseers came after them, they were drowned by a flash flood.

"Now, I would have you believe that I have no idea as to whether this comes from divine inspiration, indigestion, or a restless mind. But in any event, it may be the Lord's way of sending us a good idea. Why not open the old abandoned church building as a branch of Carvello and Rabinowitz and have Reuben run it? In addition to everything else, his presence here would be a visible sign of our confidence in the project. People would see that we believe that we intend to remain and will succeed. It would counter fears of de Navarro's treachery and give them faith and additional strength for whatever we may have to face from de Navarro."

A few days later a sign went up over the old church building reading *Carvello and Rabinowitz General Merchandise Ciudad Blanca Branch*. Samuel brought a load of merchandise from La Rosa and then headed back to Las Vegas for more. In the meantime, Reuben was building shelves and a counter and, in the midst of all this, constantly waiting on customers.

Hannah

CHAPTER SEVENTEEN

Samuel returned to Las Vegas on April 2nd. He tied up Manny, gave her food and water, and then went into the Emporium.

Mordecai, who had been waiting, called over an attractive young woman in an apron and said to the peddler, "I'd like you to meet our new sales clerk. Miss, please come over here for a moment to meet one of our best customers. This is Samuel Rabinowitz. I want you to treat him with all the respect he deserves."

The young woman mumbled, *"Sholom, bist du Sholom, mine bruder?"* Then in her broken English, she repeated, "Are you Sholom, *mine bruder?*"

With a grin, Mordecai added, "I believe her name is Hannah Rabinowitz."

Stunned, Samuel stared at the woman. It was over two years since he had last seen Hannah and he hardly recognized her. Finally he adjusted to the new reality facing him. He looked closely at his sister. She was no longer the child he had left back in Belkov, but was now a woman, with a pretty face, brown hair, and sparkling brown eyes. She resembled Momma.

Overcoming his embarrassment at his failure to immediately know her, he grabbed her with an enthusiastic hug. Tears filled both their eyes. Regaining self control, he spoke to her in Yiddish. "Hannah, did you have any trouble getting here from New York? If it is easier, speak Yiddish and I will translate."

"It's hokey, Sholom. I learned a liddle Yinglish and vant to do bedder. Dank you, but I vill try in Yinglish.

Mine bruder, ven you sended us your ledder *mit die gelt,* you gafe me goot instruction. I know deese by hart. You said I should take the Santa Fe train to Las Vegas. Den, you wrote directions of how I should get from the train station to Cohen's Main Street Emporium."

Samuel smiled. His sister was here, mission accomplished.

Bertha walked in from the backroom where she and Alfred were watching the meeting. She burst out laughing. "I can tell you what happened next. We all knew that Hannah was coming, but no one knew when. So my brother met every train."

"Actually there's only one train from Chicago so I met it every day," said Alfred, with a grin that spread over his face. "Every day at about three in the afternoon, I put on my jacket, and walked a quarter mile across the square and down the street to the station. I walked across the platform to see the time posted for the train's arrival. Sometimes I'd have to wait as long as an hour or even more; once it was three hours late. But still I waited for the 3:30 train."

"As the passengers came off," Bertha took up the tale, "he looked at every girl, especially if she looked anything like a pretty Jewish one. Then when he saw a frightened looking girl with two large suitcases..."

"I called out to that frightened little thing, "Hannah, are you Hannah?" Alfred broke in, "and then I said it again in Yiddish, 'Hannah, *bist du* Hannah? I'm Alfred.' She was so shocked to see someone waiting for her, she froze."

Hannah intervened, "Sholem, ven you tolded me dat I should not talk mit strangers, not even Jewish vones, I remembered. So I valked avay from him. He vas a pest and I vas going to hit him with mine suitcase and scream. But I felded sorry for him. Den I remembered his name from de ledder."

"Only when I explained who I was and why I was there did she calm down. She wouldn't even let me carry her bags." Alfred chuckled. "Perhaps she heard too many stories about white slavers taking advantage of young immigrant girls. Once she settled down, I took her to the store where she met my sister and Mordecai."

Bertha again took up the conversation. "After I took her home, I explained to her that it was important to learn about life on the Western frontier. I told Hannah many things about the position of women and, especially, Jewish women here. I advised her how to adjust to her new world since the frontier has no place for putting down women like Europe and back east. I said she would find many suitors waiting for her but, of course, none would be as fine as Alfred."

Impatient, Mordecai added. "I brought her into the store as a clerk as part of the joke we were to play on you, but she's done so well I think we'll keep her here." Then winking at Samuel, he added, "Especially since Alfred has never worked so hard."

Samuel laughed as Alfred and Hannah both blushed.

Bertha sensed their embarrassment and shooed everyone away. "Let them have some privacy."

Once seated in Mordecai's office, Samuel wouldn't let go of Hannah's hand and asked, "Tell me about the family and your trip to America."

"Sholom," Hannah began, changing from her halting English into fluent Yiddish. "Momma became depressed as I prepared to leave. Poppa was too, but he hid it. With Nathan and Isaac gone, I was their last child and about to leave home."

"Both gone? Are they all right?"

She paused to wipe her eyes. "They're as well as can be expected. We must bring Momma and Poppa here as quickly as possible. Momma used the clothes in my suitcases to wrap the family's precious belongings including the Kiddush cup and the menorah. Although Momma was reluctant to part with these, she was much more afraid that if they did not make it to America, they might be abandoned or destroyed and no longer remain with our family. These were her last links to her children and were surrendered to me. She feared that the loss of these would end Jewish life in our family. It was her hope for a Jewish future for her family even though she believed she might never survive."

Samuel dabbed his sister's eyes with his handkerchief.

"Even though I'm almost sixteen, Momma and Poppa were afraid to have me travel by myself. So they looked around Belkov to see who was coming to America and found Mendel the blacksmith."

"I remember Mendel and his family," said Samuel.

"Well, he and his wife Sadie have four small children and were happy to have me with them so I could help her. It was hard work but it kept me from feeling lonesome. We traveled together until we arrived at Castle Garden, where I met Cousin Abe."

"How are they?" asked Samuel.

"Everyone is fine. I stayed with them for three days, getting used to America. They are very kind and they all miss you, especially Sarah, who seemed very fond of you."

Samuel, embarrassed at the mention of Sarah's affection and impatient for further news of his parents, interrupted, "But what's happening at home? I guessed that Poppa was unable to tell me the details. I could only assume that they could not write freely for fear that the Russians might read the letters and punish them."

"Sholom, you are right. Ever since Nathan became hunted by the police, our house has been watched by the authorities."

"What do you mean? What's happened to him? Is he safe?"

"Let me go back a bit. You have been away a long time. The world in Belkov and in all of Russia is changing. It began before you left, but you were too busy working with Poppa to notice the changes that affected Isaac and Nathan."

"Where are my brothers?"

"About a year after you went to America, Isaac left home and made a long and difficult trip of thousands of miles to Israel. Once there, he went to work on a *kibbutz*, on land purchased by the great Jewish philanthropist

Baron Rothschild. But the land was worthless since centuries of Arab farming robbed it of its biblical fertility. It did not even produce enough to feed its new occupants. Jewish settlers first followed the pattern of the Arab farmers. When that failed, they tried to copy European farming techniques, which also failed. Successful farming methods still need to be developed. Isaac's letters made it clear that it would be a long time before he could send for any of us."

"But what of Nathan?"

"Give me a minute to tell you the whole story. Since you left, changes have come even more rapidly. Many young people, Jews and Gentiles alike, oppose the autocratic system. Everyone talks of reform. They have discovered what goes on in the rest of the world and are no longer content. A new world is coming to Russia. People are talking of revolution, of ending the monarchy, and even of democracy with a *duma,* an elected legislature. But for us as Jews, life in Belkov is getting worse and worse."

She looked over at him with sorrowful eyes. Twisting her long thin fingers and gesturing with her hands, her voice took on a sorrowful tone. Her pretty mouth changed from a smile to a frown. "The Ukrainian peasant boys continued their threats against us. Our family, fearful for safety, hid during the pogrom in the root cellar beneath the trap door. As Easter drew near, the young thugs boasted they had learned of the secret room. You cannot imagine how frightening it was."

As she shuddered at the memory, Samuel hugged her.

"Peasants again spread the story of a Christian child kidnapped and murdered by Jews, who drained the child's blood to make matzahs. The peasants hate the Jews so much that they believed this crazy story. Before long, drunken peasants ran amok through the streets killing Jewish men and raping Jewish women.

"Poppa went off to shul to pray for God's protection for his family. Nathan argued that this was not enough and that Jews must no longer merely pray but must take action. We barricaded the doors and windows and hid in the cellar. Then Nathan disappeared. As the sounds of violence outside the house increased, we shuddered. The thugs began battering down the door of our home. We huddled in fear in the cellar."

Fear came over her face as she continued her tale. "Suddenly Nathan and his band appeared out of the dark alongside the house. It was only due to the moonlight that we could see them through the cellar window. Catching the Ukrainian youths by surprise, they beat them with wooden clubs. The peasant boys could not believe Jews could defend themselves and quickly left with broken bones and bruises. But one never ran away. He was dead. Nathan and his friends picked up the body, dumped it in a nearby stream, and fled. Then they went into hiding."

"Is he safe?" asked Samuel.

"Yes. But, once the pogrom ended, the police investigated. They had no concern over Jewish deaths, but the death of a Gentile boy, killed by Jews, was an intolerable crime. They declared that it was a plot by revolutionaries. Suspicion fell on Nathan, who upon returning to the house, found out about the danger. Poppa gave him the twenty rubles you sent to buy another cow. The money probably saved his life. He has disappeared and we can only hope he is safe. We have heard that he has become committed to the overthrow of the Czarist government and is now hunted as a revolutionary." Finishing her story, a tearful Hannah stressed, "This change only the Russians could have caused. We must bring Momma and Poppa to America while there is still time. I am afraid for them."

Samuel smiled. "In America, you will soon get over your sadness. You are no longer a young girl but are now a woman. It will not be long before all of the eligible Jewish bachelors in the Southwest will be courting you. Alfred is already interested. Life here will be a great relief after the terrors you faced in Russia."

He told Hannah about his boat trip to America, his travels to the West, the meetings with the Cohens and the Carvellos, the opening of the store, the problems with de Navarro, the army contract, and the new branch. "With you working in Las Vegas or in La Rosa, before long we will have enough money to bring Momma and Poppa to America. As soon as possible, I will take you with me to meet my friends."

"Brother, I'm pleased to be here but I'm a little confused about all that has happened to you. I know you must leave, but come back for me soon."

"Hannah, we are together again. I am no longer completely without my family. You have been brave and strong to travel this far, and soon enough we will look into the faces of Momma and Poppa."

As difficult as he found it to tear himself away from his sister, Samuel quickly loaded his wagon. He was in a hurry to get back. His mind was anxious about two great pressures in his world: the problem of helping his family and the more immediate concerns of fulfilling the contract and defeating de Navarro.

Passover

CHAPTER EIGHTEEN

O n Sunday, April 24, 1887, Samuel returned from
Las Vegas with Hannah. As they rode up to the
store, Esther eagerly awaited them. The young
women hugged and called each other sister.

Reuben laughed. "You two could almost pass for sisters."

"I'm so happy to see all of you," said Esther.
"Although running this store is hard, it keeps me from
being lonesome."

After unloading the merchandise for the La Rosa store,
two crates remained. Samuel had pushed them to a side.

Esther noticed his actions and commented, "What
mischief are you up to? That silly grin gives you away."

The young peddler burst out laughing. "Hannah and
I have come to take you two out of Egypt. This is the time
of *Pesach*, Passover, a festival celebrated by the Jewish
people to commemorate their redemption by God from
slavery and their return to Eretz Yisrael. It is the essence
of our religion, so we reenact it every year. We have come
to La Rosa to share our holiday with you."

His hosts stared as he opened the first crate. He took
out a new set of dishes and a lovely white linen tablecloth.
"I wrote to Chicago for these. They came by train last
week." He then took a booklet from the crate. "This is a
Haggadah. The word means 'what is said.' It explains the
order of the Seder, our festival services."

Esther and Reuben looked with amazement as Samuel
continued. As he opened the second crate, Hannah broke
in, "Dees box has food for Pesach. I cooked mit Bertha
Cohen for her family and she vas gut enough to make
some for us.

"Mordecai asked if I vould vork mit Bertha on de cooking. He said dat it vas more important den mine vork in de store. Ve vorked long hours for many days cooking in de kitchen. De gefilte fish alone took lots of time." She pulled out strange looking parcels of food including hard flat crackers.

"They look like tortillas," said Esther.

"Perhaps they are related, but these are matzahs, unleavened bread," Samuel said. "Today we shall lead Reuben and Esther out of Egypt into Eretz Yisrael, the land of Israel. Come along, as we are no longer slaves but free people and we should not tarry. In order to leave Egypt quickly, we will have no time to wait for dough to rise and so must eat matzah."

A look of pride came over Samuel's face. "Last night I was a participant in Mordecai's Seder. Today, for the first time in my life, I will lead one. From the time I was a small boy I was merely a participant as someone else was the host and led the services. Today I will lead the services in my home." He looked around the room. "To this little house on the American frontier in Gentile America, I will bring Passover. God, help me make my place in my home in this new country."

"But," interrupted Hannah, "first ve must take all of the *chometz*, the leavened bread. Ve must sell or giffe it to Gentiles. Dis separates Pesach from de rest of de year."

"Why don't we just give it to our neighbor, the widow Alvarez?" suggested Esther. "With a houseful of children, she has plenty of mouths to feed. Already this holy day has accomplished a good deed."

"That's a fine idea. It is a mitzvah," agreed Samuel. "And so, with your help, we shall prepare for the Passover seder." He had Reuben don a yarmulke, explaining that a Jewish man should keep his head covered out of respect for God. Then he passed out copies of the Haggadah with its bright cover printed in many colors. On the inside, the writing was in Hebrew on one side of the page and English on the other. It even had pen and ink illustrations and many songs, prayers, stories, and commentaries.

"Hannah has brought our family's religious objects from our home. By using these today, we will continue our family's tradition."

His sister pulled out of a bag two Shabbes candlesticks, a menorah, two special platters, and a Kiddush cup. "I must write and tell Momma dat ve are using dem in our first Pesach in La Rosa. She vill be trilled to know dat ve are carrying on mit our Jewish traditions here in Samuel's home in America."

"What does it all mean? Tell me more about this holy day," inquired Reuben.

"Passover celebrates God's redeeming of the Jews from slavery in Egypt," explained Samuel. "This we reenact every year at our seder. It is the very essence of our religion. Not only are we grateful for God's delivering the Jewish people from Egypt but in addition, we celebrate His covenant with us by the giving of the Ten Commandments, the forty years in the desert, and the return to Eretz Yisrael.

"The message against slavery and the Ten Commandments are part of everyone's heritage. I have learned this from educated people I've met in my travels. In the late Civil War, Northern clergymen, especially abolitionists, frequently quoted our Hebrew Bible regarding Passover in support of their position against slavery."

Samuel paused to look around the table before continuing. "But Passover has two sides. On the one hand, in each generation, when our enemies rise up to do us harm, God with His burning wrath acts to protect us and destroy our persecutors. So whether it is the Egyptians, the Spanish, or the Russians, we must remember on every Passover our redemption by God from our suffering as well as the destruction of our enemies. But it is more important to remember that we have survived and multiplied.

"The freeing of the Jews from bondage marks one of the few times in history that a nation of slaves living under an alien master revolted and became free. We Jews look to the Exodus in a personal sense, marking our special relationship with God. For in every generation the Almighty redeems each of us."

Reuben and Esther looked on as the house was transformed. The rough wooden table was covered with a
beautiful white tablecloth. The special new dishes were in
place. Fresh candles were placed into the candleholders
waiting to be lit.

"Dese dishes are very special," explained Hannah. "Ve
use dem only on Pesach and den only for meat dishes. Ve
never mix meat mit milk. Dey are another sign of separa-
tion from the rest of the year. Dese two platters are only
for Pesach foods. The first has on it three matzahs. The
second has parsley, a hard boiled egg, a lamb shank bone,
horseradish, and *charoses,* which is a combination of
chopped apples, nuts, raisins, and cinnamon."

Then Samuel, leading the seder, explained the part that
each of these played in the Passover service. He went
slowly through the service, reading the Hebrew and
explaining in English as they proceeded. Then Reuben
and Esther alternated the English readings. Hannah, with
her limited ability to read in either language, added her
voice where she could, helped by memories of other
Passovers. As the seder revived memories of the past,
Hannah and Samuel filled the air with songs and stories
of Passover. Soon Esther and Reuben joined in.

When the youngest was to ask the traditional four
questions about the meaning of the holiday, both Esther
and Hannah were selected. They asked in unison, "Why
is this night different from all other nights?"

The answer from Samuel summarized the history of
the Jews from the ending of Egyptian slavery to the return
to Israel, symbolizing the continuity of the tradition of
passing on knowledge of the past. Then he stated, "I, as
many before me, am the bridge to future generations."

A bottle of Malaga wine, a sweet sacramental beverage
used at Passover, was opened and four glasses were filled
as directed by the Haggadah. The door was opened to
allow the prophet Elijah to enter and drink a special glass
of wine set out for him.

The Passover meal was a wonderful treat. Bertha and
Hannah had made gefilte fish, chicken soup with matzah

balls, roast chicken, and several special desserts. The food was an integral part of the ceremony. After consuming a delicious meal, they finished the seder and cried out, "Next year in Jerusalem!"

"Passover, to me," commented Samuel, "reinforces my Jewish beliefs. Every year, Hannah and I have celebrated our part of carrying on an eternal ceremony, the tradition of our people. But today, it is in my home."

Reuben, in the quiet tone of one whose strength has been sapped by memories, said, "It reminds me of a dream of my childhood, and today it was even better, because it did not fade away."

"What do you mean?" asked Samuel looking at his host, who suddenly appeared to be a tired old man.

"I am now forty years old, yet I remember the dream of my youth as though it were yesterday. It must have been more than thirty years ago, probably around 1856. I was ten years old. My grandfather, then about ten years older than I am now, would tell me of the strange customs of our family. He told me some of the stories that were passed down from generation to generation. I had to swear to tell no one. He was the first one to give me a clue as to my family secrets, as others did not approve."

He sat back in his chair, closed his eyes, and seemed to drift off into the past. "It is hard to separate my dreams from tonight. I don't really know if they are inspired by my grandfather's stories or by tonight's events. These memories seem so old that I am not sure how or why they come to me. It's almost as if I had a memory as part of an ancient race with its own customs and traditions that have been transmitted to my mind in a way I do not understand. And now my memories have begun to fade, fade until they have all but disappeared."

Esther stared. "Father, why have you never spoken to me of these things?"

"*Lita*, my darling, it is only this festival that has returned me to the past. In my youth, Grandfather told me of a festival held each year in honor of God and of freedom. It took place in a hidden storage room, whose

windows were sealed off so that no light could escape. All
of the servants were sent away. The ladies of the house
did all of the housework and cooking. A strange ritual
took place with praying and singing. We were warned
that if we said anything to the servants or neighbors, disaster might befall us.

"On the night that grandfather told me this story, I
had difficulty falling asleep. Finally, I drifted off, dreaming that I was in that hidden room. Everyone in the family
was there. They were both elated and fearful. Strange
singing was going on sounding like tonight. Suddenly a
noise came from outside. Spanish soldiers accompanied
by priests broke in. The adults were dragged away to the
Inquisition. Although I knew that the Spanish Inquisition
was long over and could never again affect us in America,
I was in terror and wept. My crying woke me out of my
dream.

"Somehow, I have never been able to determine if my
dream really occurred. I have not remembered this for
many years until your seder reminded me. My hidden
fears had let these thoughts come out only in my dreams.
I was even too fearful to speak of it until today. It is still
difficult for me to explain. I believe that if I had been discovered at this seder, soldiers and priests would have come
for me. Secrecy and fear have become part of my heritage.
Although the Inquisition is gone, the fear remains as if
my belief had helped it to continue. For me, it will never
be over." He stopped and looked over at Samuel. "I was
not apprehensive until these memories came back. For
the first time my sense of danger seemed to be offset by
the pleasure I found in your seder. Perhaps it has alleviated
my fears."

Samuel looked around the room and saw Reuben spent
by his confession. The wonderful evening ended on this
strange note. For a day they had forgotten the problems
that confronted them. The festive nature of the holiday
and Reuben's strange response pushed everything aside
until the morning.

The Dowager of the Carvellos

CHAPTER NINETEEN

*T*he morning after the Passover seder, Samuel explained to Hannah what was required to fulfill the Army contract and how de Navarro would fight them at every opportunity. "Now that Reuben has moved to Ciudad Blanca to manage the store, we need someone to live with Esther in La Rosa."

"From the time Miriam died," Reuben added, "I have been father and mother to my daughter. Not for a single day has she been left alone until I went to Ciudad Blanca."

"While on the road, I won't be around to be here with her," said Samuel.

"I am probably more capable of protecting myself than either of you," declared Esther. "While I do not fear the hired desperados of de Navarro, I do fear the wagging tongues of La Rosa. They could be much more difficult. Samuel has always been a gentleman and would not violate my trust. But as a woman in La Rosa with my father not here, that alone will be enough for gossipy women."

"Perhaps my sister could help," said Samuel.

"Hannah, would you come to La Rosa?" asked Reuben.

"If I could be off help, I vould come gladly but I must speak mit Mordecai first. I owe it to him," said Hannah.

"That would solve our problem," said Samuel.

"That would be fine to help out in the store but she would not be acceptable for long as a chaperon both because of her age and because she is Samuel's sister," replied Esther.

"Maybe there is an older woman who could stay in the house, a neighbor," suggested Reuben.

They mulled over the likely prospects, reviewing most of the people who lived in their little pueblo. Their neighbors were mostly mothers with small children. None was a close friend. No choice came to mind.

"I have it!" Reuben suddenly cried out. "Esther's Aunt Gracia Carvello might be just the one. She is the widow of my brother Aaron. Her children are grown and married. One daughter, Rachel Mendoza, and her husband, Arturo, run the family farm in Ciudad Blanca. She has little to do. But I must tell you she may be difficult to live with unless obeyed."

"I'll manage to get along with her. But will she do it for us?" asked Esther

Reuben smiled. "Years ago Gracia and I were great friends. We grew up together. I was still a young man when she married my eldest brother, Aaron. She spent many a day trying to teach me some good sense, but I was wild and would listen to no one. She'll help us."

"So let's ask her," said Esther.

The next day Reuben and Esther rode over to the Carvello *hacienda.* They rode beyond the city to the northwest, following a little road to the place where the fields of the fertile valley met the foothills of the mountains. There they came to a *rancho,* a farm owned by the Carvello family, where they had lived and worked for several generations. They rode up to the hacienda, a handsome, tan two-story adobe home, larger than average but still not luxurious.

Aunt Gracia, a tall, stern looking woman answered the door. She welcomed them. "Come in. Reuben, it has been a long time since I have seen you. There must be something you want, for otherwise you would not have come to see me."

Embarrassed at her directness, Reuben fumbled for words. "Good morning, Gracia."

Then she turned to Esther. "This must be Miriam's daughter. You look very much like your mother, my dear child."

"It is lovely to meet you at last," said Esther. Then she turned to Reuben. "Father, it was cruel of you never to have brought me to meet my aunt."

"Better a little late than never. Let us just say that my life has had a detour," said Reuben. He thought, "*Gracia has not changed.*"

The good aunt gave the first of many bits of advice to Esther. "Do not rely too much on men. They have so little good sense."

Reuben explained the entire situation about Samuel, Father Sullivan, and de Navarro.

"I have some knowledge of what has been going on here," said Aunt Gracia. "De Navarro fawns over me because he believes I have an important social standing in the city. Heaven only knows why. For this, I despise him. But I despise him even more for what he is trying to do to this poor town.

"I will be pleased to help until the project is completed. Then I must return home, for they will not be able to spare me for more than a few months. Miriam was my friend and, although you never listen to me, Reuben, you are also my friend. A man like you does not know how to raise a daughter. I shall raise Esther as my own."

It was time to leave and Reuben walked out of the house with the look of a schoolboy who had just been disciplined, but once outside the house he winked at his daughter.

The next week Samuel traveled to Las Vegas, anxious to see if his sister would come to La Rosa. As he and Hannah sat with Mordecai, the peddler explained his problem.

Mordecai looked lovingly at Hannah. "You have become like my child, a very welcome one, who has done a good job. We would miss you, Alfred especially. But you alone must decide what to do."

"Uncle Mordecai, I vould miss you and your family very, very much. You are all so very gut to me. But mine job is to help mine bruder." She began to cry. "I vill miss everyone so much."

"Hannah, just come for a visit. See how you like it. I will bring you back here whenever I come to Las Vegas."

And so it was decided. Hannah came out to visit La Rosa and remained there to help out. Although missing Las Vegas, she was pleased to be with her brother.

Soon Aunt Gracia arrived. She greeted her niece and then saw Hannah. The old woman grumbled and gave her a hug. "I now have another daughter to raise and protect." Then looking over at Esther, she added, "It is difficult for me to distinguish between two such beautiful young women. Each of these pretties will attract men who will seek to take advantage of them."

Hannah and Esther spent most of their waking hours together running the store as Samuel was away a great deal of time peddling in the country. Aunt Gracia was busy running the house. Tired from a long day's work, she generally dozed off after supper, leaving the two young women to share each other's company.

As neither had any close female friends or relations, they confided in each other. Every night they chatted in bed long after Aunt Gracia's snores began. Hannah told of her feelings for Alfred, her affection for him, how handsome he was, and how charming he could be. But then a dark frown came over her face. "I do not vant a husband who runs mit bad people in taverns. Mine husband must spend his time mit me. I do not know vat to do. I think I luff him and I do so vant to be part of the Cohen family."

Esther comforted her friend. "Hannah, you're right. Don't change one bit or you'll regret it!"

It was harder for Esther to confide her thoughts to Hannah, who after all, was Samuel's sister. But Hannah broke the ice when one evening she asked, "Has my bruder ever told you of his luff for you?"

Esther blushed. "I don't know what you are talking about."

"A person vould haff to be blind not to see the feelings dat you two haff for each udder."

Then Esther quietly shared her feelings, telling Hannah of her love for Samuel. She went on to say that neither had ever acknowledged their love for the other.

Hannah laughed. "Except ven you are selling, you two must be the shyest people in the world. Ven I first saw you together, I thought of the surprise Momma and Poppa vould haff mit you as Samuel's bride. But vonce I came to know you it was clear that everyone vould luff you."

Esther felt unable to respond. Soon each of them, filled with pleasant thoughts of love, dozed off.

A New Pattern of Life

CHAPTER TWENTY

*H*annah helped Samuel unload the wagon
after his return from Las Vegas. He said,
"I feel like a shlepper, dragging goods from
one place to another. Those are the last items for this
store. Now I'm off to Ciudad Blanca to deliver all the
stuff for Reuben."

"Samuel, Esther is vatching the store and doesn't need
mine help. Maybe ve could haff a cup tea and talk a liddle. I haff not had much time alone mit you since I came
to La Rosa."

They went from the store into the house, sitting down
at the kitchen table. Hannah poured Samuel a cup of tea
and gave him a piece of cake. Switching to Yiddish, she
continued. "There's something I don't understand. You
have been in America more than two years and yet you act
as if you were still in Belkov. You left home carrying away
all of the fears of the shtetl. But even back in the Pale,
life is changing."

Samuel wasn't sure what his sister was talking about
and looked closely at her as she continued. "I had Gentile
friends from among the peasants back home. Much of
the ignorant hatred of Jews is being pushed aside with the
new ideas of the Enlightenment that have come from
Western Europe. Somehow, the Gentile world frightens
you. Even as close as you are to the Carvellos, there still
seems to be an invisible barrier between you and Esther.
Don't run from your love for her. She is a fine woman

and is just right for you. Momma and Poppa will soon learn to love her as I do."

Samuel looked down to avoid Esther's eyes. His mind went back to Belkov where he could hear Poppa. *"Use your judgment. We will accept whatever you think best."* But before he could respond, Esther walked in from the store and the conversation ended.

At Ciudad Blanca, Father Sullivan had invited Reuben to live in the rectory. But Reuben had declined, saying, "Padre, I thank you for your kindness, but I must not leave the store unprotected. We are too close to success to allow an opportunity for one of de Navarro's dirty tricks to defeat us. Since he failed at La Rosa, he waits for any opportunity to disrupt us. If I am not here, the store could be vandalized or the building burnt down. I shall sleep with my rifle at my side."

"I cannot disagree with your determination to afford de Navarro no opportunity to commit any further evil. But I must do more to help you. I will have Louisa bring over your meals and plenty of coffee every day. I feel guilty that I am not sharing your burden. Whenever the Lord permits me a little time, I will join you. There is not much that I may do to help, but rest assured that my spirit is always here with you."

As soon as the store branch opened, the farmers discovered that there was another place to buy. The prices at the new store were lower and the merchandise better. Reuben's respectful treatment of everyone contrasted sharply with de Navarro's contempt. Farmers who had left the project regained faith and returned. While the new branch helped many, those in debt were still under de Navarro's thumb. If they went to the new store or joined the project, the threat of the loss of their land loomed over them.

One day Jose Cruz came into the store. Reuben recognized him as one of the farmers living in the area. "Senor Carvello," he implored, "I wish to trade with you and to take part in your plan to sell corn to the fort, but I am afraid."

Reuben, seeking to comfort Jose, smiled and said,
"Jose, please tell me what you need."

"I have lived here all my life and have always bought
from de Navarro. Each year I go deeper into debt, but
cannot break away. He will take my land as he has done
with others. My wife, children, and aged parents will
starve. Many of us want to get away from him and work
with you, but with all we owe, what can we do?"

"How much do you owe him?" asked Reuben.

"It's only thirty-five dollars, but it might just as well be
a million. I have no money and no way of getting any."

"I will help you." Reuben walked into the back room
for a minute. Returning, he said, "Here's thirty-five
dollars." He handed the money in small bills to Jose, who
signed a simple IOU.

With tears of gratitude in his eyes, Jose prepared to
leave. "I swear that I will never forget you and will repay
you as soon as I can."

Although he promised to tell no one, word got around.

Reuben feared that if other farmers found out about
his generosity, he would deplete his life's savings. But
even worse, knowing of Samuel's hatred of credit, Reuben
feared his anger if the peddler heard of the loan.

The following week, Jose's cousin, Roberto Escobar,
came by with a similar story, and received forty-two
dollars. Soon another cousin, Raphael Mendoza, came in.
Reuben gave him twenty-eight dollars. Then a neighbor,
Vincent de Lorenzo, came by and borrowed thirty-four
dollars, as did a friend Hector Lopez, who borrowed forty-
three dollars. Soon Reuben's life savings of one hundred
eighty-two dollars was gone.

Reuben's loans became common knowledge, and soon
an angry Samuel demanded an explanation. "What do
you mean by giving out money?"

Responding apologetically, Reuben said, "I know you
would have tried to avoid making loans, but I just could
not let de Navarro destroy those people. After all, it was
my money alone that I used."

"Don't you see," said Samuel, "that's the point. All of
my life, I have opposed credit and the evil it forces upon

both the borrower and the lender. But sometimes there is no alternative. If Yankel Cohen had not staked me to an initial supply of goods, I'd still be working in the dress factory. If we provided no credit, many farmers could not afford to take part in the plan. I guess the same is true for the poor folks caught in de Navarro's trap. I don't know whether you should have made those loans, but once you did I'm in for half. I'm your partner and we share. Here's ninety-one dollars that I saved to pay Mordecai. That's my half. Whatever you do, right or wrong, we're partners, but I sure hope they repay us."

"Thank God I have a partner like you."

Back at La Rosa, Hannah shared Esther's work in the store. One night, when both were in bed, Esther inquired, "When will your wedding with Alfred be announced?"

Hannah broke into tears.

Esther, surprised at Hannah's reaction, apologized.

"Please, don't feel sorry for me. You've done nothing wrong. I'm afraid I can't marry mit Alfred though I luff him. He insists on running mit the fast vimmen of Las Vegas. I von't share my husband's luff mit dos vimmen!"

"Have you told him?"

"I can't. Mordecai and Bertha have been so vonderful mit me. I just can't tell dem. I vas happy to get avay and come here to sort tings out." Then changing the subject, Hannah asked, "But vhat about you and mine bruder?"

"I think your brother is the shyest man in the world."

Hannah knew her brother well, and agreed with Esther. Soon both women settled into the deep sleep and restless dreams of young women whose long days of work left little time for thinking romantic thoughts.

Between watching her wards, running the house, and managing the farm, Aunt Gracia's life seemed fulfilled. In her grumpy way, she was happy, but registered concern over the family farm back in Ciudad Blanca. At the store Esther was the boss, but Aunt Gracia ran the house with an iron hand. The old ease that Esther and Samuel had in the past was now gone. Samuel knew that Aunt Gracia regarded him, as she would any eligible male, as a threat until marriage vows were taken. Her fears mirrored the reality that each believed they had hidden, and increased the consciousness that Esther and Samuel had of each other.

One evening as they were sipping their dessert cup of coffee, Aunt Gracia dozed off. Hannah was in Las Vegas to help take inventory. Alone at last, Esther looked at Samuel. "I miss the old days when father, you, and I talked through the night."

The sound of her voice reminded Samuel of the sweetness of Jacov Klingman's violin in the *klezmer* band back home. It was the most beautiful music he had ever heard. It had sounds of love, of hope, and of a future. He sighed. "For me, too, those evenings have been the sweetest part of my life. They created a home for me." Then he gathered courage. "If only I could..."

Aunt Gracia snorted, waking herself up. She cleared her throat. Samuel cringed before her accusatory glance. It was as if the *duenna* had caught him in the act of seducing Esther. She quickly shooed him out of the house. "It's time to leave. Good night, Mr. Rabinowitz."

That night he lay in his bed and wondered if Esther could be as lonely for him as he was for her. He prayed, *"Why God, do you torture me? I am but a man. I want a woman and a wife. I want to feel the warmth of her body in the bed beside me. God, why do you torment me with this cruel jest? I shouldn't marry until I have saved my family. And even if I could, how would it be possible for me to marry Esther? If only she and I could..."* and deep into his thoughts, he dozed off.

The next morning was Sunday. At daybreak, Esther, Aunt Gracia, and Samuel set off for Ciudad Blanca. Samuel had avoided selling trips on the weekends so that they could see Reuben each Sunday while Aunt Gracia visited her family and he brought more goods to the branch store.

Just outside the city, Aunt Gracia ordered, "Samuel, turn left at the little road coming up. I want to visit the grave of my husband Aaron, of blessed memory."

He turned up the road. A few yards later they were at a small, secluded graveyard. Aunt Gracia led them over to a distant corner and pointed out the tombstone of her deceased husband. Looking around the ground, she and Esther found some small pebbles and placed them on the tombstone.

"This is to indicate that a visit has been made," said Aunt Gracia.

Samuel looked at the stone. Something struck him as strange. In the corner was a small six-pointed star. It was barely noticeable. He blinked and looked closer. He could not believe his eyes.

Aunt Gracia called to her niece. "Come and see your mother's grave. I know your father is too negligent to bring you here."

They walked to another grave. Esther paused in silent tribute to her mother. Her eyes filled with tears as Aunt Gracia handed her a small pebble and they each placed one on the tombstone.

Samuel looked over at the stone; on it was a flower with six petals. He started to ask Aunt Gracia about the markings, but she quickly steered him away from the subject. They returned to the wagon and drove to the Mendoza home where they dropped off Aunt Gracia. Samuel and Esther then rode the short distance to the branch store where they spent the day with Reuben. Esther had packed a picnic lunch and they chatted through a leisurely meal. It was like old times, but too soon it was time to pick up Aunt Gracia and return to La Rosa.

Evil Abroad

CHAPTER TWENTY-ONE

E arly in the morning of June 1, Dominick Gomez, a short, stocky Norteno farmer wearing a large straw hat, ran into St. Xavier, shouting, "Padre, padre, they've destroyed my crop! I'll never be able to harvest my corn and send it to Fort Madison!"

Father Sullivan calmed the hysterical man. "What happened?"

"Late in the afternoon, six riders came over the ridge, rode into my cornfield, and trampled my corn. Masks hid their faces and they never came near me but I am sure that they were de Navarro's desperados."

The priest led the farmer to a window facing the square. He handed him a spyglass and pointed at the men hanging around in front of de Navarro's store.

Dominick looked carefully. "I'm not sure, but they look like the same desperados who ruined my corn."

"You must report this to the Marshal," directed the priest.

"But Padre, what good will that do? He's only one man."

"You may be right, but it is the correct thing to do. Please excuse me, I must now seek God's guidance to be able to help you."

The priest walked over to the branch store where he found Samuel bringing in supplies and Reuben inside the store, waiting on customers. "Please serve the remaining customers, then come to see me in the rectory. It's important!"

When they arrived, Louisa brought in a tray of sandwiches and coffee. The priest told her, "Please see to it that we are not disturbed."

Father Sullivan repeated Dominick Gomez's story and added, "De Navarro knows he must win this battle. Our plan challenges his power and he believes we must be defeated. If we lose, no one will ever again stand up to him. He knows it, we know it, and the farmers know it."

"Well," said Samuel, "what can we do?"

"Maybe it's not as difficult as you think," said Reuben. "We might just take advantage of our superstitions to defeat the devil of Ciudad Blanca. As you know, we have many superstitious beliefs about death and the devil. We could exploit the fear and awe that surround the holiday of *Dia de los Muertos,* the Day of the Dead. This holiday, based upon a Mayan Indian ritual, has become part of the Catholic religion as All Souls Day."

"That's right," picked up Father Sullivan, "it's a medieval holiday that Americans celebrate as Halloween or All Saints' Eve followed the next day by a holiday called All Saints Day. The following day is known as All Souls Day. It is on this day that the Church transferred the Indian year-round preoccupation with death to a one-day event. But what of it?"

"Well, on All Souls Day a festival takes place around a picnic in the cemetery with bread, pastries, candies, and flowers. It is then that the souls of the dead return to spend the day with their descendants. Death plays a prominent role in our life as the dead wear the costumes of skeletons and the devil." Reuben looked over at Father Sullivan. "Padre, do you have a map of this region?"

The priest pulled a map out of a drawer in his desk and gave it to Reuben, who said, "There are four main trails leading out of Ciudad Blanca. I believe that de Navarro will vary his attacks with his desperados each day to create the most fear. I suggest one day very soon we wait for him."

Late into the afternoon, the three wove their plot. On a hot afternoon two days later, de Navarro was sitting on

the portico in front of his store biting off pieces of
sausage and throwing them to Pepe. He had at his command anywhere from six to a dozen desperados, depending on who was in jail, on the run, or drunk. To a man,
they were lazy, cowardly bullies, quite willing to use violence to avoid honest work, provided they had the advantage in number, weapons, or surprise and, of course, as
long as they were paid. It was these men whom de
Navarro pitted against the farmers. The destruction of
crops continued. Now he was eagerly waiting for his men
to return from their latest mission.

De Navarro sat feeding Pepe and daydreaming of his
childhood. His career from poor boy to mighty merchant
and, soon, great landowner moved through his mind. He
was imagining that with a beautiful young wife, he was
entertaining in a magnificent hacienda when the sound of
horses in the distance shook him out of his reverie.

He saw a cloud of dust raised by returning horses that
appeared to be riderless. As they came closer, de Navarro
could see that each horse had behind him a barefoot, dismounted rider with arms tied behind his back and the
rope tied to his horse's saddle. Each horse was dragging
his former rider backward to the store.

De Navarro jumped up, grabbed the horses' reins and
cut the ropes, freeing his desperados. "What happened?"

Jose, the leader, replied, "God help us! We were
attacked by the devil!"

After all of the men were cut free, de Navarro passed a
bottle of whiskey around. "Hey compadres, take a drink
and calm down. What really happened?"

They all shouted at once. "It was the devil! The Jew
Rabinowitz is the devil!" "An army of ghosts serves him!"
"I will never go out there again!"

"Quiet down!" demanded de Navarro. "Juan, tell me
what really happened."

"Patron, it was like this. The six of us left town to
finish off the corn on the Montoya farm just south of
town like you ordered. As we cut through the pass
between the great rocks just south of here, a bunch of

skeletons attacked us from the sky. Our horses tripped and we were thrown.

"When we got up to remount, we were attacked by hundreds of ghosts. Solid as real people, they grabbed us, tore off our masks and tied our hands behind our backs. Then they took off our boots and led us to a huge bonfire in a field. Forcing us to kneel, they called for their master, the Devil. Out of the fire rose Samuel Rabinowitz. Remember you told us the Jew was the Devil. You were right. He is the Devil with horns and a tail. Holding up his pitchfork, he told us that if we ever came back to any of the cornfields, he would turn us into ghosts and we would wander through eternity at his command."

The men nodded their agreement. They cried out, "Senor de Navarro, we are leaving tonight! We are leaving this accursed place!" They took off the remaining ropes, mounted their horses, looked furtively around, and rode away to the south.

"Tontos, idiots, fools!" cried de Navarro. "Those skeletons were as solid as people because they were real people."

Only Pepe, snarling at the desperados, supported his master.

But all of the threats of de Navarro fell upon deaf ears. As he threw a chunk of sausage to his dog, he cursed the departing desperados, declaring, "Pepe, you are my only true friend."

After all, no sane man would fight the devil. No desperado would take on *el Diablo* by attacking the farmers. But de Navarro was not one to use good sense. His arrogance and anger always prevailed. Impatiently he waited for his next opportunity for revenge.

De Navarro's Revenge

CHAPTER TWENTY-TWO

*E*very Sunday the *mariachi* band played in the bandstand in Ciudad Blanca's Plaza. People moved about, eating and drinking, talking and singing, walking and dancing. For the first time, the Carvellos and Samuel decided to join the community in the festivities. Esther flitted among her newfound customers, relatives, and friends like a hummingbird between flowers. Looking at Reuben and Samuel sipping their fruit punch, she smiled to herself, *"How nice it is to have a day off with nothing to do."* Across the plaza, de Navarro sat in front of his store with Pepe at his side. He was wearing an angry look on his face, probably as a result of el Diablo, who had frightened his thugs away.

De Navarro approached Esther.

"Senorita Carvello, would you care to dance?"

"No thank you, Senor de Navarro."

Suddenly, his shouting disturbed the tranquil atmosphere. "How dare you decline this honor, you little wench!"

"Senor, I mean no offense. But since you have made yourself the enemy of my father and my friend Samuel, I do not wish to dance or to ever have anything to do with you."

His face livid with anger, de Navarro roared, "Woman, if you know what is good for you, drop to your knees and beg my pardon. The old man, the Jew, and the drunken priest cannot protect you."

Samuel watched, conflict stirring within him. As a peddler, in a class with priests and women, he was excluded from participation in frontier violence. If any boisterous cowboy, Mexican desperado, or hostile Indian challenged him, Samuel would have to withdraw and surrender what was necessary. But this was different. To allow de Navarro to go unchallenged was to surrender his manhood in front of the woman he loved.

Suddenly Samuel found himself between the two. Facing de Navarro, he said, "I don't like you. I have seen too many of your kind. You don't run this town. Your time to push people around is over. We are under the United States government with a Marshal. If you think you are above the law, go ahead and we'll see what happens! I'm not a violent man and don't want to fight, but I'll do whatever's necessary to protect Esther."

Stunned, de Navarro paused.

Marshal Williams walked up to them. "Anything the matter, gentlemen?"

"No," replied Samuel.

De Navarro turned and stormed away.

Esther, shaken, watched de Navarro return to his store. Pleased to have been rescued, she thought, *"Samuel is gallant. No wonder I am so fond of him. If only he were bolder in expressing his feelings to me."*

Soon everything was back to normal. A strange woman walked over to her. "Senorita, your father has taken ill and is asking for you. Will you come with me to help him?"

Without pausing, she followed the woman to a deserted area behind the livery stable. Suddenly a sack was thrown over her head. She was tied and tossed over a horse. It all happened so quickly that she was unable to scream before her captors carried her away.

It seemed a long time before Esther felt herself dropped on a hard surface. She was untied and the sack was removed from over her head. Soon her eyes grew accustomed to the dim light and she found she was in a dilapidated cabin. Then, seeing that the men who had carried her there were de Navarro's thugs, Jorge and Alphonse, she screamed.

Trying to calm her, Jorge said, "Do not worry, Senorita, we have brought you here to meet your true love. He told us that under the control of a rich Jew, your father was keeping you two apart."

"Yes," continued Alphonse, "our benefactor asked us to do an easy job for him for which he would amply reward us. We were pleased to help out since we have had nothing to do since we left Mexico."

"And," added Jorge, "the hundred he promised us was more than we got from our last job."

Alphonse quickly gave him a dirty look and mumbled, "Shut up, you fool!" Turning to Esther, he said, "De Navarro told us that all we had to do was bring you to this cabin and that you would pretend to protest but you really wanted to be with him."

"What are you talking about?"

"You know," said Alphonse, "Senor de Navarro, your lover."

At this Esther dropped to the floor, pretending to faint from fright. Lying there, she began to understand the evil plot. Jorge and Alphonse, who were not the brightest of men, took de Navarro's words at face value and believed that her romance with de Navarro merely needed a little help. She concluded that only her feigned unconsciousness could gain her time.

Back at the *fiesta*, Reuben asked Samuel, "Where can Esther be? I'm beginning to worry about her."

But before his friend could answer, Lupe Alverado, a customer and friend, called out to them. "Reuben, are you all right? I heard a woman tell Esther that you suddenly took ill."

"I am fine, but what do you mean 'ill'?" Reuben asked.

"I thought you weren't well. The woman asked Esther to follow her," Lupe explained, "and Esther went with her."

"Where did they go?" asked Samuel.

"I saw them walk behind the stable," replied Lupe.

Instantly they ran to the stable. Esther was not there.

"Did you see my daughter?" asked the trembling father.

"No, Senor," replied the stable boy.

"Who has come here this afternoon?" asked Samuel.

"Well Senor, about half an hour ago, the two men living behind de Navarro's store came in and had me saddle their horses. One of them carried a large sack and threw it over his mount."

"Did they say where they were headed?"

"They were riding south. I think one of them said something about a deserted cabin."

"My child, my child," sobbed Reuben.

Samuel, with no time to comfort the distressed father, instead helped him into their wagon and headed south. A small group of farmers, who had been listening, mounted their horses, as did a tall solitary figure.

Esther opened one eye slightly to survey the scene. Continuing to feign unconsciousness, she saw Jorge and Alphonse looking confused. They didn't know what to do, as she alone understood de Navarro's plans. If he could violate her, it could be made to look as though Esther was a woman of easy morals, and her reputation in the village would be ruined. Shamed, she and her family would have to abandon the store and leave La Rosa. Worst of all, any hope of marrying Samuel would disappear, for no one would marry a disgraced woman. She regretted following the strange woman in the village without saying anything. But it was now too late for that. The only thing to do was play dead and wait. There might be an opportunity to grab one of the kidnappers' guns.

Suddenly, dismounted riders with drawn guns came crashing in through the door and windows of the cabin. The surprised banditos threw up their hands.

Esther quickly rose out of her feigned swoon and ran to her father. "Father, thank God you're here." They hugged each other. Then she ran to Samuel and embraced him. He returned the hug. It felt wonderful to feel his body so close to hers. Suddenly embarrassed, she separated from him. "Thank God, you have come to save me. They were kidnapping me for de Navarro to violate."

One of the farmers said, "Enough talk. String them up!"
Another added, "We've had enough of de Navarro."

They immediately tied Jorge and Alphonse's arms
behind their backs and led them to two tall oak trees. They
made nooses with their lariats. The other end of each of
the ropes was thrown over a tree limb and the banditos
were told, "Mount your horses and say your last prayers."

"But we have done nothing," cried the two as they
proceeded to tell their story.

"Hang them," shouted the farmers.

"One moment, boys," Marshal Williams called out,
coming out of the shadows. "If we hang them, we might
not be able to convict de Navarro for kidnapping. We
need live witnesses and these two will do just fine. We've
a cozy jail back in Ciudad Blanca with plenty of room for
them and de Navarro."

The farmers removed the ropes from the necks of the
desperados. They were marched back to Ciudad Blanca
with their arms tied behind their backs. As Reuben and
Samuel rode back to town in the wagon, Esther sat
between them.

Overlooking the scene, de Navarro sat quietly on his
horse in the shadow of a rocky outcrop. He had been
preparing to ride down to deal with his prey, with Pepe in
his saddlebag. Hearing the sound of riders, he had pulled
off the trail and hidden. At first he was dismayed at the
discovery of his plot, but when he saw the farmers preparing to hang Jorge and Alphonse, he was delighted.

Then his little dog began to growl.

"Hush little Pepe. Dead men tell no tales."

When he saw Marshal Williams take the men into
custody, de Navarro's delight turned to horror. This was
trouble. His two desperados would talk, incriminating
him to save their miserable hides. He cursed Esther, her
father, and the Jew and threw in an additional curse for
that drunken priest who had started it all. There was
nothing he could do but disappear into Mexico with Pepe.

A Victory Parade

CHAPTER TWENTY-THREE

With the disappearance of de Navarro, the farmers were free to raise corn. The plentiful snow from the prior winter lay on the mountains and melted slowly, furnishing the springs with ample water to irrigate the fields. The acequias remained full throughout the summer. The powerful sun in the high desert helped produce corn stalks heavy with large ears. As summer began to ebb, the ears ripened.

In late August, the corn was ready to be picked. The farmers allowed the ears to begin drying on the stalks before they walked through each of the furrows, either popping ears off or cutting them with a corn knife. Then they threw the corn into large bags. After the bags were filled, they were dumped into a large box that held ten fanegos or twenty-five bushels. Each box was carried or carted to an open area roofed over with branches to protect the corn from rain, where the ears were dumped upon the ground. Then the outer husks were removed to allow the remaining moisture to evaporate. Once the ears were dried out, the corn was ready to be shelled. This was done either by hand or by placing the ears into a hand-operated corn sheller, a small machine that resembled a meat grinder. It separated the kernels from the cob. Kernels were then placed in sacks that held one hundred pounds. As each farm attained its allotted share, hundreds of sacks were filled.

Four days before September 9, 1887, the date set for delivery, the farmers and their families formed a procession of wagons in front of St. Xavier. Reuben gave each wagon a number. Esther and Hannah calculated the weight of its contents. Samuel led the way to the fort atop his burro, Manny. As they departed, Father Sullivan blessed each wagon in the caravan and called out to Samuel, "May your God and mine lead you as He led Moses to the Promised Land." He joined the Carvellos and Hannah on their wagon saying, "I wouldn't miss this trip for the world!"

At sunset, the wagons stopped. The riders made fires to cook food. Farmers formed a mariachi band singing and dancing into the night. Storytellers wove their experiences into myth. The colorful dresses and shawls of the women and sombreros and serapes of the men marked the event. When the women danced, the whirling of their garments merged their bright colors into a beautiful blur. The men in their finery were transformed from poor farmers into caballeros in the finest Spanish nobility.

Each day more wagons joined the caravan as the Yankee farmers joined the Nortenos. These farmers had dealt only with Samuel and found the people from Ciudad Blanca strange. But as every night was a fiesta, they soon grew to know each other. At first the children searched each other out with the curiosity they have when encountering other children. Then little by little, the parents copied their offspring. Driven by a common goal, everyone soon became friendly.

The Yankee farmers introduced their new friends to folk dances and learned the dances of the Nortenos. For the first time in many years, there was something to celebrate. They would all have a better future and, in addition, the Nortenos would be free from de Navarro's control over their lives. As Fort Madison came into view, the caravan heard army buglers announcing their arrival. Wagons came in, one at a time, up to the storehouse where Quartermaster Jones carefully weighed and inspected the contents of each sack to determine both its quantity and quality. All was as contracted.

After the grain was delivered, Jones produced the biggest sack of money Samuel had ever seen. His eyes bulged. He said, "Thank you God for this miracle. I still remember each coin I've earned since I came to this country. Can this sack of money be real?"

Samuel became paymaster to the farmers. Esther helped with the account books, and he calculated the monies earned for the corn minus that owed for seed and supplies. Then Reuben paid each farmer. Those who had borrowed from him repaid their loans. The introduction of money into the previous barter economy would change life in the region. It would create prosperity with the promise of a future.

After setting aside the money due to Mordecai, Samuel took a few moments to confer with his partners. "Let's share our new wealth with our customers," he said.

"Great idea!" said Esther

Reuben nodded his agreement.

Samuel called out, "Listen folks, there'll be a bonus for everyone. It may not be a large amount, but I'm sure it'll come in handy."

His audience responded with cheers.

Samuel counted out a tenth of the remaining profits after deducting the money due Mordecai. Handing the money to Father Sullivan, he said, "This is our tithe to God and our guarantor."

"Have you forgotten the most important thing of all?" questioned Esther. "What about the money to bring Momma and Poppa over to America."

"You're absolutely right," responded Samuel. "I didn't forget. There were just so many other things that we had to do immediately. But I'll send it right now."

He went to the quartermaster and returned with paper, envelope, and stamps and sat down to write a short letter.

Dear Momma and Poppa,

God has been good to us. Our contract with the army has been completed and we have money for everything. I am enclosing enough to cover all of the expenses for the two of you and Nathan, if you can convince him to come with

you. Hannah is fine and awaits your arrival. With the help of God, you will have a safe journey here, and in a matter of months, we will be a family again. All is very well here, and I am only lacking you to make my life complete.
    Love,
    Samuel.

Outside the fort that night, Norteno farmers, Yankee settlers, and American soldiers held the greatest fiesta in the history of Ciudad Blanca. They dined, drank, and danced. The height of the evening was an impromptu play narrated by Father Sullivan entitled, "How the Devil and his Ghostly Allies Defeated the Forces of Evil." And of course, Samuel played the lead role. Everyone laughed as the play reminded them that the superstition of de Navarro's desperados, believing Samuel to be the Devil, had led to their defeat.

After the play ended, the Norteno farmers gathered around Samuel and cried out, "The God of Moses has sent us a new Moses to lead us! You must be our *Alcalde,* our leader. Now that de Navarro is gone, you must move to Ciudad Blanca and take his place. Help us save our money and stay out of debt. Sell our crops for us every year. Then we shall prosper."

The Yankees echoed agreement.

Overcome by these signs of love and acceptance, Samuel was speechless. He knew that he had found the magic spot on Yankel's map, his home in Ciudad Blanca.

The priest toasted each of his friends.

Esther responded, "Do not be so modest, Father Sullivan. You are the one who planned all of this."

The kindly priest answered, "Yes, but it would not have been possible without your help and the help of God."

Late into the night everyone sang and danced. The night had a magical charm, brought about by the success of the venture. The Nortenos and the Yankees now had a bond of friendship. The Buffalo soldiers sat quietly in a corner, where Father Sullivan came to welcome them. The women, Norteno and Yankee alike, brought plates of food over to the Buffalo soldiers. Slowly the shy black soldiers overcame their reticence and joined the others.

Samuel imagined that he saw a group of Indians quietly watching from behind the brush on the nearby slope. He visualized Running Deer in a tree looking down. This, together with the other activities of this night, transformed the celebration into a peaceable kingdom.

Esther asked Samuel for a dance. She refused to accept his excuse that he didn't know how to dance and vigorously insisted, "Now you belong to us and to our town. You must dance with me."

As he held her in his arms, Samuel spoke, his voice quivering. "Esther, for all the time I've known you, I've denied my love for you, but I can't hold you in my arms without saying I love you and want to marry you."

"Samuel," she responded, "I've loved you as well. I have waited so long for you to tell me of your love, as your eyes told me of it long ago."

BOOK FIVE
Coming Home

Romance

CHAPTER TWENTY-FOUR

*S*amuel was loading his wagon to return to La Rosa when Mordecai called out, "Hey *macher,* big shot, you got no time for me? Already you forgot your old friend."

"I'm sorry. I've got too much on my mind." As he saw the merchant's look of disappointment, Samuel thought, *"This is the first time that I haven't stopped to talk. Mordecai must be concerned about me."* After confessing his love to Esther, he had realized that in his world, a confession of love must always be followed by marriage. But was this marriage possible? He had promised his parents to remain a Jew, which implied marriage to a Jewish woman. He didn't feel capable of marrying outside his faith. Unable to comprehend how Momma and Poppa would respond to a marriage with Esther, he knew they would ultimately acquiesce to his choice.

"Big shot, you don't know me anymore. I remember when you first came to Las Vegas. Then you were starving. Now you're a hero. You not only won the contract, but also actually delivered the goods despite everything that mamser de Navarro tried to do. You're at the peak of your success. So what can be bothering you that you can't take some time to schmooze with me? Come on into my office for a coffee or, better yet, a *schnapps.*"

Samuel followed Mordecai into his office. He looked down, too depressed to say anything. Mordecai poured out two glasses of whiskey and said, "L'chaim! To life!" They downed their drinks.

Samuel sat down, placed the whiskey glass on the table, and stared down at the empty glass, almost in tears.

"Tell me, how can I help?"

"I love Esther. She loves me. We have told each other of our love but I still can't marry her."

"Are you meshugana, crazy?" interrupted his friend. "Esther is a fine woman. Her father is a fine man. They're your best friends. What do you mean you can't marry her? This should be the happiest day of your life."

With a voice that mirrored his torment, Samuel continued, "After all that has happened in Russia and all the sacrifices my family made to send me to America, I just can't marry out of my faith."

"That's a problem for all Jews here," replied his friend. "This is not a shtetl or even New York City. This is New Mexico, the frontier. It is natural for a man to want a home, a wife and children. Here in the West it's hard to have our faith and a family, too. Maybe you've been on the road so long that you are incapable of enjoying life."

Samuel bristled. "It's not been easy. I've done nothing but work and send money home. I've never even been able to afford the company of a woman. I love and desire Esther and hate this life." He paused with tears filling his eyes. "But I cannot — I will not — desert my faith as a Jew. And I can't ask Esther to leave hers."

"You're a fool. Only a few Jews have the money to bring wives from Europe or back east. I was lucky enough to have help from my family. Many married non-Jews and lived fine lives. Some converted to their wife's religion. In other marriages, the wives have become Jewish. In some, neither changed. Try to find a solution. Talk to her."

Samuel said, "I can't deal with it. I'm too overcome. I just can't discuss it with her. Nothing in my life has prepared me for this. In the shtetl parents arranged marriages through a marriage broker. There was no such thing as romance. Although I have long wanted to be married and have a family, I don't know how to deal with it." Abruptly ending the conversation, he loaded his wagon and left for La Rosa. Glancing back, he saw Mordecai watching him leave.

A week passed. The town and its people had a new
vitality. Everyone was elated except for Samuel. Early
Sunday morning, after Reuben returned from Ciudad
Blanca to La Rosa, the young peddler called him aside. "My
dear friend, I must talk to you. I've treated you badly."

"Samuel, I do not understand."

He noticed that for the first time Reuben addressed
him without calling him Senor. "When we were at the
fiesta, I danced with your daughter and told her that I
loved her and wanted to marry her,"

"I am pleased to give you my blessing. You are like a
son to me. Only a fool would not have noticed the affection between you and Esther, even though you two thought
you hid it from yourselves and from everyone else. Is the
problem that you did not ask me first for her hand? You
may have it, my son."

For a moment, Samuel thought of how much Reuben
reminded him of his father. Then, with a look of despair,
he said, "But you don't understand. I left Russia to
remain a Jew. I wouldn't enter their army where we were
forced to become Christians. I wish to remain in my faith
and not become a Catholic. But I can't deprive Esther of
her religion. I don't criticize those who marry Christian
women and embrace their religion. But I won't do so.
It's not only my promise to my family, but Judaism is my
dearest possession. I'm not willing to give it up and I can't
ask Esther to abandon her faith. So it's not so simple."

"Talk to Esther. But before you do, come with me.
Even if you are only considering becoming a part of the
Carvello family, there is something I must show you.
Perhaps it might help solve your problem."

Samuel followed the older man over to the fireplace in
the kitchen. Reuben selected a chisel and a hammer from
his toolbox. He then carefully removed several bricks
from the fireplace wall. Reaching into the opening, he
withdrew a metal box.

"There is a tradition in my family that the contents of
this box are shown to no one except those who are about
to marry into our family. I had forgotten about it until

today. When I married Miriam, we found that each of
our parents had their own secret. Perhaps that's why they
arranged our marriage. It would allow each family to
know that their secret would be shared only where it
would be safe."

Reuben placed the metal box on the table, lifted its cover
and took out a pair of beautiful Shabbes candleholders and a
Kiddush cup used for ceremonial drinking of wine.

Stunned, Samuel stared at the beautiful objects.

Then Reuben removed a large packet of papers bound
together by a red ribbon.

"The candlesticks and wine cup were brought into our
marriage by my beloved Miriam, of blessed memory. My
mother and father gave the manuscript to me when we
married. I believe these papers have been passed down
from generation to generation for more than two centuries. I don't understand what they mean, but I believe
they contain information about my family's history.

"The memory of the past has faded over the years. At
your Passover seder, you had candlesticks and a wine cup
like these. It revived some of those old memories and
gave meaning to my strange dreams. Since you have come
to La Rosa, those dreams and memories of my family and
the old stories have become more frequent and more real.
Maybe this manuscript tells more of my family. Perhaps
the distance between Esther and you is not as great as you
may have believed."

Astounded, Samuel stared at the contents of the box.

Reuben picked up the manuscript and was untying it
when Esther came into the house from the store.

She stared with disbelief. "What's going on here?"

"This is your heritage, my daughter," replied Reuben.
"Maybe I should have said something years ago. But until
Samuel reminded me of things lost in memory, I had forgotten about this old metal box. After I buried your
mother and moved to La Rosa, I hid the box behind the
fireplace." He showed her the Kiddush cup and the
Shabbes candlesticks.

"This is beginning to look like Samuel's Passover table," said Esther. She eyed the manuscript, drew closer, and joined the others in carefully inspecting its yellowed pages.

"I can't read the language in which these pages are written," declared Reuben.

Samuel paused, looking at the pages. "That part is easy. The script is Hebrew but I can't make any meaning out of it, as the words are not Hebrew. Yiddish is also written in the Hebrew script, but this is not Yiddish either. I can make out the sounds but the meaning remains a mystery to me."

"Until we untangle the mystery, we may never know the secrets of the Carvello family," said Esther. "The only person who might know is Father Sullivan. Why don't we take the manuscript to him?"

Early the next morning, they rode to St. Xavier and showed the manuscript to Father Sullivan. He studied it. "I can read printed Hebrew, for we studied that in the seminary. But Hebrew script is a mystery to me as we had no reason to learn it."

"I can read the script," said Samuel, "but I can't make any sense out of the words."

"Well, maybe you could try to sound it out aloud," said Esther.

Samuel lifted the first page, surveyed it closely and then slowly and carefully sounded out each word.

"Does the word Ladino suggest anything to you?" inquired Reuben. "My grandparents sometimes spoke a strange language that they called Ladino. Its sounds resemble those you are making."

Samuel looked up from the page. "Long ago I met a peddler who was a Turkish Jew. He told me that his people didn't speak Yiddish but spoke Ladino. He said that they were Sephardic Jews and that this Ladino was mainly Spanish like Yiddish is mainly German. Like Yiddish, Ladino was written in Hebrew script. If Reuben is correct, his ancestors must have had some contact with Jews. Perhaps they might even have been Jews."

"To me," said Father Sullivan, "it sounds like the Spanish I learned in the seminary in Northern Spain. It's almost as if someone were reading aloud from *Don Quixote,* which was in the language of Spain as it was written and spoken more than two centuries ago. Please excuse me for a minute."

The priest left. Almost twenty minutes later, he returned with a dusty old book in his hands. "I found it, the old Spanish dictionary that I used in the seminary in Spain. I'm not sure how much I remember, but if you'll read slowly, we may find out the manuscript's secrets."

Samuel read the pages, carefully enunciating each word, repeating each of them two, three, or even more times as Father Sullivan asked. Then he waited for the priest to locate the word in his dictionary.

They worked all through the night.

Slowly the Carvello family history unfolded.

The Carvello Heritage

CHAPTER TWENTY-FIVE

'I am not aware of who you, my reader, may be,' the manuscript began. 'I will be dead long before this document is discovered, if it is ever found. Yet I hope you are my descendant, so you may learn how the vile Spaniards robbed us of our heritage.

'My name is Don Miguel Carvello. I am a Jew. Because of the ill treatment my ancestors suffered, we were known as *Conversos,* New Christians, *Marranos,* or *Anusim.* Whatever you may call me, I'm still a Jew hiding my true identity.

'My ancestors settled in Spain centuries ago. They lived a prosperous life under both Moslem and Christian rulers and were a bridge between those two cultures. Although life was dependent upon the goodwill of individual rulers, they lived well.

'After the unification of Spain under Catholic rule by the marriage of Queen Isabella and King Ferdinand, the Queen determined that all Spaniards must become Catholics. We Jews had to either convert or leave. There were between two and four hundred thousand Jews in Spain. Half left and half converted. Many of those who left Spain survived and spread throughout the world.

'Later many of those who first converted to Christianity became dispirited when they found that the same anti-Jewish hostility pursued them as it had uncon- verted Jews. This led many New Christians to return to

Judaism. Those who ultimately escaped from Spanish control went to Turkey, Italy, France, or Holland.

'Those Jews unwilling to convert were forced to leave Spain by late 1492. The Carvello family converted and became a prominent Converso family in Southern Spain. Many times I wished that my ancestors had had the courage to go into exile rather than convert. But one cannot condemn others without standing in their shoes.

'The Old Christians, as Gentile Spaniards were known, hated Jews and made no distinction between those who converted and those who did not. To them, our guilt was not only based upon our religion but also upon *limpieza de sangre,* the purity of Spanish blood. One had to show four generations of pure Spanish ancestors untainted by Jewish, Moorish, or Indian ancestry to be acceptable as Spaniards under this racist doctrine. Some questioned whether even King Ferdinand met these standards. But the Old Christians pretended that their stock was pure and that their faithfulness to the Church was unquestioned.

'With the economic success of the New Christians, jealousy among the Old Christians grew. Denouncing a New Christian to the Inquisition as a fallen Catholic could subject the accused to an *auto da fe,* a test of faith by torture. Then part of the New Christian's property could be forfeited to the informer. How ironic to burn someone to death under the pretense that it was an act of faith to save his or her soul.

'We, like other Converso families, prospered in Spain until the Inquisition made life too precarious. Following the exploits of Coronado, who conquered New Spain in 1521, we escaped by immigrating to these new lands. At first Queen Isabella refused to allow Conversos to settle in the New World. But after her death, the way opened and we went to New Spain, hoping that distance would protect us.

'At the age of twenty, my father Alfredo came to New Spain with his cousin Luis Carvello. In July of 1568, Luis led a fleet of ships to New Spain, where he was appointed

Governor of the Province of Nueva Leon. Because of his prominence as a soldier, no one questioned too closely the ancestry of the one hundred or so settlers that accompanied him, which included many New Christians.

'It was here that I was born in 1573. As in Spain, our family was successful. We moved north from Mexico City and acquired a great amount of land.

'The intensity of the Inquisition increased. The violent actions of the Grand Inquisitor Torquemada resulted in thousands of victims. The atmosphere of terror followed us to New Spain. Luis Carvello's sister's son, spoke too openly of his Jewish beliefs and was summarily burnt at the stake in 1586.

'Perhaps the violence of the Inquisition was not as widespread as it seemed, but still it terrorized the Conversos. More than the number of persons burnt at the stake, it was the threat of what *could* happen that struck fear in our hearts.

'Our family became even more guarded. When we celebrated our holy days, we did so in total secrecy. Servants were sent away and windows were sealed off. The violence led us to move further north from Mexico City, the headquarters of the Inquisition in New Spain. But just as the bloody trail of the Inquisition had followed us from Spain across the Atlantic Ocean to New Spain in 1571, it followed us northward.

'We feared informers even among our own people. We knew less and less of the true feelings of other Conversos. Nothing could have been written in a manuscript such as this, for its discovery could lead to death. Only because I am as hidden away as I am, is it possible to put my thoughts on paper. Even so, I hide them in Ladino rather than in Spanish so that they will be less likely to be discovered by unfriendly eyes.

'Each generation has remembered less of our heritage as Jews. We have no religious books, not even a Bible. So our knowledge is based upon memory and an oral tradition of each generation telling the next of our beliefs, customs, and traditions. One has to be cautious, for the transmission of information in an indiscreet fashion, even through a rebellious child, could place an entire family in jeopardy. I remember less of our ways than did my father, and he, less than his. Perhaps my grandchildren or great-grandchildren will have no memory of our ways at all.

'In 1598, when I was twenty-five years old and my brother Phillipe was twenty-three, our father purchased a large cattle ranch for us. Salvatore de Madrid, an arrogant Castilian who coveted our land, owned the adjoining ranch.

'We were sure that he suspected us of being secret Jews and was only waiting to denounce us to the Inquisition to steal our land. He was always sneaking around to see if we were doing anything special for the Sabbath or for holidays. We carefully hid our activities from him.

'We knew that it would only be a matter of time until he exposed us to the Inquisition. Once arrested, our property would be seized while we waited for a year or two for our case to come to trial. We would be presumed guilty and given little or no information about the charges until the trial. Even if we were found innocent, we would never regain our property.

'As we prepared to leave, we deeded our land to our servants to make it more difficult for de Madrid to steal. Our foreman, Juan Lopez, came to say goodbye. "Senor Carvello, of all the caballeros who have settled here, you two have been the best. You have treated us as humans. It is not fair for you to have to flee like desperados."

'"Juan, God will protect you but you must help Him. Take this letter. If anyone comes to talk to you about our relationship with de Madrid, say that he frequently visited with us on Friday with his best clothes on and stayed for dinner but would not eat pork. Tell them we were close friends. Do not protest. I know this is not true, but if you follow my directions, de Madrid will not be able to steal the lands we have given you. Give this letter to no one until the Inquisitors come to see you and then hand it to them saying that I gave you the letter for them."

'Preparing to leave, we were concerned that de Madrid might take drastic action if he learned of our plans. We

spotted him lurking nearby. Phillipe called him over. I
snuck up behind him and placed a cloth soaked in a
sleep-inducing drug over his mouth and nose. We pulled
the drugged de Madrid into a clump of trees. Phillipe
removed his pants, while I took out a sharp scissors and
circumcised him by cutting off the foreskin of his penis.

'When my letter denouncing de Madrid as a secret Jew
was delivered to the Inquisition, his circumcision would
have been all the evidence they needed, especially after
Juan told them of his close relationship to us. Trading
two Jews for one Jew-hater would have been the best thing
that the Inquisition has ever done.

'I have long wondered what the fate of that swine
Salvatore de Madrid was. What would the Court of the
Inquisition do when my letter denouncing him reached
them? Then with all of the additional evidence that would
turn up — Juan's testimony, the circumcision, and our
stack of discarded clothes — the Court would have had no
problem convicting him. If necessary, the Inquisitors
would have used torture to force de Madrid
to confess.

'We bid the snoring de Madrid *adios,* mounted our
horses, and traveled for several days to the unknown
North, looking for a place of refuge among friendly
Indians. We headed directly north rather than northeast
to Texas or northwest to California. Each of these regions
contained Spanish soldiers and priests, for there were
rumors as to the existence of gold and silver. We avoided
this danger by going to a place where the fierce Apaches
had chased the Spanish out.

'For Phillipe and me, the discovery of gold and silver
would only be our downfall, as it would have given the
soldiers reason to denounce us, to steal the precious met-
als. Like the Jews of Spain, we would only have suffered
for the wealth we brought. Even after their conversion,
when the Conversos brought wealth to Spain, they suffered from the Inquisition. The ignorant Spaniards would
soon learn that with their Jews gone, their prosperity
would disappear.

'Luckily we avoided the Apaches and found friendly Pueblos, who clustered their homes together in small villages to protect themselves. They took us into their tribe. We found it difficult to adjust to their way of life, but there was no other place to go. We married Pueblo women and settled into the life of the village.

'It has been almost forty years since we settled here. Phillipe died five years ago without any children. I have tried to raise my own tribe of Jewish Indians, keeping our ways alive for my four children and fifteen grandchildren. I have tried to pass my Jewish religious beliefs down to them. I will never really know of my success, but I have no problems with the Indians and their ways. They are good people. But somehow, I would hate to see de Madrid and the other Jew-haters win out, and they will if no Jews survive.

'I have done my best to observe our Jewish customs, remembering such things as our way of butchering. I tried to eat only animals with cloven hoofs that chewed their cud. We never mixed milk and meat. We remembered the Sabbath and the holy days by using a calendar I had created from an old, outdated one that I had brought with me from Spain. It was hard but I did my best to teach my wife and children. However, I am sure that I forgot a great deal and they will forget even more.

'In recent years, others have settled nearby. These include two hundred or so soldiers and settlers who followed Juan Onate in 1598 up from New Spain to El Paso and then to the northernmost parts of New Spain. Some believe that Onate or his wife had Converso blood, as did many of the settlers.

'I have made contact with them and have found many of our people. My children have married among them. God willing, the Jewish religion will continue on forever despite such murderers as Torquemada and Queen Isabella.

'I hope the reader is my descendant and that you are a good person. But down deep, I hope you will confound the enemies of our people and return to the faith of our ancestors.

'Miguel Carvello, April 15, 1637.'

BOOK SIX

Home at Last

The Quandary

CHAPTER TWENTY-SIX

*A*s Father Sullivan finished translating the last words of the manuscript, a stunned silence fell over the room. Samuel wondered what each was thinking. Reuben and Esther were at least the descendants of Jews, whatever that might mean. He had often heard stories of lost Jewish communities popping up somewhere. There were stories of Chinese Jews, descendants of those Jews who traveled over the Silk Road routes, or the descendants of Solomon and Sheba in Ethiopia. But tonight was not a *bubbe maiseh,* a grandmother's tale.

The priest's brows rose up on his forehead and wrinkles spread across his face. Then breaking his silence, he said, "I'm horrified over my beloved Church's part in these events. While I knew of the Spanish Inquisition, it was never real to me, as it came from books which minimized its effect and rationalized away its cruelty and excesses."

He paused, and a pained look came over his face. "When a people's suffering takes on individual human form, it becomes more than statistics and generalizations. What penance do I owe the Carvellos?"

"You owe us nothing," said Esther. "You have been a good friend and are a decent man."

"Of course," added Reuben. "If the Church has done wrong, it was not due to you."

"But as a priest of the Catholic Church, I must bear the burden of the wrongdoer. As a man of God, it is harder to atone for the crimes of my Church than to suffer from the crimes of others against me. It is easier to be a victim of the British and suffer as an Irishman than to bear the guilt of the Church, and of my Franciscan Order, in robbing Jews of their souls in the Inquisition." He rose and left the room.

Samuel was struck by this candid admission of Father Sullivan. He had never before heard any Christian express sorrow for anything done to the Jews. Not only was this a Christian apologizing, but a priest. But now Samuel had little time to think. He was concerned about the Carvellos and how they would adjust to their new identities. Elated over the revelation, he hoped that this would remove any obstacle to his marriage to Esther. No longer was his primary concern over religious differences. In fact, he was no longer sure what that difference was or how Esther would deal with these new disclosures.

After a prolonged silence, Reuben spoke. "The events of the last several hours keep running through my mind. I have gone back in time to the last few days, the last few months. On and on, back to the coming of Samuel, to the birth of Esther, to the death of Miriam, to my marriage, to my childhood, to my parents, to my grandparents, and perhaps even back to Abraham and Sarah.

"I have a memory of a past that is so faint that I am unsure of whether it ever really existed. If it is real, little remains for me to pass on to my daughter. When memory fades as it passes from generation to generation, a point may come where all memory is gone." Looking at Esther, he continued, "Perhaps, Hita, my darling child, once again I have failed you."

His eyes then met Samuel's. "Before you arrived, I was a discontented man, old before my time, with no sense of identity with my community or my neighbors. I only knew that I was not part of the world around me. When you arrived, I felt some faint stirring. Assuredly, there was no outward similarity between us. Your appearance, speech, and physical attributes are totally unlike mine. But still your arrival evoked a faint memory, like poking the dying embers of a fire.

"From my first meeting with you, a sense of kinship began. It grew when I asked you about your refusal to eat pork. Maybe this too fed the embers of my faded memory. When Mordecai jested with Esther about our names, a faint recollection of our family's effort to carry on its religious tradition emerged. Another part of my faded memory was stirred.

"When de Navarro attacked us as Jews, he accidentally found some basis in fact. Could this attack have stirred the unexpired Jewishness in my soul? Could there have been a hidden portion of memory waiting to be reignited by such an act?"

Samuel nodded and sighed deeply.

"The Passover seder woke other faded memories. It revived the dreams of my childhood. The ashes burst into flame. The fire of memory grew brighter and brighter. The manuscript returned to me those family memories which had all but disappeared.

"I have always been an outsider here. Regaining my heritage means so much to me. I'm happy to rejoin the Jewish people and to return to my ancestral faith." Then he paused to look over at his daughter. "Alas Hita, my darling, while I have rekindled the embers in my soul, I am unable to pass the flame on to you."

Samuel saw a tear in Esther's eye. Her hands folded in her lap and her dark eyes fastened on the coffee cup in front of her as she responded, "It is a custom among Norteno men to treat their wives and daughters as chattel. But my father, you are not like those men. You are the sweetest and kindest person I know and you have always treated me not only with love and affection, but also with respect. Now that I am a woman, I ask that you continue that respect. I must discover first who I am and what I wish of life."

She looked up at Reuben. "Father, I don't share your estrangement from this community. I have not been as distant from them as you have. Perhaps we are two different types of people. It may be that I am more like my mother."

Her father looked down at his own hands, which were folded gently in his lap.

"Yet on the other hand, there is much that I do not share with the Norteno community here, although I am, or at least was until today, a part of it. I am unable to share the fanatical devotion to the idols of the Church or even to participate in Church activities, as do most of the women of the village. I have different beliefs and values thanks to you, my father. I do not rebel against you but I must think through all that has happened. You have educated me to have a mind of my own. While I thank you for this, it has not made my task any easier."

Then looking over at Samuel, and casting her eyes down, she continued, "My problem with these new disclosures has nothing to do with my love for you. I love you and have always loved you. I have accepted your proposal of marriage and fully intend to marry you. We will work out any difficulties that may arise."

Her eyes rose again to meet his.

"I would never require that you become a Catholic for that would destroy you and I could not destroy the man I love. Until recently when you came to La Rosa, I knew of no faith except for the nominal Catholicism shared by the entire community. What was my relationship to being a Catholic? It was very little as a religion, but much more in terms of my friendships and my life in La Rosa. But there is no reason for these relationships to change."

She looked over at Samuel and with a warm, loving glow continued, "Your kindness and understanding over the time I've known you has helped me grow from a girl to a woman. But there are certain things that I must decide by myself such as my relationship with Judaism and the Jewish people.

"How do I relate to your need to marry and remain a Jew? Would I change my faith for you? I think I would, for I would do anything to be part of your world and to share your love and kindness. I've never known a Jew before I met you. For the success of our marriage, I must think everything through. I owe you no less."

When Samuel nodded his head with conviction she continued.

"Samuel, I have met a few of your Jewish friends in Las Vegas. I like them. They are gentle people, little given to the rough life typical of a New Mexican town. They respect their wives and daughters and all women, unlike the machismo attitudes of most Norteno men."

Then turning to Reuben, she added, "But now my father, we may both be Jews." Looking around the room, she made her plea. "If no one objects, I would like to stay at La Rosa with Hannah and Aunt Gracia. I must have time to sort things out."

Tears glistened and rolled down her cheeks. Brushing them aside, she struggled to regain control with no idea of why she was crying. She loved these two men sitting across from her. Was it the sorrow for the loss of a simple, uncomplicated past? Were they tears of joy, for now it would make possible the marriage to Samuel with the last obstacle overcome? Only one thing was certain: she could never leave the two men she loved.

A Challenge to his Faith

CHAPTER TWENTY-SEVEN

Father Sullivan could not sleep that night. Tossing and turning, he retraced his life from early childhood to the present. Although he loved the Church, the disclosures in the manuscript repulsed him to an extent matched in the past only by his feeling over Ireland. He recalled dealing with that challenge. The Church would not tolerate any public dissent, but there was no danger of being labeled a heretic.

Once inside the orphanage, he had become sullen and withdrawn, challenging the priests with hatred of the English over the hanging of his father and the destruction of his family. He had been unable to accept the Church's attitude that this was God's will. He had repeatedly been told that he might not understand it then; however, in time, he would comprehend everything and believe that its actions were correct.

Only with kindly Father Kearney had he begun to soften. The young Jesuit priest behaved more as an older brother than as a spiritual advisor. Making no attempt to argue, the priest encouraged him to spew out his hatred. The caring example had encouraged young Patrick to follow in his footsteps.

Father Sullivan recalled settling down and learning obedience. One day the priest had come to him to pose a question. "Now my young friend, it is time to decide what you want to do with your life. Choose your path carefully. I think you would make a fine priest, with great compassion. Rebuild your life from the wreckage that came after the tragedy of Ireland." The phrase, *"the tragedy of Ireland"* never left him.

He decided to enter a Jesuit seminary and become a priest. But the phrase "the tragedy of Ireland" still haunted him as it challenged a vocation that sought obedience. It took time to subdue this challenge and the subduing was never complete. Together with other rebellious youths, he took to baiting their professor, Father Mahoney. "But what of the Church backing the British?" They cried out with a hundred variations on that burning question.

One day, Father Mahoney came to class looking as though he had had a little too much to drink. As the raucous comments of his class swelled, he called out to them, "Why do you not all hold your tongues? I have something to tell you."

The clamor ceased.

"Do you not know how difficult it is for me as an Irishman to see how wrong my Church is when it comes to dealing with the British against my people and then to have to remain silent? But as a priest I have only two choices. Either I must leave the Mother Church and join the Godless rebels as many have done, or remain within the Church and deal with my doubts.

"But I cannot leave. So I stay as part of the Church. I do not have to accept the policy of my Church in this matter as correct. I need only accept her views on religious matters as infallible — matters like dogma, doctrine, and faith. Things such as support for the poor Irish peasants do not create such a conflict that the Church will declare that I have deviated from the integrity of the Catholic faith. This is not an issue that will make me into a Martin Luther. Thus, while it might make the Church unhappy were I too vocal, I would not become a candidate for excommunication."

He peered out at his tormentors. "While I cannot speak out openly against the Church's urging the Irish to comply with British oppression, I may and, indeed, must continue to work to help correct her attitude. You boys must be here to help the Mother Church find her way, to separate out the wrong message from the divine messenger. Shut your mouths and give yourselves a chance to think about what I have said."

Young Patrick Sullivan did just that. He thought and thought until his head was about to burst. While he disagreed over Ireland, he remained loyal to his beloved Church. But now what of this latest challenge? He thought about the Spanish Inquisition and recalled that the Church was not monolithic over the matter. While Spain, the Dominicans, and Franciscans had become extreme on the issue, Rome had sought to caution them and moderate their actions. It challenged their use of torture and contested forced conversions that failed to win the souls of the converted.

"But what does this all mean? Has my life been in vain? I must remain silent and be obedient, but my submissiveness must not be a surrender of intellect, rather a requisite of discipline." He thought of the many things he had sought to do and how he had failed in some and succeeded in others and he then took consolation in the defeat of de Navarro.

"My faith in my Church has sustained me. I live in an imperfect world, but much remains to be done, and I must get on with it."

Alfred and Hannah

CHAPTER TWENTY-EIGHT

*A*fter Yom Kippur services at the synagogue, Hannah was in the kitchen helping Bertha with the preparations for the holiday meal celebrating the breaking of the fast, when Bertha broached the subject that had long been disturbing her. "I find it difficult to ask you what it is that has gone wrong between Alfred and you, but I must."

Hannah looked down at her hands and began to cry softly. "I luff him and very much vant to be part of the Cohen family but I'm not villing to marry mit a man dat spends all of his free time mit de vimmen at taverns."

Bertha comforted the tearful woman. "Hannahle, this is what I was afraid of. Give me a few days, and I'll soon put a stop to that problem."

That evening when the guests departed and the children were in bed, Bertha told her husband the whole story. "After all of our efforts to get a wife for Alfred, she is rejecting him and, worst of all, I can't blame her."

"Bertha, every child thinks he or she is the center of the universe until that child grows up. I am sorry to say that you, with my help, have spoiled Alfred. When we first brought him to America, he never had to work as a stock-boy or go out into the country to peddle like the rest of us. He was always the boss's brother-in-law. So starting in at the top, he carved out this fancy floorwalker's job for himself. I didn't mind. It actually turned out to be a good idea. But for his own good it would have been better for your brother to grow up and learn to provide for himself without our help. People like us can be too good to someone they love."

Mordecai continued as his wife nodded in agreement. "He began to hang out with that crowd at the tavern down near the station. They play up to his ego as long as Alfred pays for drinks, and he gladly pays for them if they flatter him. He really needs to accomplish something so as to achieve a sense of his own worth."

"But what can we do now? I hope it's not too late."

"Well, I have a suggestion. Since it looks like the Carvellos and Samuel will move to Ciudad Blanca, let's buy the La Rosa store for Hannah and Alfred. Of course, we will not make it a gift but will resell it to them on terms that are generous. I expect this will give them a sense of pride by making them work. If Alfred's out there, he'll have to learn to manage for himself. And in La Rosa, he won't find any fancy ladies to tempt him. The only thing you'll have to do is to put their romance back together."

Bertha smiled and reached for her husband's hand. "Mordecai, I'm glad I married you. You're so right. There's nothing wrong with Alfred that a little hard work won't cure. Don't worry about the fancy ladies. We don't do those things in our family. I won't tolerate it."

A week later, when Samuel returned to Las Vegas, Mordecai took him into the office, sat him down, and said, "I have an idea. I would like to buy your store in Las Vegas and then sell it to Alfred and Hannah." He then proceeded to tell Samuel the problem and his proposed solution.

Samuel quickly accepted the proposition. "I was so involved with my own affairs that I wasn't aware of the difficulties between Hannah and Alfred. Obviously, I will have to discuss it with Reuben and Esther. Basically we need to buy a house and to stock our new operation in Ciudad Blanca. Both Esther and Reuben want to return there. It would be too difficult for us to handle both places. We'll work out a deal for the store that everyone will like."

On the next Sunday, a chastened Alfred rode out to
La Rosa to renew his courtship. He walked with Hannah
down to the riverside where they sat in a shady spot under
a large willow.

"I've been a fool. I want to spend my life with you."

At first Hannah rejected Alfred's proposal. Then when
he pressed her for the reason she blurted out, "I'm a poor
girl and I dearly luff you but I vill not marry mit a man
dat fools mit bad vimmen."

Alfred began to laugh. "Sorry. It's not you that I'm
laughing at, but myself. I was so busy with my primping
and showing off before those phonies at the tavern, who
were only after free drinks, that I failed to see that you
were the real thing. I want to spend my life with you and
only with you, my love. I'm sorry. It's not really funny.
I never carried on with any of the ladies. It was all show.
But now marrying you is the most important thing in my
life. My tavern life is over, starting now."

Hannah accepted the proposal.

Bertha threw a party to announce their engagement.
Esther came early to help out. She was intrigued with the
ketuba, the Jewish pre-marital contract, which established
the relationship between husband and wife. She began to
imagine what her relationship with Samuel would be.

Samuel, Reuben, and Esther entered into an agreement
to sell the land and store to Mordecai. Esther had mixed
feelings about the change. La Rosa was the only home she
had ever known. But she longed to be reunited with her
newly discovered family in Ciudad Blanca.

Before long, the store was sold to Mordecai and then
to Hannah and Alfred. The Carvellos and Samuel used
the money to stock the new store, acquire a home, and
pay their debts to Mordecai, but even then they had some
money left over.

It was decided that the marriage of Hannah and Alfred
would take place before they moved to La Rosa, although
Hannah wanted to wait for the arrival of Momma and
Poppa. A quick move would eliminate any chance of a
relapse by Alfred. The tavern would not only be a part of
the past but would also be at a great distance.

Reuven's Return

For Reuben, the revelation in the manuscript was the fulfillment of his life. Whatever free time he could marshal, he spent reading or talking to Samuel about his newly found ancestral faith. As often as possible, he went with Samuel to Las Vegas and took every opportunity to attend services at Temple Montifiore. Initially he merely accompanied Samuel to services and participated very little.

One day when Samuel returned to Mordecai Cohen to collect the new items, Reuben decided to remain behind to speak to the Rabbi. At first Rabbi Glick eyed Reuben suspiciously, unable to determine what he was doing at the minyan. The Rabbi inquired about Reuben's trips to the synagogue. Soon the conversation turned to the topic of Judaism.

"If it is your desire to become a Jew, it is my obligation to discourage you," announced the Rabbi. "I must reject your request three times to be sure that you are sincere."

Before Rabbi Glick could continue, Reuben broke in, "But I am a Jew. I am just trying to learn how to be Jewish."

The rabbi was stunned.

Once the barriers were broken, the floodgates opened, and Reuben told him of everything that had happened.

From that time on, the Rabbi took every occasion to explain the Jewish religion to Reuben. Never speaking down, he explained the basic ideas of his faith in plain, uncomplicated language.

"Rabbi, I want to be a full member of your congregation, a part of your minyan, and fully a part of the Jewish community now that I have found out who I am. What must I do?"

"Well," Rabbi Glick responded, "it will require your determination to join with the people of Israel."

"Do you not mean rejoin? For us as Anusim, forced converts, we have never left. Does not the long suffering of my ancestors make me a Jew? What else could be necessary?"

"Yes, but a problem exists."

"I do not understand. I have returned to my roots. What else can count after all my ancestors have suffered to remain as Jews?"

"Let me explain. Although I believe you are a Jew and nothing else is necessary, a question may be raised. Our religion is one of rules and reason. A Jew, in our beliefs, is defined as a person either born of a Jewish mother or a convert to our religion."

"That is not how the Inquisition saw it! Many a person was burnt at the stake merely for having Jewish blood," replied Reuben.

"You are correct, but how would you be able to show your Jewish ancestry on your maternal side from the expulsion from Spain down to the present? It would be difficult, if not impossible, to show your lineage for almost three hundred years. I agree that the process of conversion after all the suffering to remain as Jews may well be offensive. Would it not be wise to undergo a formal conversion and remove any doubt that could ever be raised? What is wrong with seeing your conversion as formally coming home to your people Israel, especially since you are already here spiritually?"

"You are right. For me it will not be as much a conversion as it will be a reaffirmation."

And so Reuben began his course of study, until one Shabbes he formally rejoined his people.

Reuben was very excited over the coming of the high holy days of the Jewish New Year, *Rosh HaShanah* and the Day of Atonement, Yom Kippur. The rabbi had explained to him that the High Holy Days or Days of Awe begin with Rosh HaShanah, the New Year, which lasts two days. Ten days later comes Yom Kippur.

While Esther was not as sure of her religious attitude as was Reuben, both accompanied Samuel to holiday services. They found the two days of Rosh HaShanah fulfilling. But it was on Yom Kippur, when the prayer of *Kol Nidre* introduced the holiest day of all, that Reuben was most moved.

At that Yom Kippur service, Rabbi Glick explained, "Jews have been saying this prayer for centuries for their brethren, the Anusim who, having been forced to convert, were unable to pray for themselves. These were people not free to believe. People were forced to say 'yes' when their hearts said 'no'. By making this prayer for our distressed fellow Jews, we identify with them and share their pain. On Yom Kippur, we Jews come to the synagogue not only to atone to God for our sins but also for those who cannot come to the synagogue and must have someone speak for them."

After services Reuben said to Esther and Samuel, "I have never been so moved in my life as I was when I found out that for all these centuries my Jewish coreligionists had been praying for me and for my ancestors. Could it be that their prayers played a role in all of the amazing things that have happened to us this past year? Somehow Rabbi Glick's prayer last night reached me as nothing else in my life has."

A New World

CHAPTER THIRTY

fter the Carvellos and Samuel sold the La Rosa store to Hannah and Alfred, they moved to Ciudad Blanca, which brought them closer to Father Sullivan and many others who had wanted them to come there to replace the departed de Navarro. Aunt Gracia returned home, but the bond that had been created with her niece promised a continued, stronger relationship between Esther and Aunt Gracia.

In Ciudad Blanca, people called Samuel their Alcalde, their leader. They wanted him to keep the contract with the federal government and insisted that he act as their bank to help them remain out of debt. Samuel, who for so long had hated credit, found that when honestly dispensed, it could be used to help move people out of poverty.

He hoped that Momma and Poppa would soon be on their way but doubted that his brother, Nathan, would come given his involvement in the revolutionary movement. Samuel eagerly awaited a reply to the letter he had sent home with the money.

A week later, a letter came from Belkov.

Dear Sholom and Hannah,

Thanks be to God, your letter of deliverance arrived with plenty of money to get us to America. While Momma has been preparing to leave for some time, we still had to sell our belongings. I think one of our Gentile neighbors will buy the house and everything in it. It will be hard to part with our cows. With all of our children gone, they have become our family.

At last we are ready to leave Belkov. As difficult as life has become, it is painful to leave. It is the only place we have ever known as home. It was where we were born and grew up. It was the place where we were married and had children.

We are used to the ways of shtetl life, but still, with our children gone, nothing remains here for us. So we must leave. No matter how bad the Russians have become, it is hard to say good-bye.

Nathan has not left Russia but is in hiding. He must have heard we were leaving as he snuck into town to say good-bye. The Russians have set a price on his head, so he had to be very careful and could not stay long. We think the Russian police have been spying on our house and as much as we love him, we were happy to see him go safely back into hiding.

He has rejected your invitation to come to America with us. We are not sure that it is his inability to get out of the country or whether he feels obligated to remain with his comrades. Nathan has grown a beard and dresses like a peasant. We have heard that he is living with a farmwoman. He has become a hardened man, embittered against the Russian rulers, and committed to violence. While he speaks only of the Revolution, I think deep down he regrets what has happened to him but as always, Nathan is unwilling to express any sorrow. I fear they have changed him and can only hope and pray that he has not forgotten his God and his people Israel.

Two weeks ago a letter came from Isaac. Life was improving on the kibbutz but they are still quite poor. His letters reflect their difficulties, but are filled with hope. I believe he is saddened at his inability to ask us to come to Palestine. We wrote him that we were leaving and asked him to write to us in America.

I end this letter hoping we will see you soon. Our dream of America is at long last coming true. While fearful, we look forward with love to seeing the two of you

*and meeting your friends the Cohens and the Carvellos.
We will never be able to thank you and your friends
enough for obtaining the money to get us out of Russia.*

*For obvious reasons, we will post this letter just as
soon as we cross the border.*

Love,

Momma and Poppa

Father Sullivan was sitting with Reuben and Samuel in
his study when he heard of the letter and inquired. "I
guess your parents are on their way. Did you not tell me
that your father is a dairyman?"

"You might call it that. We had two or three cows and
sold their milk."

"Have you considered that he might do the same work
in Ciudad Blanca?"

"But is there such a thing as a dairy here? If people
need milk and don't own a cow, don't they just buy from
a neighbor?"

"Well, perhaps the time is ripe for that to change," said
the priest. "Ciudad Blanca is becoming a big enough town
to require a real dairyman. There is some indication that
we need higher health standards, especially for our children, and a professional dairyman might provide that."

"Poppa always dreamt of a few more cows. Then he
could produce and sell dairy products other than milk,
such as butter, cottage cheese, and sour cream. He hoped
for a horse and wagon. All of these could be available for
Poppa should he begin a little dairy in Ciudad Blanca.
Maybe the store could start a dairy. Then Poppa could
begin life in America by selling his dairy products from
the store."

Samuel left the priest and returned to Reuben at the
store. He discussed his dream of creating a minyan with
Reuben, who was excited at the idea. A thought struck
Samuel. "Perhaps with me, you and father, we might look
for a minyan. But where could we find seven more Jewish
males? With Alfred in La Rosa there would be four of us."

Mulling over the idea, Reuben suggested, "I think there
might be one or two men hereabout who might seek to
reclaim their heritage."

Suddenly it struck Samuel! "Arturo Lopez, the Sephardic peddler I knew from Yankel's loft, wanted to go west with his consumptive father where he could use his knowledge of Spanish! If the two of them were able to come, we might have six members of a minyan. I will get a letter off to Arturo at Yankel's to sound out their availability."

Then on his next trip to Las Vegas he explained his plan to Mordecai. The merchant suggested, "There might be a Jewish peddler or two out your way. I'll keep my eyes open and see what I can find out."

When he returned to Ciudad Blanca, he told Father Sullivan of his plan. The priest suggested, "Why do you not seek out any Jewish soldiers you might find at the Fort? The good Reverend would be pleased to help you."

Two weeks later Samuel presented his idea to Rabbi Glick. No one was more enthusiastic and helpful than he. "Obviously, it will be a long time before you could build a congregation that could afford a sanctuary and a rabbi. But in the meantime, I would be delighted to help out. Since you come into Las Vegas frequently, I could meet with you on a regular basis and advise you. I could come and visit you, maybe once every two or three months and help you with a student or circuit-riding rabbi. But we're getting ahead of ourselves. Let's just get a minyan first."

Samuel smiled, "One day we will have our minyan and maybe even a small congregation. What a wonderful goal."

Since the disclosures in the manuscript, Esther had tried to resolve her confused feelings as she ran the La Rosa store until Hannah and Alfred took over. She spent a great deal of time either by herself or talking to Hannah or Aunt Gracia, working through the problems of her identity. One morning she told Samuel, "Now that I have discovered that I come from Jewish ancestry, I must determine what that means. Ultimately everyone must make a choice. My love for you is an undeniable part of my life and probably the most important part of my choice."

Samuel thought, *"What will my relationship with Esther be?"* Each day he waited and hoped for her decision.

After the discovery of the manuscript, Samuel's concerns changed. Now he was less concerned with what marrying Esther meant. He was unsure of what the dramatic effect of the revelation would be on Esther. Now she was a descendant of Jews, yes, but he was unsure of what that meant to her. To Samuel the whole New World was a place where everyone had to choose.

Esther's Resolution

CHAPTER THIRTY-ONE

eeks passed. The world had changed. The Carvellos and Samuel moved to one of the stores on the plaza in Ciudad Blanca. At first the City, which owned the property, wanted them to rent de Navarro's abandoned place of business, but with all that had occurred, Esther was reluctant, so they rented another store. They settled into the new premises quickly, using the money they had received for the La Rosa store to equip and stock the much larger one. They also bought a new home.

After Alfred spent a few weeks in La Rosa, Samuel noticed a great change in him. No longer solely concerned with his impeccable appearance, he had rolled up his sleeves and did all of the heavy work, never allowing Hannah to lift a box. *"Hard work agrees with him,"* Samuel mulled. It was as if the cardboard man on the wedding cake had stepped down and become a real person, a mensch.

The next Sunday, Esther's cousin Rachel Mendoza invited her to her daughter's birthday party. Here, she found herself seated with Rachel and another cousin, Louisa Alvarez, the daughter of Uncle Jacobo Carvello. The three were engaging in much good-natured chatter, when Louisa said, "Esther, what's happening with you and your Jewish friend, Mr. Rabinowitz?"

Esther blushed, but before she could reply, Rachel broke in. "Well, so what would be wrong with that? Everyone knows that our family has Jewish blood."

Louisa snapped, "Our family is descended solely from Castilian Spaniards, all of whom have always been good Catholics." Then she stalked off.

"It's all right with me if she wants to keep up that pretense. God knows we've done it for generations. We all act as if the Inquisition is still out there waiting to pounce on us."

Esther looked over at her cousin. "I need a friend," she asked. "I have been away from Ciudad Blanca too long. I do not know my family. Would you help me and respect my confidences?"

"My dear, it would be my pleasure to be your friend. Do not worry, anything you say will go no further."

So the young girl proceeded to tell her cousin about the manuscript.

Rachel absorbed the entire story without once interrupting. "I've had some idea about our background, but I never knew about Don Miguel till now. I think it's amazing."

"But what about Louisa?"

"She's just old-fashioned. I love to tease her about her silly idea that we all descended from Spanish nobility. There is a concept called limpieza de sangre, the purity of blood, which has been carried over from Spain. To fulfill this concept, a person must have pure blood for at least four generations. Obviously, the Spaniards determined that the impure blood was that of Jews, Moors, and Indians. There are no pure Nortenos. We all have Indian ancestry. In addition, it is doubly stupid for a member of our family since we have Jewish ancestry. But the pretense still continues."

"How do you know that?"

"Our family, as well as the others of Jewish descent, has a tradition of keeping certain customs that have passed down for hundreds of years. We also have kept our secrets over the generations. It is not safe for that tradition to be shown to outsiders. For this reason we resist attention from the non-Converso world. In each family, certain members are told of their secrets. My father, Aaron, was told of our heritage by his father.

When my father was near death, he took me aside and told me a story that I never fully understood until today when you told me of Don Miguel.

"In every generation, the message was carried through someone believed to be safe enough to entrust with the family's secrets. I have heard that when your father was a young man, the family regarded him as too immature to know its secrets. But when the marriage with Miriam was arranged, she was entrusted with this knowledge. Her sudden death and your father's departure to La Rosa took you away from the family. Your leaving kept you from learning about your identity."

Esther sighed and watched her cousin carefully as she continued.

"Some of us, like Louisa, deny its very existence, yet it was her father who circumcised all of the male babies. If she was such a good Catholic, isn't it strange that her father circumcised her three sons? None of us uses animal blood. We eat only certain animals, which we slaughter in a unique fashion. Many of us still light candles on Friday night and follow other Jewish customs. When I was in school in Albuquerque, I had Ashkenazic Jewish friends and was amazed to learn of the many customs which we held in common.

"But our family was very careful that these secrets were not told to everyone. Someone might give us away. I have talked to many here who have Jewish blood. We Conversos regard our heritage in varying ways. Some, like Louisa, hide their background and engage in total denial, purporting to be of pure Christian ancestry. Denial and hypocrisy are not my approach to life, so for me that route is out.

"A few others take the opposite view and seek to return to the outside Jewish world. They call themselves Anusim, Hebrew for forced convert. They regard themselves as descendants of Jews who were forced to convert during the Spanish Inquisition and regard themselves as if this had happened personally to them. They seek either to return to the Jewish community or to practice their brand of Judaism in secret. I have heard that your father is seeking that route of return. Only a few have been able to do that, although it is not unusual for these people to find spouses for their children among Ashkenazi Jews and to return in that fashion.

"That is a way that is too difficult for me. It is hard enough to be a Norteno without adding the difficulty of being a Jew. But I am comfortable with the fact that I have Jewish ancestry. Now as open as I am with you, I would still never speak this way to an outsider. For us, the Inquisition is a part of our lives. It remains alive in our minds as if it were real. To tell others might subject us to scorn and danger, so we keep a shield between the rest of the world and ourselves. We remain Conversos, openly participating as Catholics and secretly carrying on certain Jewish customs.

"For some, the tradition has worn too thin and is lost. They have become true Catholics. But most of us keep some of our secret ways, although we may have forgotten why. Our memory has grown too faint. Most of us accept the fact that we are Conversos. We regard ourselves as Catholics of Jewish ancestry and remain with a confused feeling of what this really means, as we know we are not like other Catholics."

Esther left the luncheon in a daze. The past so recently exposed to her had been a closely held family secret. She realized that she had Jewish roots from both her parents. Unlike her cousin Louisa, she was not willing to lie about the past. She felt no problem regarding her membership in the Catholic Church. She had neither her father's hostile attitude nor her cousin Louisa's unquestioning acceptance of the Church.

The following Friday after Shabbes dinner, Esther sat with Reuben and Samuel. They looked out at the dusk of evening, relaxing and enjoying one another's company. Breaking the silence, she said, "I have spent the last several days thinking and making decisions. For the first time in my life, I feel like an intelligent human being capable of deciding for myself, and I like that feeling."

Samuel held his breath, thinking, *"Maybe I will learn my fate. Time has seemed to be endless since the manuscript has been read. I fear what she will say and yet I must know."*

"First of all, Samuel, I am now ready to marry you."

He gasped in happiness and clasped her small hands in his.

"I want to be your wife and would accept your faith were that necessary, but it may not be. With the recent disclosures in the manuscript, I have discovered that I am of Jewish descent, although our family has hidden that fact under their nominal membership in the Catholic Church. Indeed, our family tradition, based upon what I have learned, is that we are Conversos, whose acceptance of Catholicism may or may not have been legitimate. I may even be a Jew and not a Catholic. I will have to sort it all out."

She released his hands and turned to her father. "But what is it that I wish for myself, not based upon my love for Samuel, for my father or even for my ancestor Don Miguel? For many years my life in La Rosa was an existence in a lonely world of its own. Until Samuel arrived, it appeared I was destined to live out my life in my father's house. I knew that the life of the village would not be the life for me. I knew that I could not marry a macho Norteno peasant."

Samuel got up from his chair and walked to the door. He watched the last of the day's light leave the sky. He looked at Esther, whom he loved so dearly.

She continued, "When Samuel came, something happened. I found my own self in his kindness and gentility. This he showed not only to me, but to everyone. Those long evening conversations created a new world. Perhaps it was within me, only to be brought out by him. I treasure the ability of people to talk and think together and to enjoy each other's company. I felt that I had a mind and a personality. My life took on a new meaning. In the time since Samuel came to us, I forced myself to learn and grow. I decided I wanted to be a full person. I did not want to be just a girl, who serves her father and her husband.

"Samuel, I want to be Jewish, not only to be your wife, but also to live as the Jewish people do, with gentleness, kindness, and intellect, appreciating the good things in this world. I find that for me this world of kindness, consideration, and intellect is what I want. When you first came to La Rosa, I knew nothing of Jewish ways and the Jewish faith. Little by little I have learned some of the Jewish practices and customs. I have no problem belonging to that people. Samuel, I have come home."

Samuel took Esther in his arms. She had created a home for both of them.

Epilogue

*A*fter Esther accepted Samuel's proposal, life became hectic. They wanted to wait for Momma and Poppa's arrival to have the wedding, especially since Alfred and Hannah had been unable to because of the move to La Rosa. The next month passed quickly. As Samuel believed his parents would soon arrive in Las Vegas, Esther accompanied him to meet each train whenever they were in town.

On one hot afternoon they waited for the train. As usual it was late and an additional half hour dragged on. Samuel was nervous about Momma and Poppa meeting Esther. Suddenly he saw a train in the distance. As the train pulled into the station, he watched the passengers disembark.

Then Samuel saw an old couple cautiously step off the train. "Momma! Poppa!" he cried. Running to them, he wrapped his arms around his parents. Tears streaked down his cheeks. Like a little child, he kissed his mother and wept. "I never thought I would see you again."

Momma remained speechless, kissing him over and over again like her child of old. Weeping, she mumbled, "Sholom, Sholom, I can't believe we are here. I'll never again let you go."

Poppa said, "Sonnelle, it's all right. We're here and we're safe."

Then Samuel brought Esther over to his parents. "Momma, Poppa, I want you to meet my friend Esther. I have written to you about her and her father. They are my dearest friends."

Samuel was trying to get the courage to tell of his
impending marriage when his mother in Yiddish asked.
"Bist du de schoene maidel du hust chasone mit? Is this the
pretty girl you wish to marry?"

Then she walked over and kissed Esther.

Both Esther and Samuel looked over at Momma.

"Don't be so surprised. Hannah wrote me about you
and Esther. She told me about how wonderful Esther is
and what a good wife she will make for you."

Samuel brought his parents up-to-date about what had
happened since his last letter.

They returned to the Cohen home where they met
the family.

The next morning they departed for La Rosa and visited
with Hannah and Alfred. That Alfred charmed his mother-
in-law was not unexpected, but when Hannah told
Momma and Poppa that she was expecting a child,
Momma shook with excitement. "The fact that I have lived
to be reunited with two of my children and soon I will have
my first grandchild is my fondest dream come true."

Too soon it was time to leave for Ciudad Blanca. They
arrived at their new home where the Carvellos and Samuel
had settled in. Insisting upon helping out in the store,
Poppa said, "I have never spent an idle day in my life."

Father Sullivan came by and suggested that Poppa set
up a small dairy in the store.

Samuel said, "Let's give it a try."

Poppa agreed. "I'll make a list of what I need to start."

After Momma and Poppa's arrival, the day was set for
the wedding. It was the event of the year as the entire
Jewish community of Las Vegas and many non-Jewish
friends had been invited. Also many guests came from La
Rosa and Ciudad Blanca, as well as from the surrounding
countryside.

Five months later Momma was staying with Hannah,
helping out with a new baby girl. Poppa had developed a
small dairy business as part of the store. While not yet
profitable, it was at least breaking even. It would take
time for the people of the town to become used to this

radical idea. The store itself was doing very well. Nobody even mentioned de Navarro.

In Ciudad Blanca, Samuel had gathered a small group of Jews. They met and prayed together. Samuel invited his Sephardic friend from New York and his aged father to come west. A month later, they had arrived. Poppa, Reuben, Albert, and Samuel were the basis upon which they hoped to build a minyan. In addition, the two men from New York brought them to six, more than half-way to their goal. An old friend of Reuben's began to show an interest in his Converso background. Sometimes there was a Jewish soldier, once even two from the fort. An occasional Jewish peddler was encouraged by Samuel to remain in the area. But they had not yet reached the desired minyan.

A year later everyone had settled in. Both the La Rosa and Ciudad Blanca stores prospered and the families dependant upon them had grown. Momma now had two grandchildren, Hannah's little girl and a son of Samuel's and Esther's. For the *bris,* the circumcision, they all returned to Las Vegas.

Rabbi Glick performed the circumcision accompanied by the rituals of the bris, celebrating the covenant of the Jews with God. The guests retired to a celebratory meal.

Father Sullivan began, "This is a good day for all of us to count our blessings. Samuel and Esther, I see your child as the happy culmination of all that has passed since Samuel came here.

"I'm growing old and will soon be returning to my God. When I was a very young man, anger burned within me for what had occurred in Ireland. That anger went beyond the English and affected my relationship with my Church. I raged against the part the Church took backing the English. Then I protested against de Navarro and the exploitation of the Mexicans. But, it was only when I learned the truth about the Spanish Inquisition that my anger reached its peak. But God saw my suffering and sent Samuel here to help heal my pain. Little did I know the extent of God's mission when de Navarro raided the store."

Mordecai asked, "But how, Father, was Reuben and Esther's leaving the Catholic Church and returning to Judaism a divine mission for a Catholic priest?"

The priest responded, "The actions of the Church in secular matters are not exempt from error. God, hearing my suffering about His beloved Church, gave me the opportunity to help redeem two kidnapped souls to their rightful place. Somehow this has made all well in my world. God has made amends for the failures of His Church."

Esther took up the conversation again after a few moments of quiet followed Father Sullivan's words. "I'm grateful for a wonderful family. My extended family and all of the people in this room have given so much to me and contributed to my sense of belonging in Ciudad Blanca."

Poppa responded, "I'm happy just to be in America, a place where all of these different people can come together in the same space for a bris! I have never enjoyed a meal so much."

"You're right," agreed Momma, taking a break next to her husband. She had spent most of the afternoon running around serving everyone. "We are safe here and we have our grandchildren. I only wish my other two sons were as well off."

Samuel paused, took a sip of his coffee, and began, "When I started my journey four years ago, Yankel Cohen gave me a map of the United States and told me that somewhere on that map was a place destined for me. He was right, and that place was bashert, predestined. I found it and it is here.

"As I survey my world, I have concluded that while the Messiah has not come, and there is not yet a peaceable kingdom where the lion has laid down with the lamb, my world is a wonderful place, and I can ask for nothing more."